Ten Golden Fields

Your Little Piece of Forever

Wen Henagan

AuthorHouse™ LLC
1663 Liberty Drive
Bloomington, IN 47403
www.authorhouse.com
Phone: 1-800-839-8640

Contact at: whenaganace@gmail.com
In association with: www.marketgoodstories.com

Original cover art by Stephen Botka
Look Stephen and me up on Facebook!

Published by AuthorHouse 08/04/2014

ISBN: 978-1-4969-2988-4 (sc)
ISBN: 978-1-4969-2987-7 (e)

Library of Congress Control Number: 2014913526

This book is printed on acid-free paper.

Contents

Foreword

In the temporal world, nothing outlasts forever. However, it is true that many enduring works of art and writing linger a long time in the hearts and minds of adoring humans. It would be very fine indeed to create some piece of literature that has a chance to endure for awhile.

So this unknown writer would like to place a small bet with you, Mr. or Ms unknown reader. My wager to you is this: In five years after you read and thoroughly enjoy the (virtual) pages inside this book, I challenge you to mail me then, and honestly declare that not one character do you remember, not one plot do you recall, or not one line of dialogue has stuck into your head.

If I lose this bet, I will do something for you. It may not be much, but it will be something. That's a promise. But first, let me make an earnest promise to you: You are going to remember this book. You will remember its name. You will probably be able to recall three or four characters. And you will remember some plots. You will do this well into the future. Five years is not too long a time for your fond thoughts of diving into "Ten Golden Fields" to linger and press against your memory banks.

I can declare this because I have created something special here. It's a genre of fiction that may be hard to place, to define. The stories are relatively short, maybe one or two of novella length. Two fit into the mold of flash fiction. You can devour a story fairly quickly, and (another promise) you will come back for seconds because your mind will declare, "Run that by me again. How did that happen?"

As a lifelong reader and analyzer of writers and their works, I wanted to make stories that even I would not forget any time soon. In "Ten Golden Fields" there are ten hugely different, character diverse, plot driven tales. In the stories there is the gentle tug of some paranormal or futuristic element. I have tried to do this in the easy style of my favorite writer-Steven King. When there is some paranormal element that comes into the tale, it is so natural, one may say it's thoroughly expected. In stories that take place in the future, I have tried to make the science so palatable, it's like you are chomping gently on a delicious pastrami and cheese sandwich. In short, the science does not get in the way of either the plot or the characters.

Admittedly, this is an ambitious assignment. But I want to double-down even more. I want this to be "Ten Golden Fields" Volume I. So what would a Volume II look like? Its essence would be similar to the quality and diversity of the first volume. But in Volume II, I have in mind something weird and special: I will compose the first five stories with as much care and daring as before. But the second group of tales, those will be written by hungry writers desperate and weary of trying to get their good story published. I will entertain offers at my web site, and in time, five great tales will be picked out from five thoroughly unknown writers, but these are people with something to say and the talent to get it across. Why shouldn't they be recognized?

Isn't "Ten Golden Fields" an excellent venue for that? Who knows if there will not be "Ten Golden Fields" volumes well into future times?

It's my sincere hope that readers who like good but short fiction, will find my book to be entertaining. I want the cast and characters to truly ring out with zest and verve, as they are certainly capable of. I want readers all over this globe to peer into the future with me, and come out asking questions.

In fact, that is what I call the mark of a very good writer. He writes his fiction, but it seems so real, so engaging, so vivid, that it's not like fiction at all. It makes the intelligent reader ask questions of himself, of the world, and its often peculiar realities.

Have a great read. And be prepared to lose a certain bet five years from now.

www.marketgoodstories.com

(Prof) Wen Henagan

Writing this near Baekseok University, in Cheonan South Korea

Now here's a generation conflict! And it's all the fault of one good-hearted U.S. President, along with those various benefits the upcoming Revolution in biomedicine are on the verge of producing. Real people, real *old* people, have to learn how to play a new kind of game ...Hey! They're pretty good!

Old Farts Marriage Parlor

When Larissa Pennyman arose early in the morning, she always surprised her sleepy-eyed progeny from the act of simply slipping into her favorite orange and blue jogging suit without any groans of strain. And when she returned an hour later, always sprinkled with little sweat dots, they seemed equally stonily bemused noting the easy way she untied her shoes. Did they expect her old vertebrae to make crackling sounds when she bent over?

Any light jokes those two children chose to make from time to time, bore not the faintest bit of humor. She'd been forced by some moral imperative to allow the two old farts to move in with her and everything between them was stale, almost unhealthy.

"What are you looking at now?" The mother seal bark had its usual bite.

Freddie Pennyman never smiled at his mother. These days, every time he said anything it bordered on grim. This easily dovetailed with his round face which resembled a stout ham hock. "Nothing mom. It's just that I noticed how you reached down to untie your shoe laces on those bright green jogging shoes. Why don't you get some slip-on shoes? Then you won't have to worry about straining your back."

Rissa flipped one shoe then another over her shoulder. She heard the familiar 'plop' as they landed in the box she'd set up behind the couch. "Freddie let's always get our facts straight. And the first one is that it's your flimsy little discs that go out of whack with the slightest mention of work, not mine. I run circles around you most days. So drop the shoe talk. It puts me in a bad mood."

Freddie dipped his head and wrinkled his face. It was loose and white with furrowed lines splaying unevenly in every direction. Fortunately big sister Lanna picked that moment to rescue any shards of his pickled pride. "Mom, you just are writing the book on being haughty. Quite frankly, Freddie and I are getting tired of it. You might feel good right now at this moment, but remember you are 110 years old. When you most need us, we might not be there."

Rissa let out the best huffing sound she could muster. Suddenly she clapped loudly and sauntered over beside the couch. "Fine children you are. But you fit the mode so very well of the *BSL* bunch. Say it again to me what that means. I know how much it ticks you off."

Lanna easily matched the naughty huff her mother had conjured. "We are not Blood Sucking Leeches Rissa. We are your kids." Lanna paused and removed the earpiece. "The kids who have had the good-or bad luck- to have lived long enough to need their mother more than they have at any other point in their ridiculous lives."

Rissa jabbed a finger into her daughter's chest. "You'll be so lucky to make it to a hundred. Being a *Hundy* is a gift Lanna. We are hanging in well, as you see every day. But you guys," Rissa waved despairingly. "Well, I simply won't touch that subject again today. As you said, it makes me haughty."

Rissa arose and reached into the refrigerator for her water bottle. Two liters every day was her rule, even if sometimes her bladder seemed about to pop. It was all too easy to eye the two plump strangers moving around gingerly in the den. How long had they lived here, wrecking Rissa's perfect retirement abode? In the first five years they'd argued endlessly about the stupid politics that led to Lanna's and Freddie's retirement evisceration. "We weren't the only ones in our generation to be fooled Rissa. We believed the guys. After all, President Roy had a Ph.d in economics."

Rissa always went back to her stock in trade. "But I remember what the Silver Octopus said, and I believed *him*. Why weren't you paying attention when he warned about the dangers of privatizing your precious social security money? Now, you pay the price, and a big one. Living with your very old mother, and you hardly even offer to pay for any groceries."

The two always lost the argument, always had to retreat in silence and defeat. Their mother was dead correct. The difference between them was entirely a matter of funds. They had none. She had enough for general survival-and then some. Everyone knew that situations much like this were common all across America. This kind of discussion ranked in first place concerning the American social scene. It was what people talked about as another century was about to ripen and turn. The aging of America was an expected, known factor. But the generation gap between the very old, and merely elderly had taken an entirely different turn from anything predicted even fifty years ago.

As she galloped out toward the solitude of the darkened den, Lanna shouted: "By the way call up Vinnie. His mug lit up the screen."

Yeah, thought Rissa. Ole Vin. He might be just the ticket on this morning with nothing clearly set. She punched a number on her videophone. "Come now." It was all that was needed. Words tend to be excessive when a woman is dealing with some guy who is a shade over 112. Launch too many words at Vinnie Wasserby and you'd get that load plus more stories right back at you. His ageless tongue nicely matched the condition of the set of porcelain teeth he had put in when he was a young man of 88.

He ambled over from two blocks down the street. "You caught me on a slow day," he said through the lanai screen. Vinnie never came in through the front door. He knew right where Rissa would be. Out on the lanai hiding from those two kids of hers.

He poked at the screen door and that bamboo cane made the usual rattling sounds as he let it scratch across the stone floor. "Didja hear what happened over in Tampa?" Vinnie asked. His voice came out still manly enough, but the quirk was right there, making Rissa always think he was really a big toad in disguise.

"You mean about the rising tides? Yeah too much sea ice melting. Hard to believe it's really happening." Rissa had the hot water ready and poured a half cup over a packet of green spiced tea. Vinnie wrapped ten fingers around the ceramic cup, as if it might leap away any moment. "My beautiful beaches. Turning into mangrove swamps. Terrible. Just awful."

He sipped thoughtfully, keeping both eyes fixed upon her face. She knew something was strange even before he spoke. A poker face was one thing Vinnie Wasserby most surely lacked. When his brain was ticking full speed, those brows arched over and the crows' feet around his eyes took full wing. Thoughts telegraphed to perhaps give warning of something Vinnie had dreamed up.

"I got an idea, Rissa. It's not really about making money, although we would. Money never hurts, and at our age, who knows if we have enough?"

Rissa half chuckled, suspicious of Vinnie, but still had to ask: "What's this 'we' part. I heard you distinctly say, 'we.'

But Vinnie plowed on, ignoring the question. "My plan is partly about finding a good use for that old office building over in central Tampa. That recruiting agency moved out, maybe I told you. Now, it's just costing me taxes."

"And the second part of your plan? What's it about Vinnie?" Rissa took her hot chocolate cool. This made her plainly weird in the sight of her children, but if Vinnie had ever noticed, he never uttered a peep about it.

"The second part of the plan is to give us something fun to do. It might be really challenging, or it could turn out to be easy."

Rissa half smiled. "There it goes again, this time you said, 'us.' What do you want to involve me with at my age? We're both *Hundies* with change to spare. A plan?"

He nodded. "This plan has been kindling in my head for quite a spell. It gets our kids out of our houses. I've thought of a way fair and square to them and to us."

"Really?" Rissa stirred her cool chocolate drink twice. Her ancient heart beat twice in one space. Roaming free in her own house again. What a nice thought.

"And the kicker is," Vinnie leaned in close as if relaying a secret that affected world peace. "The kicker is that other *Hundies* are gonna like it too. Maybe so much, they'll follow our lead. We'll be like the pied pipers of our generation, blazing a new trail for other *Hundies* like us."

Rissa smiled and blinked twice. "Ok, I am intrigued with this master idea of yours. Do tell me more." She placed her full facial load directly on that grin that had plastered itself over every wrinkled line. What was it about this man's face that almost paralyzed her? She almost enjoyed watching the way those facial lines broke out. If his great oval face were a wheel, the age lines going in all directions would be spokes.

"It's best if you read it, see it, feel it. In my best decade, maybe you didn't know I could put together a killer proposal. Hope you agree with me that I've still got the touch." He reached into a vest pocket and pulled out a *digi-root*. "It's all right here. Pop it into the drive and tell me what you think."

She nodded and accepted the *digi-root*. Something in there was making Vinnie awfully animated. "And Rissa," he added not quite whispering, "This time I won't hurry you. Take your time. But know this: ole Vin ain't joking about the 'us' part. You and me forever." His smile was as soft as it could be. She'd never heard his voice come down to a whisper like that. Something must really be up this time.

At least two times over the next couple of days while Rissa watched the fantastic presentation on 3D Vision, both Freddie and Lanna intruded, and they vented their disapproval of this viewing with abnormal huffing and stomping around before leaving the room. Rissa didn't have to ask why. Vinnie wanted to start his idea off by going after the obvious, a fairly extensive review of the radical implementations of former President Alberto Senesco, the Silver Octopus. Of course, from his vision, the present generation of *Hundies* had taken flight. Without that vision, there was little doubt any of them would be alive today. To the *Hundies*, Senesco harbored the best qualities of ole George Washington and even Abe Lincoln.

Senesco was already an octogenarian when he was elected U.S. President, and his busy eight years as Chief Executive was a tremendous windfall of benefit for elderly Americans. With his leadership, Medicare rules had been greatly loosened. Expending every ounce of political capital the Silver Octopus opened the doors wide and allowed the older generation to partake of that fantastic revolution in advanced medicine and age reducing therapies. Senesco made it possible for healthy oldsters to apply for grants that paid for *telomere lengthening*, skin restoration, *cell ion flushing*, and *therapeutic cloning*. In the end, Medicare received the tab and the hundreds of billions that were adding up left those to pay for it, the shell-shocked younger generation. They didn't appreciate it one bit either. So they did what disaffected Americans always do, they voted in huge numbers with their hearts and their feet.

But while the glory days lasted oldsters found their health suddenly vibrant from such things as weekly injections of *enzymatic bonded reservatrol*. So for the last five years of Senesco's term at the helm, if one listened intently, there was the slow gurgle of millions of half clogged veins and arteries flushing clean. Although he died too soon, in every way, by every method available, President Senesco paved the way for a new class of people-*Hundies*-to spring into the American social scene. For the first time in human history, scientific theory had mushroomed into fact and practice. Even with long life, however, they were not a terribly happy bunch.

After eight years, those legions of enemies Senesco had made, eked out enough wins to force great changes in the halls of power. The cannon shots rang out-the reversal of insane and costly policies was at hand. The next sixteen years became known as the time of Chuckles I and Chuckles II. For the Seniors who had benefitted from Senesco, they watched the news with great sadness and some trepidation. The Chuckles tag team happily exploited the vast gulf of the American generation gap, siding with every younger taxpayer who didn't want to pay all those taxes. So came the decoupling of the Great Medical Revolution of the 21st Century.

The Chuckles' team promise was so simple; let those who want to pay, so pay for the benefits of longer life. Just don't make everything so damn free. So came about the long expected major restructuring of Social Security into a Private Corporation. The government would happily stand by and watch as the magic of private markets allowed every kind of fund to gradually work themselves into great profit. The idea was good, simple and it had every neat sound bite. The only problem-it didn't work.

So it was that the *BSL* generation came into creation-angry, exhausted from working until age 72, and cash-starved.

There was only one thing for them to do to avoid living on the streets or in cheap hovels. They could move in with their parents, the very same old folks who were not aging so fast, who were not dying in droves.

Of course Rissa knew of such facts, and she never tired of going over them again. But Freddie and Lanna had both supported the Chuckles twins in those days. Rissa always had the high moral ground of arguments that never ceased on this topic, and she pounded them over the head with it.

In the Pennyman home, as in millions of homes across America in this strange era, the generation gap was far more than an abstract concept; the generation gap *was* the daily strain of life.

And so Rissa had considered Vinnie's proposal. She marveled at his twin proposals on the *digi-root*. She leaned toward saying 'yes' to marrying him if only because it was the necessary thing before they could try and implement the business plan. It was indeed incredible in every respect. And he wanted Rissa to be a part of this undertaking? What would be the energy requirement for such an idea? Did she have enough? When she was ready, she met Vinnie on her lanai.

For five minutes she just stared his way and played with her cool hot chocolate cup. His strong nose seemed to have lengthened in this extreme old age. It harbored pits and pores that a gnat might fly through. But his eyes danced like a thieving leprechaun. At some unseen signal, he simply reached both hands across the table, and their fingers together formed a gentle arch. Inside this temple, all their hopes and dreams, unspoken, for words were not truly sufficient items for expression for them. "Thanks for saying, yes!" He smiled much too broadly.

"Well, we are off to the right start. My ex-husband never could read my thoughts."

She ran her fingers across the knobs of his over-prominent knuckles. She saw that the texture of her own hands almost matched his; rough and stiff. No amount of medical procedures she'd endured all those years ago could turn every part of her body into Cinderella. But for what had happened, she was grateful enough.

"So this plan of yours does involve us. I studied your idea carefully. And yes, it may be fun. But I don't care if we make money so much. What I most want to behold is the look on their faces. I cannot wait until we drop the bomb on *them*. Shall we practice in secret?"

They both laughed until tears streamed, two very happy *Hundies* who had the audacity to think they had any chance at all for a remake of the typical dysfunctional American family of the late 21st century.

It was simple enough for the four of them to be in the same room at the right time. Tina and Tim, Vinnie's progeny, rarely went anywhere on Wednesday night. They enjoyed the virtual church services their local church provided, and by eight were in the habit of munching on peaches or bananas to prepare for bedtime. Vinnie and Rissa easily sauntered into the den. When Vinnie put up three small picture frames in different places and sat down directly beside Rissa, it got the twins' attention.

Vinnie reached over and put Rissa's hands in his lap. Tina slipped on her bifocals and took a closer look at one of the pictures. Five seconds later, she shouted: "My God Dad, this is you and Rissa at a wedding parlor. Is that a ring you are giving to her?" Tina got her own question quickly answered when Vinnie held up Rissa's left hand.

"Yes, that's right Tina. Aren't you happy for us?"

She couldn't say a thing because her mouth remained splayed wide. Instead she groaned in her brother's direction. Tim moved over closer and took a seat. "Dad, why are you getting married at your age? You are fantastically old. What benefit is there for you?"

To that, Vinnie Wasserman arched his big head toward the ceiling and hooted. Then he laughed like some madman. "Benefit? My kids, what concern is it to you how I benefit from marrying this lovely woman? But just for kicks…how about the benefit of…my general happiness? How's that one?"

Tina and Tim gave a quizzical look to each other. It was not farfetched at all to assume they not only thought alike, but at the same speed. "And may we ask Dad, are you going to live here or over at her house?"

"Ah yes, my kids, the matter of housing. I had hoped you would bring that up. My darling Rissa and I want to live here!"

For many moments only the old grandfather clock near the kitchen made any sound. Then Tina ventured forth cautiously: "So you and Rissa will share your bedroom?"

"That's our business my daughter, but I'm quite sure we will want the entire house to roam around in. Some days can be hot, and I like to keep the air conditioner turned up too high as you know. We may want to strip down every day to our bare panties."

An instant scowl came over two 84 year-old faces. "That's an interesting thought Dad," said Tim, "but don't hold it too long. I'm sure Tina was just wondering how we can all co-exist very well all living here together."

"Well," said Vinnie with the drawl he did not possess, "We want to live here by ourselves kids. You two will have to move out the day Rissa moves in."

Tina reached for her pill box as Tim swooned, almost losing his balance in the chair. "And that will be when, Dad?"

"Next Monday," Vinnie's voice boomed. There was no wheezing component this time. Everyone knew this was words truly uttered.

On the way down the street, walking to Rissa's house, they held hands and laughed so hard each one was wiping the other's face with some Kleenex Vinnie had filched as he gloriously exited his doorway. They reached Rissa's front door and tiptoed past Ranger the collie, who could get too excited and go into a barking frenzy.

"Ok, this is your house so you quickly set up the picture frames just like I did at my house. The cameras in them are preset when the frame gets into a still, vertical position."

Rissa had to call Freddie and Lanna into the living room. Their mouths gaped when they saw the couple sitting almost in each other's laps and holding hands. "How do you like our photos?"

Neither person made a move to look. Had the twins already called ahead to warn of the impending tsunami?

"How do you like my ring, Lanna?" Rissa made her voice as curly and coy as the raspiness would allow.

The retort shot out: "You're too old for this mom. Shame on you Vinnie for using mom like this!"

Vininie glanced at Rissa and that was enough: They exploded in torrents and gales of laughter and almost bent double. When Rissa had recovered, she walked over to where her kids sat nervously, faces red but quizzical at such a comical sight as two people at least 110 years old having that good of a time. "I see you've been chatting on the phone already. It's ok my two beautiful, darling children. I won't ask you to move out."

"That's great mom, because we've been through this before so many times. If not for you, we'd be two old homeless people, right there on the streets with so many others."

"Of course we don't want that, do we Vinnie?"

He nodded in the manner of a kindly old man. "But Rissa, do tell them about the good chance they will have… of other people staying here with them."

Freddie almost knocked his milk cup off the armchair. "What people?"

"Well most likely, Tina and Tim, that's who. But it won't be a bother because you are all such good friends. It will be an easy transition. Same neighborhood even."

Lanna rubbed the loose skin on her triple turkey neck. "Don't get funny mom. This is not hilarious to me and Freddy. Give me one reason why Tina and Tim would even want to move in with us?"

"You want one reason Lanna? It's very simple. Shared expenses. There's no way you and Freddie boy here could come up with the rent fee. But if four of you put together your funds, you could meet the rent."

"You'd charge your own kids rent, knowing we can barely make ends meet now? How heartless of you Larissa Pennyman!"

"Call it payback my dears. I am well aware that you and Freddie boy have been in discussion with that separation attorney who comes on tv at the most annoying times during good movies. Separation attorneys are vile, slippery eels who call themselves lawyers? They fleece you guys so that you can legally separate your elderly *Hundy* parents from their assets." She had begun to wag the finger and the voice had risen to a high strain. "And you wonder why we call you *BSLs*? In case you've forgotten that stands for *Blood Sucking Leeches."* Rissa paused both for effect and to catch her breath. "Therefore in light of those developments and the fact you two have been sucking at teat since you were 72, the rent will be $1600 a month. If you can persuade Tina and Tim to live with you, that's only $400 a month each."

She turned sweetly to her new husband. "Is there anything you'd like to add, dear?"

Slowly he swung his head away from the two fuming faces just across the way. "Not a thing Rissa. You said it for both of us."

Outside the door Vinnie pecked his new bride on one lip. "Step one is done. You were magnificent. The example has been properly set. We take what the cameras collected in both our living rooms and let it tell the story on the world wide web. Now we officially say that *Old Farts Marriage Parlor* is off on the right foot."

Vinnie was able to be a whirling ball of energy for four hours at most before he fell out. He would be expected to doze for at least a couple of hours in the middle of the day. Then, he'd take a cup of coffee and zoom up to his study, where he put together the main parts of *Old Farts Marriage Parlor Online.*

In the last phase, his office building that sat in a small strip mall in the heart of Tampa, was convincingly converted to a wedding chapel. Four marriages could be performed simultaneously, along with four small wedding receptions. As for their office, the bosses, Mr. and Mrs. Vinnie Wasserby, commanded a good view of the main highway from the third floor. Vinnie made sure Rissa's desk was exactly like his, made from oak and planked sturdy enough to hold an elephant.

He was most happy the online business concept for his company was approved for the Second Tier of the WorldWide Internet Sphere. He hadn't expected First Tier Approval, but Third Tier Approval might have been a problem. Search engines usually didn't go down that far. People were much too impatient for good results in their queries.

It was easy enough to get part-time ministers lined up. All the ministers were *Hundies.* The people who worked to cook the meals for receptions, however, Vinnie wanted to be from the *BSL* generation. Almost all of them craved jobs, no matter how menial. Rissa happily signed off on this. She had gone to both Lanna and Freddie and told them they had a job if they wanted it, but they immediately turned her down with scorn. Rissa made a mental note: Up the rent another hundred at the beginning of the year.

Vinnie's first strike was to go to every person in or near his neighborhood, knock on their door, and give them an introductory *digi-root.* From this, they clearly got the idea. He asked them to talk about it to five others, to spread the word: *There is a way to get back your privacy, your life, and to do it with grace and be fair to boot. Do as we do! Do exactly as we do!* It's ok to copy in this case. Word spread fast and far. The *Old Farts Marriage Parlor* became a hit.

Rissa never got used to how hard and how fast her customers wanted to pump, not shake her hand after their marriage. Usually they asked the same question: "How did you think of the idea about the concealed cameras?" Every newly married *Hundy* couple told Rissa they were going to have the most *fun* setting this part up. It might be even more fun than getting married, almost everyone said. Rissa could see them rushing back to their home base, inserting the marriage photo into the special camera-studded frame, and practicing their lines on the unsuspecting *BSLs*. It was Vinnie's idea to sell those special frames right on the site. Customers loved it. They lapped them up.

Rissa was sure she'd never forget the newly minted couple, Gary and Rhoda Palmer. They were happy clients in that first fiery week of operation. Gary was a young *Hundy,* only 102, and his bald pate shone like a small lantern that day up on the marriage stage. Almost at once, he bounded down from the stage, just after kissing his bride, and sought out Rissa. "When I put the video on your site I want you to laugh as hard as I will when my four *BSLs* get informed of the new deal Lois and I are offering them. It's gonna be the same as what you and Vinnie did! We are gonna make some extra rent money, live in peace at my house, and watch with great interest as our kids actually have to do something in life besides leech off us. It's gonna be great! Thanks for saving us, Rissa. You and Vinnie both. Thanks for being brilliant!"

That was also Vinnie's idea: the suggestion to clients that when they have both records in the *digi-root*, safely collected from the frame cameras, they be sure to place them online. Vinnie wanted millions of people, especially *Hundies* considering marriage to their preferred soul mate, to see as many of these incidents as they could stand.

BSLs no doubt would react with distaste and disgust. At the opposite pole the *Hundy* generation would look on with great interest and no doubt pose the question to themselves: *Would this actually work for me? Could I solve my problem this way?*

As business shot forward it did not take long for Vinnie to shut the office door and motion for Rissa to take a chair. Vinnie seemed to lurch everywhere these days. Rissa noticed his back no longer could hold itself ramrod straight. He wiped his face with a handkerchief. "Rissa, it's great what we're doing out there. You can tell by so many happy faces." He held up a photo printed from an internet article. "This was taken up close by some person unknown to me. Take a close look at my face. What do you see?"

Rissa leaned forward and peered. "Nothing. It's you and me and one of our clients. Everybody is smiling."

"Right, and that is my point. That's the best smile my old face can muster. And while we are talking about my face may I describe it for you. A goat has a nicer looking face than I do."

Rissa wanted to grab his hands, but held back. She took another look. Her husband looked the part of a 112 year- old -man. The picture of course, could not capture his energy and vitality, but Vinnie Wasserman at 112 would have won no beauty awards. "So what's your point? You are not good at feeling sorry for yourself."

"My point is-no more pictures of myself in any form are to be taken if it can be helped. I'm not a good visual representative for us Rissa. But you on the other hand, are fine for the job. Just look at you."

She took the picture, held it with both hands. What she saw was four *Hundies* of which she clearly looked the best. Larissa kept her hair short and colored light brown. The facial restoration she'd opted for at her retirement had held up nicely. She had full lips, nice eyes and low grade wrinkles. She could stand erect. When she smiled, an honest, open personality revealed itself. She wore no eyeglasses.

"Ok Vinnie. I see your point. I'll be the one up front. You do what you do best. You can be the genius behind the scenes. But do show up at the marriages as much as you can. I do not want to take all the credit. Without you around people shovel far too much adoration my way. In the long run, it cannot be good for me."

About once a week some long limo pulled into the parking lot and nice young people assisted Rissa into a false, temporary world of comfort. She came to know the exact locations of the major radio and television stations because they all wanted to talk to her, to see her. They asked her questions, almost all of which she'd already hashed over many times in her 110 years of life. It was easy. It was fun. She felt her world turn upside down in a good way. How many 110 year- old-women could say that?

But of the magazine interviews, she insisted they be done in the office so Vinnie could participate. If there were no cameras, no pictures, he would sit in his fat, thick leather swivel chair, often put his feet right up on the table, and yak away like the astute businessman he was.

Hundy, You've Come a Long Way Baby! Scope on Seniors; AARP; these were a few of the major magazines and Blogs that came calling. Rissa greatly enjoyed hearing Vinnie preach the gospel as he saw it.

"I never did get the facial restoration therapy. Actually, they told me my face was too far gone at that time. But Rissa over there met the requirements and you see what it's done for her. I'd put her up against any 110-year-old woman in the world when it comes to good looks."

When they agreed to do the interview with the major editor from *Health and Fitness* they were asked at what age they underwent the telomere lengthening procedure. "I was just about to retire," said Vinnie as if in fond reminiscence. "President Senesco went on television and announced Congress had agreed to fund that procedure and about ten others for Seniors who qualified. To qualify you could not have major problems at the time, could never have had cancer at any time in your life, and your telomeres could not be at the nub. Not being a scientist or around science, I had to do some background on telomeres. I was shocked to find out that they were important aspects of our chromosomes and as chromosomes divided over a lifetime, parts of them got shorter and shorter. This turns out to be one of the great consequences of aging. Lucky for me, mine were not frayed down to the nub at the age of 68. So I got the procedure and it's helped my cells to stay nifty enough."

"Yeah I did that too," said Rissa. "But I think the cell ion flushing was so important. After one month of that I honestly felt like I could go climb a mountain. I've paid for it ever since the Chuckles twins took away the benefit."

The interviewer leaned back in his chair and lofted a softball question to Vinnie. "Do you think there will ever be another one like President Senesco?"

He shook his head boldly. "No never. He came onto the scene at the perfect time to get things done for us. And he was a six-foot-six grizzly when he wanted to be. He was smart enough to compromise if it got him most of his goal. Of course, it's no secret that after he left office the Chuckles Twins wrecked everything for those younger than us. The precious gift we have enjoyed in our old age will not be there for our children, grand-children and great-grandchildren. The desire to pay the taxes to fund the programs is not present in younger Americans anymore. If they make it to our age, it'll be mostly on their own money."

Vinnie had employed Ricky Beeson, his great-grandson to be marketing manager for *Old Farts Marriage Parlors* springing up all over Florida. "Vinnie I put the check into the account. Did you notice?"

"What check?" Vinnie had just blended a fresh grapefruit and a fat, juicy orange. He'd stopped eating lunch in favor of a giant slush drink.

"For the franchises in Florida. You've yet to tell me what to do about the requests in Alabama and Georgia. Don't wait too much longer. People are getting impatient."

Vinnie muttered something and gulped down a frozen draught. Ricky stood there looking at his PDA watch. "Oh and there's a gentleman from Japan who dropped by without an appointment. He's right outside."

Vinnie put the cold glass down. "Well Ricky, let him in. That's a long way to come and talk about....what does he want to talk about?"

"It's a surprise Vinnie. You are close to your next birthday and so this is my little present to you." Ricky glided over to the door, opened it and there stood Mr. Nakamura, from Tokyo, Japan.

He came in and bowed to both Ricky and to Vinnie. Vinnie recovered quickly from his shock by recalling that the Japanese were not people who liked to shake hands. So Vinnie made no quick moves in his guest's direction.

Ricky pulled a chair toward Mr. Nakamura and he sat down in modest fashion. "I am happy to be here," he said in acceptable English.

"We are happy to have you in Tampa." Vinnie moved a gnarled hand through the wisps left on his head. "What is the nature of your business with me, sir?"

"It's very simple Mr. Wasserby. I am betting that even in Japan there will be a demand for a service like this. We like your name. We like your concept. We don't think anything needs much change, even given our very different culture. Our problems with the generation gap for the extreme elderly are similar to yours. We would never illegally take what's yours and steal it. So I offer you something, for the right to use *Old Farts Marriage Parlor* just as it is in English, with the attending concept that has brought you so much success. I offer you this and if it's ok, we can get the papers done easily enough."

Mr. Nakamura pulled an envelope from his suit pocket and Ricky looked first. He whistled softly and showed it to Vinnie. Vinnie made a snorting sound and put the envelope down. "May I shake your hand Mr. Nakamura. You are going to make a lot of older people in Japan very happy."

For the next thirty minutes every face beamed in the upstairs office of Vinnie and Rissa Wasserby. When Rissa came in, Ricky had already escorted Mr. Nakamura back to his hotel. Vinnie was walking around in circles with half a glass of Irish whiskey bouncing around the edges. "I want to congratulate you Miss, uh Mrs. Washerbeeee. You've achieved something never before seen in the hishtory of mankind."

Rissa pulled him down violently into his seat. "Vinnie, you are about to trip all over yourself. Whiskey before your afternoon nap time? What's happened?" Her face was screwed up like a question mark as she sat down in her chair opposite his and she immaculately folded one leg over the other.

"It's nothing Rissa. Nothing much. Just that Mr. Nakamura from Tokyo stopped by and left something for us. Right there in that envelope. Take a look."

When Rissa did, she made sure to count the zeroes by poking fingers at them. Someone had come halfway across the world to give Vinnie and Rissa a gift of two million dollars.

Ricky Beeson had come up with the idea for a kind of Old Farts Re-Gathering. Newly minted couples, of course, very often posted the actual reality of the scenes in the living rooms and dens, when they broke the news to the *BSLs* living with them. People all over the world now watched the stunned expressions on the soon to be deposed leeches. And most couples had practiced their lines they were going to use. Some were so funny as to go viral on Tier One WorldNet.

So twice a month, selected couples came to a certain studio the company had leased, and everyone put their chairs in a circle. Rissa functioned as the host and tried to direct questions in an orderly way.

"I saw how you and Gloria handled giving the news, Johnny Sandifer. Would you tell us how things went that night?" Rissa wore a long, bright yellow silky dress. She made certain the ugly thrust of a new set of varicose veins in her upper calf were not made available for review.

Johnny Sandifer nodded in the direction of all the guests as he and Gloria held hands. "Yes, be glad to Rissa. We were particularly blessed in our house with a total of seven really ornery *BSLs*. Three of our kids lived with us, the oldest 86, the youngest 80. Four of their kids lived with their parents. The oldest one is still fifteen years away from retirement and is saving zero money for when that happens. I was spending all my social security and digging into what little funds I had left of an annuity to keep everyone in food and insurance. My natural blood pressure kept spiking from all this stress, and when I overheard the kids talking about the stroke I was certain to have, that's when I had enough. Gloria told me about your service, and we jumped at the chance. She had a similar problem and it was only logical. But it still took your example to get us over the hurdle of indecision."

Rissa nodded and smiled. "But it's what you told your *BSLs* that has our attention. What exactly did you and Gloria tell them?"

Gloria came on eagerly. Her round face and large eyes offset, hair plastered in pure silver. "We did this at both houses. Used the same lines. And as you saw from what the cameras recorded, we held perfectly straight faces when we told 'em."

Suddenly she stood up, wagging a finger at the *BSLs* she'd so enjoyed shocking that night. "Kids," I said, "You just do not understand the pent up sexual drive we have. We may be over a hundred but we still want sex. And Johnny and I don't feel comfortable doing it when so many people are around. We need more privacy." Then she smiled broadly. "And besides, after sex it takes a while for us to put our clothes back on. So we might watch tv for a couple of hours before hopping back in the sack again. How can we do this with all your eyeballs around?"

Everyone howled. How many *Hundies* watching on their computers were still doubled over from laughing so hard and maybe rolling around on the floor for a minute or two? Was it really that funny? Yes, thought Rissa, it really was.

After action-packed sessions like this one, it was common for the super high speed server to get hiccups. *Old Farts Marriage Parlor* was collecting its fans by the thousands, more and more every day. The *BSL* generation was beginning to pay attention. They must be seriously disturbed, annoyed, and petrified by now. What were they going to do if they kept on living and *Hundies* employed this kind of tactic against them?

At home just before bedtime, Vinnie stood before Rissa in the full glory of his favorite boxer shorts with no shirt. His pectoral muscles were flat as pancakes, and both nipples had partly disintegrated. "Rissa, we need to talk about a honeymoon. We can afford it. Call it a combination birthday gift for me and honeymoon present for you. Where would you like to go?"

She flicked off the television. She already knew the next line, knew exactly what Bogey would say. What was it about *Casablanca* that kept her coming back to this station that played extreme oldie movies?

"Paris. It's made for romance. I know you and me are not exactly into deep romance, but the feeling is what I'm after, not dreams that will never be."

Rissa's fine poetic answer went over his head. "Fine with me. I'll tell Ricky to make the arrangements. We'll go next week. Is that ok?"

Rissa very often thought of this encounter. She had no idea that Vinnie's eyes were failing him. The special contact lenses he had to wear after Lasik surgery was no different from millions of others. But even the second cornea he'd been given had played out. What he saw all too often was a blur of action and colors. He would never have admitted to Rissa that he could barely make out her features now. Vinnie might lie awake at night and try to recall his bride's pretty open face, but when he woke up the next morning his poor eyesight could not bring the package into any semblance of focus.

⌘ ⌘ ⌘

Rissa was not in the office when it happened. At the funeral and beyond, the nagging question persisted: Could she have possibly prevented this accident? Or was it simply Vinnie's fate he'd depart this way, not by cancer, or tumor or fatal heart attack, but by a simple fall down the stairs? Vinnie was in a lathered hurry that morning. No one was around to tell him to slow down and he'd forgotten to grab the walking cane from the basket beside his desk.

When he took the first step to go down the steps from his third floor office suite, his foot caught the edge of the concrete step. Instead of flipping back on his butt, his momentum made him tumble chin first. The severe concussion broke blood vessels thinned from so many years.

It was the stroke from the accident that killed him. Rissa could accept that easily enough. But she was surprised to discover that when his spirit left, so did her desire to make the business work. And besides, these days, her varicose veins were secretly killing her. Ricky Beeson could man the oars but she'd have to appoint a *Hundy* to take her and Vinnie's places. There was no shortage of people to consider. She'd get around to that when she could.

Some weeks later, Ricky brought a list of forty suitors to Rissa's attention. "After you finish your mourning," said Ricky, "you may want to take a look at this."

She took the list and smiled. At her age, seniors understood the unstated dictum that when one spouse left the scene, love of the departed was not something that got too much in the way of starting over. It wasn't like the movies such as Scarlett O'Hara was forced to do. If you were a *Hundy*, time was a luxury item. You picked the best man for the job and got on with life. But this wasn't going to happen.

Rissa was not going to start over with another man. In truth of fact, it was a tremendous fluke she'd even done it with Vinnie. If not for his ineffable optimism, she would just have gone on and let those kids wear her down. She would've had the expected stroke or heart attack and they would have finally taken over.

This was Vinnie's old house, now her own, and she enjoyed tromping around everywhere, taking in the occasional whiffs of his physical presence that existed part in pure memory, and maybe, part in invisible essence. Old rocking chairs weren't moving on their own just yet, but sometimes when she sat in his favorite chair sipping on her cool hot chocolate, she saw little swirls in the liquid ripple and wave for no good reason. It made her smile and remember.

This would be enough for Larissa Pennyman. It would be enough to last a lifetime.

THE END

Shall we endure another Korean conflict? Let's hope not. In the lives of our characters here, two from North Korea, one from South Korea, and one from America, are revealed personal disasters of the first magnitude. And that's just from war on its first day....

Play Toys

Sergeant Young- gun Lee didn't want to be here. He found nothing virtuous about this place, and his rank and 'exalted' position promoted not a whit of honor within himself.

The stark barren landscape exactly matched the negative intake of energy that washed into his soul every single day. Going outside on the back side of the mountain was a necessary if hazardous exercise. Even if he had the permission of his Colonel to make the five kilometer jog from time to time, the cadre of special guards out there made it an unpleasant thing. Young-gun full well knew he was in the sights of their machine guns every step of the way. But if he did not get out of the guts of his mountain from time to time, he was afraid he'd go mad. And the shape of his lungs from breathing in so much granite dust-that was another issue entirely.

Young- gun had already been through an ordeal the first time he served his country. He'd seen far too much nastiness, participated through orders for a lifetime of injustice against simple, common people. The nameless cadre of local leaders had grabbed him again after he'd been free from serving the state. It had only been eight months and there was little he could do. To refuse them meant certain death. They'd promised him something 'extra.' This was it.

After new training with the biggest guns his country possessed, he graded out as 'excellent.' They all applauded him the last day of that special camp. When the commandant pinned the award on his lapel and uttered the words, "*front line*", Young -gun's smile eroded. The last time, he'd been lucky. He was based along the border with China. Idiot defectors never shot at you. But on the DMZ, it could be a different matter. But wasn't an assignment in the bowels of a fortress, tending to one of the 3,000 monster guns deterring war against the South, an honor and a blessing? They all said so.

After months of living in the guts of chewed out granite, his best friend had become *Little Dragon Tooth*. Young- gun's position was the soldier furthest forward in the bunker. He was the official *shell loader* of the five man crew. The others did their jobs behind him, on the other side of the conveyor belt. He could hear them, yell back at them, but only see their shadows. Anyway, they would never be *chingoos* with him. They were from the coast, fishermen before and now soldiers of a kind. And they were at least five years younger than Young- gun. Age was the very first arena of consideration as males sized up one another in Korean society. So at mealtime, the members of his squad might nod his way, but never actually said much to Young-gun.

It made for lonely times so he easily turned to *Little Dragon Tooth*. He spoke to the huge gun, caressed it like a lover. And the 185mm howitzer gun seemed to hang on every word. Such loyalty provoked Young- gun to polish the great bronze barrel twice each week, and he knew the commanding officer of the squadron approved. Within the bowels of the mountain that directly flanked the great uncertain zone where a desperate peace had become standard for the last sixty-seven years, there were no big secrets.

Their routine was to drill realistically twice a week. The scenario was always the same. The dogs of the South had teamed up with United States forces, and had begun the attack. If the gun was ever used, Young- gun's main job would be to insure the old shell had properly expelled itself, and the new shell was lined up perfectly so as to pop into the great breech of the 185mm howitzer. The timing of the gun firing and the opening of the outside door was crucial. The special gun was designed to quickly roll out on a rail line once it was loaded. Then the outside corridor opened suddenly, hopefully too quickly for the enemy to know precisely where to attack. *Little Dragon Tooth* would fire, sending its incendiary shell propelled by a special booster agent, somewhere out toward the great city of Seoul. The concept was to play a jack-in-the-box game. Shoot as many shells as possible for as long as possible. They were never told about the end game. But there could only be one result-certain destruction. His own death for the sake of the State was something only in the back of his mind. It could never advance very far. The simple fact was this-nobody, not a person alive, truly cared if Young-gun lived one more day on this cruel earth.

Young- gun felt it was his duty to know everything about his job, it was all he had, and he was pleased to discover that Colonel Bae was a teacher at heart. He recalled one of his first questions to the short, quick-moving chief officer of this bunker. "Why Colonel," asked Young gun, "Don't we load more than one shell into the breech at a time?" The Colonel smiled politely at his Sergeant and draped an arm over the surprised soldier's shoulder. "We used to do it that way Sergeant. But the eyes in the skies keep getting better. We can't keep the gun outside for more than ten seconds. They will coordinate our exact position. So, there's only one shell required."

But most of the time he spent with *Little Dragon Tooth* was a massive waste of hours. He was required to be on duty, and yet that meant, if no drills were scheduled, to simply sit in one place, in his chair beside the gun, and daydream. He looked forward with unusual gusto to the times when he was allowed to bring the enormous barrel to level twice a week.

How many times had he inspected it in the short time he'd been stationed here? Sixty? Seventy times?

He preferred not to dwell so much on his former life. It was, by any account, a colossal failure. The one thing he could claim, despite his wife leaving him, despite his father and brother dying from starvation, was that he'd been a good and faithful soldier. Even so, he'd never really enjoyed being a nameless cadre serving the Kim dynasty. But also there was nothing elegant about going back and living again in the impoverished Central Province region. In his childhood he recalled intermittent groves of trees. Now the barren brown earth offered the feeblest of nutrition to any seed that fell there.

On the edge of that home land, spines of small mountains rose up and it was there Young- gun once roamed. He knew of every crack, crevice and ravine where there might be ginseng root. So he was able to live well enough when times became impossible for others. So many around him died and were simply dumped into unmarked graves by the soldiers unlucky enough to draw that sickening duty. Young-gun could never decide if he was luckier or smarter than the dead ones. In the end, it was an abstract question. He was stuck here for the forseeable future. He could only complain to *Little Dragon Tooth.*

Certainly the young man felt shards of guilt that rippled sometimes across his perpetually tired mind. If he had been able to share some of the money he'd gained with his father and brother, they may have lived. But in his black caution, he trusted no one. If they ever gave in to the soldiers' tricks about gathering information that implicated anyone in an illicit activity, they would have come for him and dragged him off to a nameless grave. What was left of family ties in North Korea were the sickest of rotting cords. Trust had long since become an unredeemable commodity.

He'd been at this new domain, *Black Dragon Fortress 3*, for six long months. He had ceased to marvel at the engineering ingenuity that had created these hell holes. These small mountains held solid granite cores. Yet machines had bored right through. Like true clever patriots, the engineers always began to dig from kilometers away. This had the advantage of keeping the Southern spies guessing about the ultimate location of the end of the bore. The huge long range cannons were hauled in on the darkest, stormiest nights as the tunnels were being finished. But lately, a new generation of howitzers had come online. The army brass needed smarter, loyal, ever fearless soldiers to man them.

Young- gun relished drill time if only for the waves of praise his good work generated. Colonel Bae adored detail and in this pissy boredom, it was something Young-gun could generate. To the others in the crew, Colonel Bae often raised his hands to their faces, as if to slap them hard. But in actual fact, he never touched them. His words, however, cut deep. Thus, they kept together night and day, avoiding both Colonel Bae and Young-gun as much as possible.

One day at the end of another successful exercise, Colonel Bae came right up to Young-gun as the squad stood at attention in the dim red light. "Do you know where that last shell was directed?" Young gun had no map in his head, but he knew the answer. "Yes sir, I know! It's going to hit close to the main train station in the downtown area of Seoul!" Colonel Bae smiled and simply said, "Yes! You recall that from your initial study some months ago. Impressive, Sergeant."

If the Colonel ever truly contemplated the carnage and destruction of Korea's greatest city, he never showed an inkling of regret in these drills. But sometimes the odd thought washed over Young- gun. What would it be like to be on the receiving end of one of *Little Dragon Tooth's* fire shells? Young- gun had no concept of what Seoul was like. He'd only been to Pyongyang twice in his entire life. It was a city, and he despised cities. Even so, how many people might die if even one of these shells exploded, washing great waves of fire and sound through the valleys of streets between the huge buildings he'd been told stretched for endless kilometers, a city without end?

So another toll of weeks passed, and it was after a routine polishing, Young- gun was told by Colonel Bae, they would practice rolling the gun out on its rail and conduct an actual firing sequence. This was something new. Up to now, the wheeling out had only been simulated. Young-gun sucked up his oats and out popped the question: "Why," he asked, "Are we choosing this time to wheel it out? Shouldn't we practice this more often?" The baleful glare lasted only a moment and once again Young-gun knew for certain he was the Colonel's pet favorite in this hellish place. "Because tonight the weather will be terrible, and who knows about the future. We are here for a good reason aren't we?"

The day after the successful drill, Colonel Bae strode up to Young gun again. He told him to level the barrel. Inspection time again. Most unusual and out of place. Colonel Bae used his flashlight and patted the back of his hand all along the barrel. He mumbled the word, "sheen" several times but never looked directly at the curious Sergeant. "Everything once again seems in order Sergeant, Good job."

Young gun snapped his boots together and saluted. "Thank you sir." Colonel Bae turned, but then wheeled back suddenly. "By the way, when is your scheduled leave?"

"Sir, if I work for six weeks, I am guaranteed one week's leave."

The Colonel nodded slightly. He already knew such a thing of course and it was reflected in his Sergeant's quizzical look. "I do look forward to helping you enjoy your countryside refreshments, but there could be a hold this time." The Colonel should have stopped, but he wanted them all to know something was up. "Some kind of National security problem I'm told. I don't know much. It may be nothing."

Young gun gulped a liter of air all at once. "National..security..?"

Now the Colonel stood ramrod straight and met his Sergeant's gaze straightway. "Yes. It may turn out to be nothing at all. Right now, my very good sources are not worried. So if they aren't worried, neither am I. But just to tell you."

But Colonel Bae knew otherwise. He wasn't about to pulverize a good soldier's morale too soon. To set the stage for such a great disappointment seemed sensible. Besides, to hurt one Sergeant's feelings was nothing in light of the true gravity of a bad situation getting steadily worse by the hour.

Eagerly, Colonel Bae made his way back to his secure office. It was small but well equipped with the essentials of communication. And right now, he was desperate to know one certain thing. A message should be coming to him from Pyongyang any minute now. His old friend and colleague Colonel Park was well placed in the security apparatus of a special division of army command. He'd called earlier, and they'd exchanged pleasantries. Then, very casually, Colonel Park had told his peer that from now on, all communication between them should be in the special code they'd cooked up a few years ago. Back then, it had been like a joke. But it was no joke now. Colonel Park might be tucked away in some office, but given his sensitive post, the sharing of classified knowledge of any kind, even with Colonel Bae, could mean his neck. They were executing officers for much less these days.

Colonel Bae was missing the tiresome but safe times of Kim Jong-il. The inexperience of the younger son was a common joke in officer circles, whispered quietly and with few smiles. But in his time as Dear Leader, he was still letting both the South and the Chinese push him around. While the North's people went from one ruinous crop failure to another, Kim launched his precious missiles and threatened to rain fire on the South with nuclear bombs. And what was the result? Laughter. The world laughed at the antics of the "Little Penguin." Cultural values very dangerous to ignorant people were seeping in from everywhere. Rice from every kind of do-good society from abroad, fed too many hungry people. One of those boiling bubbles from this dangerous caldron must have escaped the pot and exploded, augmenting a dangerous situation. But how dangerous was it?

Expect to hear from me again at 1600 hours. The words were encoded from Colonel Park in that special way the two had dreamed up in those days when they were raw, dumb, young officers. Well maybe not so dumb after all. Colonel Bae tapped his fingers on the formica desk where he'd compiled countless reports for the regime. Colonel Bae's eyes kept coming back to the one solid lead, his friend Colonel Park had known about. Code 44 was in affect. Nothing like a code 44 had ever come across his desk. It stood for *Imminent Threat to the State.*

The Colonel removed his officer cap. It was always hot in here. No matter how he tried, he could never get anyone to make the ventilation system work as it should. Thus his scalp these days was producing atrocious amount of white flakes. And the whole mess itched as if an army of fleas had taken control of his head skin.

He glanced at the few framed photos occupying a bookshelf. It was best for officers to be married so as to get ahead quickly, and if Han-rim Bae had ever made a mistake it was to marry his present wife. She had quickly become an embittered officer's wife, wanting, always wanting things. At first he spent his entire salary on her whims. At least she'd produced no children, and he knew, from his own loins no children would spring forth with this woman. But at the photo of him with his two brothers and mother, Han-rim smiled. It was a picture of the one time he'd been on a ship. His family had never fished and it would have been strange to love the sea. And Han-rim always thought the ships of his country were no better than fat, quacking ducks, easy pickings for advanced technology. But of this massive artillery piece, Colonel Bae knew it struck fear and terror into the heart of the enemy. They had little defense for it and no stomach at all for what it could do. They knew it. But did we have the will to actually turn it loose? He hoped he'd never encounter that time, hoped he would be long retired, and someone else would have the grave responsibility to actually fire it.

A computer clicked and Bae knew that Colonel Park now was using a very secured email to transmit messages. It was back and forth to the old notebook for decryptions of the old made-up code he would never have recalled otherwise. His hands visibly trembled.

...Fools and asses...Kim was almost killed. He's bled a lot and went unconscious. He was hauled in a stretcher past this very office about twenty minutes ago. But here is our fate old friend. Some kind of secret plan has been implemented. From some kind of automatic pilot protocol regarding Kim. Some nameless ally

of Kim has cleverly begun the cascade of events. One of our border units is at this very moment engaging elements of the South's forward army brigades. It's supposed to not escalate too much since it's in a remote part of the DMZ. But the South went into full mobilization at once. We have no one in charge of the facts! Pray to something Han-rim! Even if it's to the old gods with cracked and obscene faces! Pray hard we don't have to issue further orders. In fact, no one, nobody I know, is in charge. And we are risking battle!

Han -rim stared at the screen and nodded at nothing. An assassin? More than one? Kim had fought back hard apparently, preventing his certain death this day. Colonel Park seemed in shock. What he didn't know was perfectly amazing. Han-rim groaned within himself. Was Kim really dying?

Colonel Bae could not know it, but at the exact moment of these tortuous thoughts, the monitors at Central Command in the Defense Complex of Seoul, screamed a warning: *Approaching helicopters coming at full speed, already in violation of DMZ.* The generals quickly met and in a few seconds had given the command: These were the reinforcements for the brigade that had incredulously crossed into South Korean territory after a brief but terrific shelling. It would be the call of the South Korean government to defend their own land. But American forces were standing by in full support. After the last election in America, the coup of the right wing was complete. Now the prize of eliminating the so-called truce between North and South was within reach. If only the North Koreans would keep coming. Let them try was the fervent hope of America's right wing leaders. This could be the kind of war America needed to get back some tarnished prestige. It was the secret belief of the American President. American armor and South Korean fervor! It would be an unbeatable combination!

And the South had prepared for this very moment for so very long. There was no way their leaders or generals were going to interpret what the North Koreans were doing now as a minor border incursion. What was the reason to spend so much money on giant muscles if they were never flexed?

By the time Colonel Bae deciphered the next encoded message, he wondered why his brain felt numb, even if the rest of his body percolated with electric energy. Was he surprised that same nameless numbskull lackey of Kim's had ordered four of the best attack helicopters the North possessed to support the unit that had incurred into Southern territory? He wondered how he would feel when the news was delivered in a few minutes of the imminent shooting down of his helicopters and the subsequent death of such highly trained pilots. He was trying to come to grips with the fact that *he full well knew* the North was starting this new war and it was all because The Young Stud, the Dear Leader, totally lacked the ability and balls of his Daddy and Grandfather. He'd masterminded some numbskull plan in the event of his assassination. This apparently, was the plan.

... Our story will be that it was Kim who gave the orders for this attack, fearing he may be dying. You can guess at this rationale my old friend. If it is said that it was an assassin from the South who managed to kill Kim, the waves of national patriotism to fight can be generated. There's nothing like a little fighting to promote national unity! And so for us, you and me and all the others like us, the question is this: Might we disobey our direct orders if we have been attacked, even if we stupidly provoked it? No or yes, you may search your own heart. And let's hope our superiors don't fire all 13,000 guns at the same time. I am grateful that the nuclear bombs are so well hidden. I doubt the lackeys in charge know how to get them. So we will shoot at them some with our guns and they will shoot back with theirs. We cannot go too far

into the South. They'll slaughter us. Colonel Park knew what the results of the final scorecard would be. Colonel Bae closed his eyes, made his mind go blank. He knew too.

⌘ ⌘ ⌘

Seth Sykes had never met his aunt in the flesh. They'd talked a few times by Skype, and Seth had been impressed with the firm way she held her husband's hand. And when Sarah Shim's eyes met her husband's, Seth remembered telling his mother: "Uncle Ray had to go a long way to meet his soul mate. Even so, I am happy for him."

But now, Seth was border-line in shock. From the moment he walked into to the posh apartment in downtown Seoul, Sarah Shim had been a study in extreme grief. Seth held her hands, wiped her face. She hugged him constantly alternating in two languages, the words unclear, but not their visceral meaning. Now he knew why he'd been escorted from the airport by someone he'd never met and who could speak little English. Neither this person or anyone else had texted or called Seth to tell him the incredibly bad news: While Seth was in transit to South Korea, Uncle Ray had keeled over in his study and passed on.

Sarah needed Seth more than he could know. Her own family had never approved her marriage to the American fellow, even if he'd been successful by any standard. She had almost nobody to talk to, no one to send her grief and feelings toward, and for two hours now Seth had endured. At last a bit of clarity: "Thank you nephew. You helped me so much just now. We have a lot to do."

Seth had to eke out the essence of what had just happened. Apparently, Uncle Ray, one week out of the hospital from a battery of heart tests, had simply collapsed, and taken his last breath.

Uncle Ray's first stroke had been a major surprise. It was his heart that was weak everyone thought. When Gloria Sykes, Seth's mother, asked if he'd like to go to Seoul, Korea and spend time with Uncle Ray as he rehabbed, Seth jumped at the opportunity. His studies were going nowhere. He felt continually jumbled, confused about life. To go somewhere exotic might be the best medicine just now. But he'd walked into a beehive. And he had no idea what to say, how to behave.

⌘ ⌘ ⌘

Young- gun and his mates tumbled from their bed cots at the inglorious hour of 5 a.m. They dressed quickly and were assembled in a tight line when Colonel Bae strode forward. His boots shone, even the star on his cap seemed to glow in the awkward light from the generators. He had a mountain walking cane with him and he tapped it on thousands of tiny granite pebbles. "It seems comrades" he said slowly, his eyes colliding with five other sets, "that we have been attacked. Our helicopters have been shot down. We retaliated by attacking with our artillery along the coastline in the northwest sector. The enemy not only tried to knock out our artillery there, but they have lobbed rocket salvos not 5 km from this very position." His stern eyes made contrast to the charges who stood before him. Some mouths refused to close, stayed agape with astonishment. A few faces turned down, casting morose stares at shadows they would never meet.

"I am expecting an order any moment from the High Command to commence firing. This is no drill. We may all die today, but you will have no time to think on it. Just do your duty. It's all we can do. Now, get to your posts."

⌘ ⌘ ⌘

Of course Sarah Shim didn't sleep again, not even a few winks. She regarded herself in the mirror: Who was this wreck of a person? What her eyes beheld bore the face of some absurd demon, red, wrinkled and vile. And what was she asking of her nephew-in-law, this quiet young man she barely knew? Yet she had little choice and in fact knew now his appearance here was a godsend. She understood nothing about how dead bodies might be transported back to the United States. Cremation for the Christian-leaning Ray Sykes was not an option. At least Seth could speak the proper technical English to the authorities, English that would be over her head.

She glanced at her watch. She hated to rouse Seth this early, but they had to get on the subway and go for quite a distance. Even if they had to be the first patrons on the train, it would be better that way. No amount of make-up could make her look beautiful again, of that she was convinced. But maybe not too many people would care to risk a glance her way. That was what she hoped.

Seth had never been outside Aunt Sarah's apartment. Mostly, he had stared out the window at the panorama of the city. Uncle Ray had bought a luxurious suite downtown. He'd become a truly urban animal and this greatly pleased Aunt Sarah. But all this verticality made Seth feel lost. His land was Alabama, flat, watery and coastal.

Seth saw the maze of streets, and he knew about Seoul's intricate subway system. As of yet, he'd not taken a step on the first train. Certainly in Mobile, Alabama, no such thing existed. Seth had never been transported anywhere in a train of any kind. His was a world of automobiles.

Aunt Sarah had roused him muttering something like, "*Bali, bali!*" Just before he had raised himself up on the sleeper sofa she mumbled, "Hurry!" So without breakfast and zero caffeine in his veins, Aunt Sarah herded her nephew to the already busy crosswalk. There was a bakery across the way and the coffee and bagels made him feel reasonably human. The jet lag had combined with his poor sleep on the sleeper sofa. Nothing in his brain seemed well connected.

Already at 6:30 a.m. the cars honked and cursed at one another. Wild herds competed for precious space so to make the next turn of signal lights. Seth silently berated himself for doing no homework on his destination city. He'd counted on Uncle Ray to answer questions.

The odd pair walked briskly down a sidewalk. Aunt Sarah had jammed her arm into a crook of his elbow, and Seth walked at top speed so as not to be dragged along. A cool May breeze sent a small army of goosebumps down each arm. The sun lay behind a thin layer of clouds. And then, Seth heard something like a sonic boom. At once a layer of thick red, like cherry jello, rammed itself across the sky around and above him.

When fullness of the explosion surrounded Seth Sykes, he uplifted, as would some tectonic plate placed suddenly under maximum stress. At his apogee, he flailed both arms as his face turned first skyward, and then to its side. But his arms were not wings. He sailed downward from perhaps ten feet, bashing his head first on a car fender, then on the sidewalk embankment. Vaguely, his eyes tried to match the screams with Aunt Sarah's general placement. Hearts were weak in his clan, and when he spied Sarah Shim, his own heart skipped too many beats. Her hair was on fire. Little balls of pure fire puffed up here and there for no good reason, and she hopscotched between puffballs, her voice stuck permanently in full scream mode.

Seth wanted to think viciously, to get up and take action as any pure bred American male would, but instead he simply sat there like some full prop against a car fender. Seth pondered something he could not rid his mind of, that being, the surreal juxtaposition of sounds of fire and thunder against the highly refined screaming of thousands of shocked citizens. Even if his mind had dulled to nothing, two eagle eyes tried their best to transmit data. In this video game manipulated by a genius webmaster, bodies ran to and fro, some burning and twisting in throes of pure agony; car engines exploded; tall buildings swayed though none had yet crumpled into full ruin. In his own lap, a strange red liquid congregated, and when he swiped a hand across the vast irritation on his scalp, the hand turned bright red as well.

Seth sat unmoving, like a dumb ungulate and vaguely he wondered where his aunt had gone. She was screaming right over there by that doorway just a few seconds ago. But he was dazed, lame with inaction, and perhaps in those moments some people must have seen her, hauled her away from this sea of fire. He hoped she would live.

If only he knew more. He tried to form questions, first the easy one. What city was this? He knew it was Seoul, in South Korea. Who was attacking them? He studied the matter by cocking his head just as another explosion sent more cherry jello sliding down a nearby avenue. As to who this sorry enemy might be, his mind remained curiously void.

⌘ ⌘ ⌘

Colonel Bae felt his mountain shudder. Already his battery had fired three times. So far no direct hits by enemy fire on their position. His face registered further surprise when the email box beeped. This time there was no code-the message had launched itself in the full glory of the Korean language.

It has happened. What everyone feared internally and no one dared mention. The Great Miscalculation. And the leader can't lead. He'll be lucky if he lives. Whoever is in charge must be aghast about the enemy's vigorous response. What choice did we have?

Then the mountain heaved and groaned and in the next instant Colonel Bae heard the familiar blast come from what his Sergeant had dubbed *Little Dragon Tooth.* Good, thought Han-rim. That brave little sap of a sergeant got off his sixth salvo. He's setting the best example for the rest of them. He's not afraid to do his duty. As for me...what am I going to tell the men if I get the chance...when the enemy hits us directly and they silence our gun? How much longer will that take? Then he opened a drawer and put on his gas mask. The air would not be fit for breathing much longer. Pebbles were already flying around the room. Granite dust could shut lungs down even faster than poison gas if there was enough of it. All too soon, that would be the case.

⌘ ⌘ ⌘

Seth Sykes managed to stagger to his feet. Aunt Sarah, the only person he knew in this limited world, had been removed. In fact, now no one roamed these streets. New explosions farther down the street made heavy and short rings in his ears. Seth saw fire leap and flash. He felt the roils of heat every time another shell landed. It was as if some oven turned itself off and on, and he had no knowledge of how to get away.

Seth meandered in the general direction of Royal Mast Towers. At least he recalled the English name of Aunt Sarah's apartment tower. He moved like some zombie in a Stephen King thriller. Something seemed wrong with his eyes. The illusion he fought was that his brain told him he walked in a straight line, but he kept bumping into debris on the street that seemed to be *over there.*

Then a tremendous whoosh overhead. A sea of fire splashed red and orange and the tops of two large buildings fell into the street. The blast again knocked Seth backwards. He found himself once again resting almost on the hood of the car he'd just left. And his shirt smoked. He ripped it off just as the flames devoured it.

⌘ ⌘ ⌘

Young- gun could see just well enough to know that the robotic arm that picked up the shell for insertion, still functioned well. His gas mask filtered the worst of the bad air, but between the gas fumes the great gun emitted, and the massive swirls of rock dust generated from the mountain being pounded by enemy guns, his breathing dragged.

Then it happened, the moment of dread. *Little Dragon Tooth* had just fired again, for the tenth time. As it rocked in reverse on the rails, sliding backward into the cavern for reloading, a blast hit the mountain side very near the outer steel door. Young- gun crumbled instantly onto the rocky cavern floor. He crashed on his right side, ribs striking first, and when he stood up, his hand instinctively covered the injury. But a smell had wafted through his gas mask, one that made him quiver in fear. He made sure the outer hatch had closed as well as it could, then he pressed an icon on the digital display to lower the gun barrel to level.

Instantly shouts and screams came from the back. "What are you doing?" The young stupid turks shouted in unison. Young- gun had just enough time to inspect the end of the barrel, and then they were on him. It didn't hurt so much when they kicked him in the face. But on those ribs that must be cracked, he groaned until tears streamed down his face. The idiots! If they fired the gun again, not only would *Little Dragon Tooth* die, they all would.

⁂

Sarah Shim walked through the demolished office door where nameless compatriots had dragged her, until they had beat the fire from her hair. Now her disastrous hair matched her face. But Seth was nowhere to be found. Had the explosion that almost killed her, blown him to bits? The others tried to hold her back, but she begged, "Just for a short time I need to find my nephew. He must be so lost."

Seth had found a corner he liked. He sat down there, wondering about everything. Who wanted to kill him like this? And who was that calling his name? He poked his face around the building corner and there was Aunt what's-her-name running to embrace him. As she released him another savage barrage a few blocks away sent a van sprawling high into the air. Seth watched, as if in slow motion, as it crashed onto the roof of some unlucky phone store. Another fire shot flames high into the vastly polluted air. Seth wondered again about this war: Who hated them this much?

⁂

Colonel Bae intervened. His ultra- patriotic crew was apparently under the assumption that Sergeant Lee was practicing sabotage on their gun. Why else would he lower it without approval?

"Get your hands off this man!" His voice boomed, even as the mountain shook again and loads of rocky pebbles fell on their dusty brown caps. "Speak Sergeant. Tell me and your comrades why you lowered our gun."

Young- gun collected his breath and spit gobs of blood and mountain dirt at the feet of the idiot crew. "Yes sir. I will. Just as the gun was pulling back, after that last huge explosion, I smelled something unmistakable. Even through the gas mask I smelled it."

"Smelled what Sergeant? Tell us now." His comrades stepped backward sensing shame in the air.

"A part of the gun barrel got soldered to another part. Perhaps three or four centimeters of the alloy melted. The barrel must be ruined for shooting our shells. It's my guess, but you can look for yourself. Right at the tip end. Something the enemy had fired, a pulse of fire or heat, jolted our gun just before it could be pulled back. If we had fired the gun again in this condition..well...it would most likely…."

Colonel Bae glared with disdain at the four cowering soldiers. They had huddled together as if to make some kind of plan. Colonel Bae ran fast as a mongoose toward the barrel's end. He shone the flashlight urgently and came back nodding, offering his hand to Young gun. "It is as you say, Sergeant, maybe even worse. The barrel is now uselessly fused."

For many moments six men stood in silence, listening intently while the mountain around them disintegrated. Theirs was not the only gun lodged in this mountain. Many others were too. And in each cavern a theater exactly like this was playing out.

"Soldiers," said Colonel Bae whose voice stayed just above the thunder almost hurting their ears now. "We cannot evacuate. In a war time situation like this, our own commandos seal off the back exit. You can guess why. Of course, we can't go out the front door either. We'd be instantly killed by the enemy." He cleared his throat and fought back shivers of anger that would have made his face red and threatening. No, he must somehow be a father figure just now to these men who were so young and unknowing. "I will release weapons to everyone here. If we get the chance, we fight. If there's a cave-in from continued bombs and rockets, well...each man is then on his own." He paused, put both arms behind him. "I'm sorry for this. Someone has miscalculated. We must live or die with the results."

⌘ ⌘ ⌘

Sarah Shim herded a thoroughly disconnected Seth through city streets abloom with the colors of Hell. When she got to Royal Mast Towers, the elevators refused to function. They trudged up five flights of stairs and she manually opened the door to her apartment. "Lay down Seth. Let me get you some water."

When she tried to hand him the glass Sarah saw he'd found two pencils on top of a desk. He had them in his hands, one pencil fighting the other. From his mouth came little puffing sounds, as if Seth had reverted back to a small child. One pencil knocked the other one away. "These are my new play toys Aunt Sarah. I left my good ones back in Alabama." Something in his re-wired brain created this calm delirium. He was now somewhat comfortable, sitting on her bed, imagining pencils for toys.

Sarah Shim gave him the water and watched in amazement. She transmitted thoughts directly his way: *Play with your toys now Seth. And our menfolk and the enemy's menfolk are playing with theirs right now too. How they play with their play toys! What pleasure they take performing a duty to shoot, bomb and destroy things precious to us!*

Seth saw the scissors in her hand and seemed to wonder about them for only a moment. When all the hair was gone, she looked at herself and cackled softly. Compared to the thousands of dead people right out there on the streets, it wasn't so bad.

Seth smiled at his bald aunt only once and fell back into the silky sheet. Aunt Sarah had given him the strongest pill she could find in her collection, and she stroked the nasty cut that still tried to bleed. She had his bowling ball head wrapped up as well as she could, and gently, she moved it into the depths of the cotton pillow.

For Seth Sykes it was a proper time for dreams. Not that they made sense in this odd morning time rest period. Even so, he curled up and drifted somewhere. In a dreamy soup of thoughts, he wondered about people who screamed and burned and everything around him exploded for no good reason.

THE END

Ghosts aren't real, are they? Maybe the word 'ghost' should not even be used. Isn't it a word relic left over from a superstitious past, one we've left behind completely? Hmm..in these pages there are some new shades of grey worth exploring...

Burr Man Rising, LLC

As long as Sophie Sater lived in Mountain Home, her thoughts rarely turned toward the entity called Burr Man. It was only when she moved to Utica, into the comfortable life of a university librarian, that paradoxically she dwelled more and more both on Burr Man and the experiences of her late mother.

Because of such strange and unexpected thoughts, Sophie talked longer than was necessary as she assisted Portia Howard, who had mentioned that she was President of the Western New York Paranormal Society. Yes, Portia had said giving Sophie a quick glance, we deal with a great many incidents which turn out to be paranormal.

"Are you seeking new members?" Sophie's query caused Portia to stop flipping through the book she was examining, and peer deeper into young eyes that seemed far too mature for the early twentyish young woman with the mild Southern drawl.

"At this time, we are indeed. But we have not advertised such. Have you anyone in mind for us?"

To that, Sophie nodded quickly and smiled as Portia dug around in her purse for a business card. "Email me first and we'll see what happens."

After that, in dreams both Burr Man and Gina Sater dropped by often. Her mother, Gina was a lonely, impetuous, unemployed teenager when she realized she'd been made pregnant by Howie Hollard. Howie possessed the best Mohawk cut in Memphis, as well as ten slick fingers. At the local arcade, he ruled over every game and his haughty, loud manner caught Gina's attention. But Howie could not possibly transfer these skills to fatherhood. Thus, he was the first person to bail as Gina advanced in her pregnancy. In desperation she phoned people she barely knew. A long shot came through, a first cousin who lived in Mountain Home, Arkansas. His profitable dry cleaner business was able to snap up a bankrupt competitor and Gina's timely call gained her a much needed bus ticket out of Memphis.

In Mountain Home she hid the baby bump by wearing old, floppy dresses much too large for her. Gina barely slept some nights; the nightmare of a virtual child having a newborn baby roiled in her brain even in the light of day. So it was when Isabel Bingham came into the shop, she lingered. Gina's shy, soft spoken nature and gentle oval face contrasted sharply with Isabel's bold outward manner. Isabel Bingham had learned from her mother, Stella, the value of standing up for herself. Almost three hundred pounds with a round piggish face to match, Isabel had few friends. It was after the third visit, when she dropped off brother Henry's best Sunday shirts for dry cleaning, that she said; "My mom makes the best fried chicken around. You can come over on your day off and try some if you want to."

In that pallid summer, when even the crickets' and katydids' sharp evening tunes dulled to nothing, Isabel confided to Gina that she pined for adventure, for excitement, anything to spice up the long days. So one afternoon it was no accident that they headed outside of town in Isabel's pick-up truck, weaved down one road then another, and eventually turned off into a seldom used gravel lane. At the terminus squatted a surprise-it was no less than a mansion, a black specter of oak and pine planking, hiding in the late afternoon shade provided by covens of tall, gnarled pecan and hickory trees.

"It's our family's old place, Gina. And there's a secret in there. Want to find out what it is?"

And so, Gina related to her daughter before she died, it was that very day when the Phantom of Burr Man rammed itself into the life of mother first, and later, into the daughter. Gina had waited until she was certain Sophie also had the gift. "I would never have told you this story if you turned out to be normal. But you're like me." Sophie recalled the sigh and crestfallen look her mother made when she said this. So Sophie listened, captured fully by her mother's reluctance, and the imprint of that meeting never dulled in her mind's eye.

So it was that Isabel walked Gina into the heart of the old mansion. Isabel's big head craned itself on her short neck, bobbing loon-like, her eyes searching like an owl's, switching on and off with every creak, every whisk of bat wings. Gina gingerly reached out to hold her hand, but Isabel knocked it away. The place was old and badly run down, but the roof had held firm. Even so, small creatures, warming up for the impending nightfall, turned corners too swiftly to be identified. Gina heard the buzzes, swishes and tiny shrieks, and something like low wind moved around her ears.

Some furniture remained from a previous time, uncovered and heavily ripped. A row of stern people glared down from pictures taken an eon ago. Isabel roamed the first floor in a full circle then gathered her breath. Slowly they plodded up long steps. Second floor. Then the third. At the hallway's end, Gina stared down through a sturdy old window. Something parted the bushes directly below. It must have come up from the ravine that bent steeply down just in back of the house. Almost at once, a hissing, a blast of air, and a regurgitation of sound like vomit stuck in the back of a throat.

Stupid, stupid Isabel! Why had she come here? *It* must have slipped up the stairs, floating more than walking. Gina felt it, a pulsing of dangerous dark energy. It sucked like a straw, gathering fear that had walled up immediately to protect the precious aura of life. Something roiled, formed right there, a bare yard from Isabel's elbow. She turned, reacting to the expression of terror on Gina's face. Isabel fled all of six feet. She huddled against the window frame and then shook it hard.

"Burr Man, go away! Go away!"

Burr Man indeed!

Stupid Isabel knew of this phantom! Isabel wanted to play! Something deep inside Gina flexed its muscle. She knew what they faced. There was a real beast here, not of this world, but maybe it wanted to be. Now they had landed in its domain and Gina could see no solution of exit.

Gina willed herself for maximum control. Fear! Burr Man sucked it down and Isabel offered a feast. Burr Man hovered there, a photoelectric fury, its black and red pulses rippling and reverberating with so much energy that even the window pane quivered to the point of exploding. He was amazingly ghost shaped; kind of like a large furious man whose bedsheet draped from head to toe. Then he extended both arms over his head and bellowed.

The entity morphed and in seconds he was now a man-like thing with flesh that peeled off in patches, as if the skinny white bones underneath were rejecting such a gross covering. His eyes shifted to red saucers that had black points in the middle and they shone with hatred at the unwanted visitors.

As Isabel screamed and clawed at the stout oak studded window pane, Gina wondered where the big, nasty burrs came from. As Burr Man's wretched stinking skin peeled away, on each piece forest burrs had stuck. Gina knew about these burrs. She must have picked out a thousand of them from customers' clothes. Burr Man floated closer and suddenly his bony claw came down. In a raging display of photoelectric fury, Gina felt the energy burst across her face and she collapsed. Burr Man towered over her crumpled form.

Isabel turned to fight. She shrieked in little pants, like a terrier cornered by a wolverine. Her fists connected on nothing. But when Burr Man ripped at her flesh, clear red bloody marks formed. Burr Man tore away the top of her dress. It ripped away the bra strap and when she tried to cover the two bobbing orbs, Burr Man sunk metaphysical fangs into the nipple aura. Isabel almost crumpled, groaning in pain, but her stout legs did not fail.

Neither Burr Man nor Isabel had noticed Gina's calm arising from the messy floor. Gina felt as if she were floating, was mildly amazed at her calmness. She ran her fingers across her face and pulled away two large burrs that had stuck on strands of hair, after falling from Burr Man. But they melted like meek fog when she tried to take a closer look.

Then Gina closed her eyes, invoked something deep inside that was good and wonderful and raised her hands. An amber door at once rippled into existence. Right there, a bare two feet from the roaring battle between beast and person, an invitation for beast only to enter. As it was meant to be from time immemorial. The only way to grapple with its best and proper destiny was to enter the doorway.

Burr Man immediately knew. The energy shift met his great disapproval. He backed away from Isabel. He lunged toward Gina, who merely stood closer to the rippling door's entrance point. Something bobbed inside the entity, like a man trying to pop out and fly away. But the black essence held it back. Burr Man shook his head from side to side as if trying to clear his thoughts. Then his essence folded up on itself, much like the way Gina folded clothes at the cleaners. He fell back half a step, the eyes rounded into full red saucers and then came a final roar of rage resounding in the topmost hallway of Bingham Mansion. Burr Man vanished right before their astonished tear-encrusted eyes.

Gina sighed as she concluded the incredible tale. Gently, she stroked her daughter's full gift of rich brown hair. "Of course Burr Man might certainly have killed Isabel that day, or me, if I had stayed knocked out on the floor." Gina kissed her daughter's forehead and whispered. "But something woke me up, a kind of tapping on my shoulder. So I got up. I made him go away. I made the light. Burr Man didn't go into the light door, but it was then that I knew for sure that I'm a ghost whisperer." Gina paused and dimples rippled at two points on her pale, gentle face. "Sophie you are too. You are a ghost whisperer. But never feel alone. I think there are many of us in this strange and remarkable time."

Isabel and Gina agreed never to speak of the incident. They hashed out a neat story about an accident in the heavy brambles as they played some girlish game. The family generally believed it. What else could have happened? And the best thing to spin out of pure disaster: Invited to a family dinner, Gina cast her pale, green eyes upon Henry Bingham. Sophie herself had never understood at all how the sour, balding fellow appealed to Gina. But his words and manner could have been Romeo's very own as far as Gina was concerned. Henry Bingham had at last struck a bullseye right into the heart of a beautiful and tender damsel. He would have her, for better or for worse. No woman so far in his thirty-five years of life had blinked twice at his chunky face. But here, with this Gina Sater, a teen-age beauty, was a woman who found Henry's blandish charms nearly irresistible.

As in any small town, when an older, well established man takes a young and tarnished woman for a bride, people talk. After the marriage, Gina quit the cleaners. She had no choice. Her cousin explained as well as he could: "Most of my customers are pious church-goers. They think Henry is crazy taking you in like this, with your family condition showing. It's clear to most everyone-the baby is not his. It don't matter to me Gina, but I'm a businessman first. Besides, Henry's gonna take good care of you. Right?"

At the marriage, it was obvious Henry had gone over his mother Stella's head. It wasn't just that Gina was pregnant from another man. Stella had checked around, had found sources in Memphis that soured her on Gina right from the start. Gina had paranormal talents. Stella was determined to keep that kind of dangerous nonsense out of her family. Now it had intruded in a most disgusting fashion.

The tension only escalated from there: Gina's difficult pregnancy and even more precarious delivery; Henry's unofficial expulsion from the country church he'd attended since boyhood. Worst of all- the income situation. Stella had always controlled the purse strings for the entire family and now she made Henry in charge of the timber operation of the family's dwindling pine and oak reserves. When he made the family money, she paid him, otherwise he went without.

Gina noticed this of course. The continuing family pressure and Henry's general inability to deliver much income, weakened her spirit. Slowly Gina Sater fell apart.

Just after she told the nine-year-old Sophie the story about her experience with Burr Man, and how Sophie should never be ashamed she too was a ghost-whisperer, the doctors discovered the advanced cancer of both ovaries.

Gina was dead six months later.

Daddy Henry. It was what Sophie had always called her father. Now he was all she had left. The other family members handled Sophie much the way they handled their hounds. They wanted to keep her out of their homes and in general, out of their tidy lives. But when Stella fell to her knees one Sunday afternoon, both hands pressing hard on her chest, heaving mightily for oxygen that could no longer be imported, her subsequent death shocked the family and made them forget Sophie. At least until the scene at the funeral parlor unraveled nerves already severely frayed.

While Uncle Jared and Uncle Glen were quietly conversing, at the very foot of Stella's casket, Sophie came right over and joined their circle. She didn't bother to wait for acknowledgment of her existence right there, under their very noses. "Uncle Glen, your mother wants to know why her favorite gold brooch is not around her neck. She told you clearly she wanted to be buried in it. Is that right Uncle Glen?"

Glen Bingham had perhaps uttered ten words in her direction in her entire tenure within the Bingham family. Now his jaw line almost collapsed. "How do you know about that? You been snooping around conversations you ain't been invited to little girl." But Sophie stood firm, a resolute fourteen-year old outcast who glanced first toward the casket and then directly into Uncle Glen's most baleful glare.

"You mother asked me to ask you. She's standing right over there in the corner. But you can't see her."

At once older brother Jared grabbed Glen and hauled him away. The family convened an immediate conference in an adjoining private chamber.

"Henry," said Glen, "What the hell is going on with that step-daughter of yours? She's claiming momma is standing over in the corner right by her own casket, asking about a gold brooch. What do you say to that kind of crazy talk?"

All eyes turned toward Henry Bingham, and Isabel's especially, held a steady twinkle. Jared, the oldest and tallest, folded his arms and waited.

Henry was in no mood to be bullied. True, for most of his life he dearly loved Stella, and he appreciated how tough she had to be to raise five children with no husband. But when Stella had completely rejected Gina like she had, so thoroughly and without good cause, something wilted deep inside Henry. He'd always loved and cherished Gina, even up to the very end when he promised with all his heart to take good care of Sophie. If not for Stella's ridiculous intransigence, Gina might be alive this day. That was what Henry believed.

Henry walked right up to Glen, noses almost touching. "What do I say about Sophie's question to you about the gold brooch? Is that what you want to know?"

Glen nodded suspiciously, pondering what advantage he thought he had.

"Here's what I say brother. Why don't you go home, get the gold brooch out of your drawer, and go and put it on momma's neck before she's buried. Apparently, that would make her very happy."

Isabel grabbed Glen's arm. "Come on. I'm going with you." On the way out she managed to kiss Henry upon cheeks still red from nervous rage.

⌘ ⌘ ⌘

Sophie sat rigid in a straight-backed wooden chair as a semi-circle of curious peers gawked in her direction. She was the most interesting prospect the Paranormal Society of Western New York had come across in a long time.

Ann Junie, of course, knew a lot about Sophie. As the club secretary, she was the first one to read Sophie's biography, which for them served as a kind of informal application. Sophie had been offered a librarian's post at Cornell University after making high grades at the University of Missouri. But what stood out for Ann Junie, as it did for the other seven members, was Sophie's unique encounters with aspects of the darkest arena of the paranormal. It was an area only one or two of them knew much about.

Ann Junie got in the first question. "Sophie you are very young to have seen so much, but it's your family that is profiting from the so called Burr Man phenomenon? Is that correct?"

"Yes. It's very true. I'm not happy with them making money from it though."

A tall man leaned forward in his chair. "Your mother told you about her encounter several years ago."

Sophie had placed both hands onto her lap. A glowing calmness came upon her. "Yes, once she did. She told me every detail. But as I got older and with her death, it began to only seem like a dream. Like I'd only imagined that she told me. So I went back there with a discerning friend just before I shipped off to the University of Missouri."

A tall red-headed lady who'd introduced herself as Ruby asked: "I read about your encounter. You are direct and eloquent if I may say so. It reminds me of a few horrendous encounters of my own. But can you say how did this your own encounter with Burr Man differ from your mother's?"

When Sophie made direct eye contact with Ruby, she noticed at once how the woman's strange dark eyes flashed with extreme interest. It was as if every word Sophie uttered here today would be recalled and fleshed out again and again.

"My own experience was very different from my mom's. First of all, I knew what to expect. The way he looked did not surprise me very much. I kind of wanted to size him up to tell you the truth. This was just before Uncle Jared had concocted his scheme to try and commercialize Burr Man. You all, of course, know all about that. By and large, he's been successful. Burr Man is making the family some much needed income."

"So what happened," Ruby chided gently. "Just tell us without looking at your notes if you can."

Sophie allowed a smile to play around the edge of her lips. They were so interested. It was a rare thing for Sophie to have a captive audience when she wanted to talk about anything along this subject line. "Gary Gray and I roamed around the old house for more than an hour. When Burr Man came, he must have detected at once Gary and I had no fear of him, and so he stood a distance from us, just watching. Even so, he was spectacular. He seemed bursting with electrical energy, shining bright then dimming, like a Christmas tree with a short in the lighting. But the eyes glowed red with small black spots in the center. He just floated there. We saw no arms or legs that day. Burr Man made no sound, he only glared balefully toward us."

"Probably because he could draw no energy from you two. This Gary Gray must also have been a ghost whisperer." Portia Keel spoke up. Sophie knew her from the news. She was a television anchor in Utica.

Sophie suddenly snapped her fingers. "Oh and it's easy to see how he got his name. He always has these big forest burrs stuck on him, like he's been trekking through the Arkansas backwoods or something before he shows up here. I saw them clearly. They were all over the entity. Pretty bizarre. That alone could scare people."

Now someone asked what everyone was thinking. "Did you make the light, like your mother did, to send him along?"

Sophie paused, trying to get back the feeling when she raised her arms in silent expectation on that long ago afternoon. "Yes. I did do that. That's when he made the only noise of the encounter. It was a kind of grunt, not an explosion, but you could see his eyes changing then. They got redder and something seemed to move around inside that black essence. He expanded some. He grew taller along with being agitated. It was obvious he hated or feared the light. He never took one step toward it. Most entities seem almost glad to. Not Burr Man."

Someone whispered: *"Demon*. He's a demonic being." Sophie turned to Ruby again.

"I could not tell exactly Ruby, if he was or he wasn't. How would you know?"

Ruby stood. She came to more than six feet and bore the ruggedness of a backwoods lumberjack. Her long beak of a nose flared and she half turned to the group as well. "Demonic beings would never consider going into the light. And that's twice. It was offered to him by your mom and by you. The same result suggests Burr Man is not a spirit choosing to remain on the lowest astral planes of earth. It's something else. We know these things to be possessive and evil in the extreme. It's a dangerous thing your family is harboring Sophie. And they have no clue what's going on. The real problem could be down the road. Left unchecked, Burr Man might attract others. Things could get out of hand with this game your family is playing with the profit motive."

Sophie shrugged. "Well there's little I can do about that. I do speak to Henry every now and then. He even wants to start to send me some of his earnings from the terror tours, as he calls them. People pay a thousand dollars each, and there's a group of ten or so that go in. If there's no encounter, there's no charge. But most of the time, there's an encounter, Henry told me. They limit this to only one group per month."

Ruby kept the floor. "We here at our Society are of the same mind most people with paranormal talent abide by. And that dictum is simple enough: *After Death Spiritual Entities* of every stripe do not belong on the lowest astral plane and should not be encouraged to stay. Ghosts have always exercised their free will to stay and linger, we know, but it's not a part of the natural order. Now, we have the numbers behind us to banish them to go where they ought to, into the light. But if the being has a demonic core, such as Burr Man surely must, there is an even greater imperative for it to be banished by whatever means."

Sophie's eyes darted away from this strange woman and toward the others. No one stirred. They watched her carefully. Above all, she wanted to join them, she absolutely required their unique companionship to help lock out the loneliness, the fear of being so special. They wanted Burr Man banished? Ok, it was fine by her, even if she had no clue how to go about such a task.

She breathed hard and said. "Sure Ruby. You guys, I will help you all I can. I'm with you on this. Demons should not be allowed a free ride on our earth. Let's get rid of every single one of them. Beginning with Burr Man."

⁂

Jared Bingham could get up every morning, shave, stare at a fifty-five-year-old face that had faced up to its responsibilities, and knew he had come through shining. After Stella's sudden death, the family faced its gravest crisis since Fred Bingham died lumberjacking on a steep, slippery slope. The oak tree that fell the wrong way, splitting his head wide open, guaranteed no family member could gaze one last time at the father of five at his final wake. Everyone had wailed for Stella. How would she cope? Now the family lands would be at her full disposal. How would she handle it?

Stella's solution was to be the full time matriarch of her brood, and this continued even as the children became full grown men and women. She gave out the assignments as fit each person's abilities. They had to make money for themselves and the family. It was capitalism at its peak.

But one thing Stella did not take into account at all was the desire to do work. It had been assigned to Jared, for example, to handle the family's dairy farm operations. Jared had learned to hate cows of every description, and yet, he had to be around them day and night seven days a week.

It was no surprise to anyone that the first thing sold off were the dairy cows and all that assorted equipment. The new varieties of fast growing pines were taking their time making good roots in the mostly hilly land, and what little lowland oak and hickory were left, held out mostly in the hard-to-reach ravines and crannies of steep rock ledges.

So how in hell would the family get money now? They had met more than once, implored Jared to come up with something. The bank account would not hold out forever and no Bingham worth his salt would swallow his pride and go seeking a job in town.

So Jared was forced to think 'outside the box.' His research led him far and wide, and when he noted how it was that almost all the great, spooky places on earth had lost their ghosts because of the actions of the breed of people known as 'ghost whisperers', he conjured up the idea of using the old Bingham Mansion as the last true bastion of one of the best ghosts on the planet.

Jared knew this was an absolute fact. Like all the Binghams, he'd had his little private sortie in the mansion. As a goofy teenager, he'd gone in with the Willis brothers, and they had screamed and yelled in the heart of the mansion, just daring Burr Man to show his face. When Burr Man came, he descended in a whoosh of hurricane air. Henry fell to his knees, gasping for breath. When he turned around, Butch Willis was screaming at the top of his lungs. Burr Man had him by both feet, was dragging him toward the stairs. Jared bolted up and grabbed the arms. For one crazy moment, Butch Willis was a play toy, being stretched unbearably in one direction then another. Jared's muscles prevailed. He'd often thought about the metaphysical unreality of that moment. How exactly could Burr Man do anything in the physical realm, like touch objects and grab objects, when he himself consisted of material of the non-material realm? When the three boys at last had made it back into the bright sunlight, the Willis brothers ran for the hills. The brothers sometimes spoke to Jared in whispers about 'that spooky place.' To Jared, it was a day never to be forgotten.

So what was so bad about making money from Burr Man? As far as Jared knew, Burr Man had never killed anyone. He came across as a violent ghost, but Burr Man did not have much true muscle power. Jared wondered, how many people were out there in the big wide world who wanted to be spooked, so badly scared out of their wits, that they would pay good money for the experience? And what would his church say about making money from something that had to be of the Devil?

Now he knew the answer. And he was the business manager. Each family member had their own assignment in the company called *Burr Man Rising, LLC.* For the last six months it had worked even beyond Jared's wildest dreams. There were two important ideas as Jared saw it, for the good times to continue: One, there must be no videos or pictures *ever*. They had to keep the cameras out of Bingham

Mansion. What Burr Man was, what he looked like, how he behaved, must only be passed from mouth to mouth. Once people saw how he looked from photos, how could he be original any more?

The second item so crucial to a long term operation was to keep out any ghost whisperers. Jared well knew most of them believed that they were doing right, banishing ghosts right and left, allowing them to head off into the light of heaven, or wherever it was they went. That important job went to Henry. He was in charge of taking measures and issuing directives that would keep them out. If Burr Man were to vanish in the haze as it were, choosing to go off into the light rather than stay in his home at Bingham Mansion, it would ignite another full-blown family crisis.

⌘ ⌘ ⌘

Of all the members in the Western New York Paranormal Society, Sophie came to know and admire Ruby the most. It was after they'd met a few times in the quiet of Ruby's neat back porch, that Ruby had shocked Sophie: "I'm a killer at heart, Sophie. I can't explain why but there's nothing I like better than to mix it up with the really bad ones-the demon's daddies if you will."

They'd been watching the snow fall, big flakes with no sound paddling around in the air before joining their brothers in the growing snow pack. "So you're really an exorcist." Sophie had already learned it was best not to stare at Ruby Gellerman. She only stared right back, with an intensity Sophie found uncomfortable.

"Not in the religious sense. Demons never really were banished by the rituals any priest put forth. It was a war of attrition. Some priests just outlasted the demonic spirit. It could find easier pastures to graze on without the annoying human around."

"So by what means do you kill the enemy?" Ruby smiled. She seemed to appreciate Sophie's metaphoric stabs into the English language.

"I have my own special way to get the job done. If I told you, as a total novice, you would go blank. But it works without my having to spend a lot of precious time invoking ridiculous abra-kadabra mantras, like the kind you get in movies and such."

After a moment, Sophie resumed questions. "Have you always been like this Ruby?"

The answer came too quickly. "Yes. Even in other lives I was a born vanquisher, a banisher, a killer of things I found offensive."

Sophie had never considered such a thing for herself, although her mother once swore the two had already led a full life somewhere in France a long time ago. Sophie laughed at her mom's imagination in those days.

"You know what my next line already is Ruby, so don't keep me waiting."

Ruby turned her head directly on Sophie's tender face. Ruby's eyes glared as if she were recalling something imprinted in a rarely used well of her mind. "In the age of the Inquisitors, I did my part."

"So you tortured innocent people."

"Yes, Sophie. But torture in the name of God was an accepted practice, fully sanctioned by the Universal Church of that era. And I was a priest who did exactly as I was told, and believed exactly as I was told."

"Like you said, Ruby, you crave order, must always have it."

She dipped her head, and the voice lowered a notch. "Then as now. It's why I go after demonic things. Their order is of another realm. They are interlopers here."

"But you enjoy making the light and sending off ghosts too."

Ruby sighed. "Not so much any more. I let the others handle the typical rabble rousers. My specialty has become cornering the After Death Spiritual Entities that have an attitude, and every now and then I get to wrangle with a demonic entity. It's going to happen with Burr Man. Do you know how?"

This was what Sophie had come for, to hear out Ruby's plan. She listened and became excited for her new friend. What an adventure to come! More and more often when Ruby was happy, Sophie felt easier about herself. Sophie hoped that Ruby's actions would not spell doom for Henry. He'd become more and more dependent upon the monies the family were taking in from the Burr Man spectacle. Could Ruby really pull such a feat off all alone, the banishment of Burr Man from this realm?

✠ ✠ ✠

Han-sel Han worked for the entire Bingham family, but it was Henry who'd hired him. And for that, Han-sel was deeply grateful. He'd moved to America from Korea five years ago, had invested all his money in Taekwondo schools in the Memphis area. When the economy flipped on its side, Han-sel knew at once he was really the village idiot. People stopped coming for training. Everything dried up. He went broke faster than a whipsawed kite.

Instead of starving he moved to Mountain Home. A new job beckoned. Han-sel and part-timer Nathan reviewed biographies on exactly who and what kind of people were part of the tours. So once a week, Henry quizzed them to see if they knew important details about the client crowd coming into the mansion.

"How do people usually regard you Hansel, as a foreign tourist?"

"Yes, that's usually my line." Han-sel had quickly grown used to his name being mangled badly by southern people. He just told them to call him Hansel.

"And you can easily keep an eye on say, this customer who's coming in with the next group, a fellow named Dye. Jim Dye. What's your take on him?"

"Oh yes, Jim Dye." Hansel recalled his research easily enough. Anyone remotely thinking about banishing Burr Man with their New Age mumbo jumbo had another think coming, so long as Hansel Han was on the job!

"I think Jim Dye is a zero threat. He's a big guy, but big and dumb I'd say. He's just coming for the thrills. He paid in cash too."

Henry had too much time on his hands these days. He was playing mind games with the hired help more and more often. "But what would you do if you caught Big Jim Dye making the light door for our Burr Man. If the light door swung open because of Jim Dye, what would you do?"

"First I come up to him and kick him lightly on the shin. It would hurt but not too much. It would probably break his concentration and the light door would go away."

"What if he fights with you?"

Hansel laughed. These days he didn't mind smiling broadly. At last he'd been able to purchase a gorgeous set of new choppers. "Ha! Fat chance to that! I have the quickest three punch-kick in the business, Mr. Henry. If I hit you with it, you'd blink once, then be on the ground."

Henry smiled and Jared chuckled. They both admired Hansel's talent, integrity and loyalty. Since there were no cameras in the mansion it was up to Hansel to faithfully report everything that happened. How scared were the clients? Did anyone faint? How long did it take for Burr Man to come? How many encounters with Burr Man were there? Were any customers too shocked at what they saw?

Hansel saw her name on a list of incoming guests-Ruby Keller. She paid with a cashier's check and claimed she'd already been to Europe to check out their scary castles. But Ruby Keller said she'd wasted her time and money since the ghosts were no longer there. She urged the keepers of Burr Man to keep a close eye on him. Don't allow him to be banished. Keep out the ghost whisperers at all costs.

Hansel nodded and stared at Ruby's photo. He fully agreed on that point. But here-this Ruby Keller- was one homely woman. No wonder she felt attracted to ghosts and was unmarried. Who'd want her?

Hansel held no fear of Burr Man. He'd watched the ghost on more than a few occasions. It seemed furious at humans for some reason. And Hansel detected a kernel of unnatural hatred within Burr Man. And of evil things, Hansel had some experiences, totally unique to his own upbringing.

His own dear Grandmother had been one of the most sought after Shaman in the hill country of Korea. Guiding people to spirits was her business. He'd spent summers with her as a youth. The town was Andong. It was in the middle of the mountain spine that ran up and down the Korean peninsula. People believed in the old ways in Andong. Women who were spiritually sensitive, who had the talent to conjure up spirits, to hold them steady, to make conversation with them, were in high demand. Such were her talents. She still occupied a tender place in his memory banks of childhood.

She was always in some kind of attitude of prayer, Hansel recalled. She preferred to pray in a sing-song numeric chanting style. She thought that certain numbers used over and over again in her mantra, helped evoke the spiritual entities to her side. Her clients might be anybody: People who sought some closure with dead relatives were common. But she'd told her grandson about one couple who were worried they'd never have a child, and they wanted to meet some of their children who'd long been dead from past lives. She went on to describe in exact detail how the long ago children sprang up from some metaphysical mistiness, and how the mother fainted outright. The father remained sitting bolt upright, nodding at this or that comment. Then it was his strange duty to relate what they'd said to the mother, who remained on the floor during the entire visitation.

She was so kind and sweet to Hansel. When he watched her in action he was astonished at the changes. From his own much loved Grandmother, she could morph into a whirling dervish, barking out commands like a fierce general, speaking in dialects Han-sel never knew she understood. But she was gone now and sometimes came to him in dreams. It was not enough, these shreds and scraps, but Hansel was not one to dwell in pure memory.

One week before Ruby made a circuitous trek to Mountain Home, Sophie contacted Henry by video phone. He looked good-at least most of the flab of chin had vanished. His bald pate shone nicely, even if both grey sideburns had lengthened. "Hello dear. How's the library business in New York?"

"Fine Henry. You know me, I do like books. And by the way, thanks for the money you've been sending me. Looks like you and Jared are onto something."

Ruby had admonished Sophie not to speak directly on the subject of the business, but to lead Henry in that direction, as if it were his own idea. "We thought Jared was nuts at first. But actually after I supported him, the others came around. What have you heard about our little business venture?"

Sophie did not have to exaggerate. "Well, Henry, we have hundreds of magazines and newspapers, and sometimes I can read about your business operation. If you wanted to I'm sure you could get a reporter from Time Magazine down there."

Henry smiled broadly. "That's nice to hear but no thanks to the wrong kind of publicity. Actually in fact, there is a waiting list of three months now. We don't want to overwork our Burr Man or scare him off. So we limit things to one tour per week."

"How many in the tour," asked Sophie casually.

"We have no more than twelve. It's a big house you know, and we can scatter them all over the place. Surprisingly, most of the time Burr Man comes through for us."

"Are the people really all that scared Henry? I mean I read where they spend a thousand bucks a head to get in there. How can Burr Man really be that mean?"

Henry pursed his lips. Maybe he hadn't intended to talk this much about business. Had Sophie gone one step too far with that last question? "Oh don't worry about our ghost. He's just scary enough. If you see him, you cannot forget him. So far, no major heart attacks from the guests. But you should see their faces when they come out. I really think we are gonna make it in the entertainment business. We just have to keep our Burr Man happy."

Sophie paused,and smiled. "Henry, I do miss you. "And I have not yet thanked you for using all of mom's insurance money on my college education. For that long silence I truly apologize. You're a good man Henry. I just wish mom were still alive."

Henry blinked. He made a move toward his back pocket handkerchief, then decided better. "It was my duty Sophie. I promised it to your mom on her deathbed, ah, in her last hours."

"Let's talk more often Henry. The drought has been too long this time."

She wanted to end the talk, but Henry held up a palm. "I want you to come back here for a little spell. Some things have changed Sophie. Check it out and see what I mean. People are not so against you as you might think."

"Well, I don't know, but just for talk's sake, suppose I could dart down there. I'd love to see this fantastic ghost of yours."

Henry half closed his eyes, the lips shut tight and a frown instantly creased across both brows. "I can't promise you that....There could be a problem with....booking and maybe with policy too."

She tried to turn suddenly jolly, hoped Henry bought the act. "Hey, don't worry Henry, I understand how booked you all are. But what's this policy thing? I'm family like you just said. Aren't I?"

He blinked and stared at this daughter-woman. She was Henry's and yet not always his. The paternity thing had always bothered him; perhaps it was pure male instinct that made him dwell far too much upon Sophie's true, biological dad. Henry had seen his photo in a high school yearbook. A young punk nobody. Henry opened his eyes again and descended into the reality of his deepest feelings. "You are my only child Sophie. But that skill you inherited from your mother is one greatly feared by Jared and the others. We don't let any ghost whisperers into the mansion. You must know why."

"I do know why. Goodbye Henry." Instantly she regretted the terminal attitude that had sprung up so quickly. That's just the way it was, she mused. Everything seemed fine, and something always came up to ruin springtime. It always did.

⌘ ⌘ ⌘

There was no good reason to mark Ruby Keller as a troublemaker. They'd reviewed her application; she seemed to Henry to be no worse than a snooty, rich New Yorker. Perhaps she'd never worked a day in her life, and she seemed adept at traveling in some of the world's stranger places. Now that she was here in Mountain Home, Henry was even less interested in Ruby Keller. She was a gawky, talkative ostrich yakking about ghosts and castles to her newest set of friends. Ruby, like the others, thought Hansel was a paying ghost tourist and Hansel obliged. It was part of his job to blend in with them, so that when he went into the mansion with them, they'd not have the slightest suspicion he was really a company plant.

They were gabbering all at once to guide Nathan. "Where did Burr Man come from in the first place?"

Nathan almost yawned at the question. He heard it from every group of course. But he had to seem as excited and interested as they were. He fought off his growing boredom lest Henry bitch again.

"We suppose Burr Man sprang into existence when three people were murdered in the mansion. That was over sixty years ago. Those murdered were two male Binghams and one unrelated fellow, possibly a friend of the younger Bingham. It was never established by the police at that time and the family had clammed up."

"Yes, we can see from the old pictures you have blown up on the wall here that all three guys were shot from behind, shot in the head. Who'd want to kill them like that?" Nathan noted the good question came from Mary Hill, a noted mystery writer. Maybe she'd come here for some new material.

Nathan shrugged. "The Bingham clan was very closed mouthed about innermost family dealings. At that time they were engaged in some kind of hill feud with the Macy clan across the deep ravine from the mansion. Adding to the mystery, was the young Benjamin's friend who was present and also murdered. Rumor at the time had it that this guy whose name may have been Jerry Cassel, was a gay man and lived at the mansion solely to entertain Benjamin."

"Oh my!" Ruby sighed, withdrawing a bit. "So two of the victims may have been homosexual? What a scandal for that time!"

"So they just all three killed each other. That's a bit far fetched." The skeptical Bea Hatcher would turn sixty next week.

"In fact the investigation was botched by an inept Sheriff and his half drunk Deputy. The Deputy or some people on his staff happened to be kin to the Macys. This tended to cloud things. Nobody could say what happened to the Chinese handyman who also cooked and chauferred for old man Bingham. Everyone wanted to ask him what the hell had really happened, because it was so obvious he knew a lot. But he'd disappeared. Never a trace found of him."

"Looks like a pretty organized murder," said Hansel quietly. The others turned in the direction of an obviously non-native speaker of English. "I'd vote for a well planned killing, and the only real suspects would have been the Macys. Weren't they involved in some kind of long-running feud you said, Nathan?"

"Right, but no proof ever came from the sorry investigation. So that's why it all turned out this way people. We got a full blown angry ghost, three dead bodies, and nobody ever once bothered to ask the right set of questions."

The guests had settled around Nathan in a semi-circle and at this summary of events, they looked at one another and nodded gravely. Hansel smiled glancing at Nathan. That part of the story had the same effect every time. It set the stage nicely. An impenetrable mystery about to be made even more insane when Burr Man arose from the depths.

They were hauled to the mansion at exactly 6 p.m. and each person clung to his assigned partner as they entered the front door. One by one Nathan reviewed each pair's marching orders: "This is your part of the house. Don't stray away from those three rooms. Watch and listen carefully. You have your headlamps. That's the only light you get. Don't fall asleep. It could be dangerous for you if Burr Man comes upon you like that. We don't want anyone hurt tonight. You all have signed the waivers anyway. If he gets particularly rambunctious, well…we've told you how to best get away from him."

Hansel and Ruby were the last pair to go in. Nathan had paired the two together because it was Hansel's job to secretly go around and inspect what was happening to the others. Ruby, Nathan felt, would not complain and would not mind if her partner left her alone from time to time. She'd been around ghosts before in the times when they inhabited the old castles and moors, and judging from her looks, Ruby Keller might be the first person to scare Burr Man back into hiding.

Slowly they meandered toward their target. Hansel and Ruby were to occupy the bedroom on the first floor and the adjacent parlor and enclosed porch. This was the room of the missing Chinaman, the butler to the grandfather. In fact, as Ruby rifled through the chest of drawers, she came upon towels and headbands with Chinese words. Just as the family had promised, very little had changed from the light physical renovation of Bingham Mansion. Good, mused Ruby. That always helps.

After two hours, Ruby watched curiously as Hansel eased away. He told her he had a headache and he needed to shuffle around a bit. Fine by her. She took the materials from her handbag. Nathan had gone through it but found nothing unusual. Of course he would not. She would never advertise those things that were required to begin the banishment of the demon entity Burr Man. She poured water into two different cups, sighed and began the mixing. She breathed easily as a few strange shadows passed over the wall. She only hoped Burr Man did not show up too quickly, before she was ready for him.

Hansel made the rounds quickly. The tourists were settled in and waiting patiently. When he padded silently into the former butler's bedroom, his radar instantly shot up. What the hell was this woman doing?

He came right up to her, and she quickly put down everything on the chest of drawers. Hansel's feet were spread apart, hands flexed on both hips. "So you are a ghost whisperer. You surely fooled all of us. You are not allowed to stay and must leave at once."

"Maybe you guess wrong," she purred.

"Not at all am I wrong. You have been putting together some concoction that you hope will attract Burr Man to us. Then you will try to get rid of him. Don't lie to me. Admit it."

She stood up, a hard muscled woman fairly towering over the short Korean man. "So I admit it. You plan to tell somebody?"

"No," said Hansel. "I plan to stop you, to kick your butt right outta here. First, I'll be polite. Please leave the premise, Ruby Keller, or whatever your real name is."

Ruby slid over to the dresser, placed her precious goods carefully back into the purse. "I can't leave now. I'm too close to finishing things here."

She whirled into action. A long leg kicked out, crashing into Hansel's windpipe. But he'd flashed those incredibly quick hands, mitigating the blow. He half turned then spun and his trained right foot bashed hard into her exposed shinbone. Ruby grunted, wanted to grab the damaged area, but knew better. Instead she came at the strange little man with force of fists. She battered his body, then his face. Hansel blocked expertly. He grimaced when a couple of fist shots glanced from his cheek bones. Now it was time to finish this fight. He focused on her face.

Hansel figured to break her nose. Hell, it looked half broken already. He came in, hands and feet feinting, then the hard shots. His third and most powerful punch crackled off the top of Ruby's nose and its force drove pieces of bone deep inward. A sliver of such bone slashed through both nerve and artery.

Ruby Keller grabbed her neck as if shot. She gurgled and burped as she fell to her knees. Then she writhed on the hardwood floor. Hansel watched in awe as Ruby twitched and made light groans. Suddenly, nothing more came out.

He shook her again and again. "Move lady! Move around!" But Hansel had done his duty all too well. As her body stilled in death's final entrapment, Ruby's *After Death Spiritual Entity* uncoiled. It came spinning away and it hovered over a grieving Hansel Han. It watched as the living human cried and sobbed over this unjust, unforeseen death. She wanted to touch him, to assure him this was no mortal sin. Then she looked around and floated through the wooden ceiling.

Jared convened a meeting and had been careful not to tell them anything in advance. Nobody touched their water, expecting the worse kind of news. Jared's long haggard face told them volumes. Something terrible had just happened.

"One of our guests died last night. Not from Burr Man. Hansel tried to stop her from banishing Burr Man. One of his punches smashed nose bone tissue, and apparently that's what killed her." Glen launched into a cursing spree but no one else said a word. All eyes turned to Hansel Han.

Hansel's head hung low; it was his time for utter humiliation and possible banishment. But when Jared nodded his way, giving him permission to tell his side of the story, the family's tenseness loosened a frame or two. He told them everything of course, but the hardest part to relate was about the one errant punch that was a couple of centimeters off. It was because of fighting with the only light coming from two headlamps. He'd misjudged just a bit, and he had to punch hard. The woman was very strong.

"I beg of you family." Hansel plunged to his knees. "Please do not have me arrested!"

Jared helped him back to his feet. "Don't worry you're not going to jail just yet. If you do, we all might end up there." Jared patted a still sobbing Hansel and then gave his most sober stare at the family sitting still on the leather sectional. "Hansel had the good sense not to arouse any suspicion that night. He told the other guests that Ruby had to leave early because of a sudden migraine headache."

Glen cleared his throat, wanting to stand, but instead just placed both hands nervously across both knees. "And the lady's body? I hope it's not just laying there right out in the open."

Henry turned back to Hansel. "Tell them where you stashed it."

He wiped his eyes again and muttered indistinctly so that everyone was forced to lean heavily in his direction." It's under some loose floorboards in the butler's closet. She's laying right there on the old stone foundation." Then Hansel reached into a bag he'd placed on the floor. He pulled something out and the family recoiled. "I had lots of trouble getting her body to fit in that space. This came off her head."

"It's a wig!" Rosa shrieked. Everyone now turned to stare at the youngest sister. Rosa's speech impediment forced her to mostly use sign language, and so this exclamation from her was surprising in itself. Why was she so surprised Henry wondered. Ruby had disguised her entire identity in order to get inside.

Jared reached for a piece of paper and held it high. "Just got this report in from my special private investigator. Paid him twice his normal fee if he could get the information in to us tonight. He did come through and so we find…that this Ruby is really a Ruby Gellerman, and she's from somewhere in New York."

Henry said, "New York's a big state. Which city?"

Jared ignored the question, intent upon his own thoughts. "So the bigger question seems to be should we spend more valuable time finding out who this lady really is, or should we deal the body over to the local authorities?"

Henry half raised a hand. "Since most of this is my fault because I did not check Ruby out thoroughly enough, I want to apologize to my family for being such a big screw up. I will request Sophie to find out as much information on Ruby Gellerman as she can. Of course, I won't say much about the details. But Sophie is in a good position to help us. She's already in New York, part of the family chain, and as a librarian she can access information bases without raising suspicions. When she gets us more valuable information on Ruby Gellerman, I'll report it to you all."

Jared watched Henry with a cool eye. No one on the leather sectional flinched. "Ok Henry you do just that. But be careful dispensing information to Sophie. In the meantime, let's get a posse together and at midnight we'll leave out and go into the mansion. We can't waste any more time with a dead body laying around. Only Heaven knows if Burr Man will be offended by it. I just hope he doesn't take any wrath out on us tonight."

They strode into Bingham Mansion huddled together, and all four head beams shone brightly. Hansel led the group straight to the butler's closet. In two seconds they lifted up the loose floorboards. For ten seconds four pairs of eyes stared down into the empty space.

Henry shoved his way toward the front of the pack. He reached down and pulled away a fluff of bright yellow cloth. "No blood down here but this should mean something. Was she wearing anything yellow that day, Hansel?"

"Yes sir. That's a patch from her shirt. It was mostly yellow with blue flowers."

Glen suddenly spun sideways when a cool wind eddied up around his face. The bright glare forced the others to recoil, to cover their eyes. He spoke quickly, the question came out edgy, far too quiet for him. "So where's the rest of the shirt? Where's the rest of her?"

Then everyone felt it. A light moan, a sliver of sound so vague, it could have been old air gushing up from below. All four men immediately resisted the primal urge to bolt. For many seconds, with ears fully cocked, the group listened and waited for something terrible to happen. But it didn't happen.

"Well," said Henry, "If she got up on her own, why did she cover the wood planks back? Could she have been faking Hansel?"

Hansel's voice was dry, cracking like brown leaves underfoot. "No sir, no chance. I tried CPR on her. Couldn't get her breathing even after ten minutes. She was turning ice cold when I put her in here."

The men folk of the Bingham clan could only stare; each grim face asked silent questions that held no good answers. They left as they'd come inside, huddled together, striding away quickly, working hard to keep dignity intact.

The next group of visitors came only one week later. Jared had moved the date up, curious to know of the effect, if any, Ruby Gellerman's death in the mansion might have on Burr Man.

The answer came like a heavy anchor splattering a shoreline. Burr Man appeared to the group. But he was a shattered remnant of a ghost. He came right up to each guest and raised his hands in imploring fashion. His face roiled with emotions that seemed eerily human. Even so at times, he would retreat to the ceiling and roar loudly, the red saucer eyes fiery receptacles of hatred. But it did not last. He came back, jetting almost into the very faces of the astonished guests, seeming to ask a question his lips could never form.

Isabel related her favorite story more than once. "Tears!" she shouted. "Mr. Roland Bogan who paid his thousand bucks told me it was tears rolling down those bloody, disorganized cheeks of our Burr Man. What could I tell Mr. Bogan? That such a thing was impossible?"

Jared knew this to be true. He'd heard from each of the ten guests, and of course, had thoroughly interrogated Hansel. Something was so wrong with Burr Man. Was there a connection with Ruby? "Henry!" Jared barked. "What of Sophie, your daughter? Did she find out anything about Ruby?"

Henry got right up, walked over to where Jared stood. "Sophie said she checked the records, and nothing came out for a Ruby Gellerman in Utica. As for the rest of New York, she couldn't say."

"Fine detective your daughter," Glen made a finger that pointed hard toward Henry.

Henry cleared his throat to continue: "Sophie does not know what kind of family crisis we have, but she said she'd like to help any way she can. She's asked to come down for a visit. She wants to be a part of this family. Said she greatly misses our company."

For several moments, the family merely tapped fingers on wood, stared at the wall, or grunted wordless signals. "How, exactly can she help us Henry? You got any idea how?"

Jared waved an arm and the budding feud stopped for the moment. "Ok, so Henry you call her back and tell her we're thinking about it."

Miss Helena David stood on the porch of the Bingham House, and it was here they at last removed her blindfold. Henry had picked her up in Branson and spent most of the day driving her here. She'd not been told much, only that her fee would be $500 for just a few minutes work. The family required her specific talents for a certain chore. Isabel had made more than a little sense that afternoon when she stood up and talked. This was part one of the "Isabel Plan," as Jared was now calling it.

Miss David had not been told where she was. She'd only been asked to try and discern how many spirits might be about on this day, what might their nature be, and anything else that might come about.

Henry and Jared walked her up and down the stairs and into most of the rooms. She stopped often, her nose quivering like a good bloodhound's would. Sometimes she jerked her head around, as if a bat were flying by. Henry watched as wavelets of goose bumps scooted up and down her sleeveless arms. The family knew that Burr Man had no compunction about appearing in broad daylight, but on this day they could only pray his apparition would lay low.

At the fireplace on the second floor she made a firm notion. "Enough, I've had quite enough. Let's go outside."

In a bright patch of sunlight Isabel, Rosa and Hansel waited. Miss David came right up, unsmiling, her eyes moving from person to person like a searchlight.

"It's no wonder people don't live here. It would be quite impossible as you all must know." She turned and almost waved at the old house.

"There's as much negative heavy black energy here as I've ever come across in fifteen years of doing this. I am getting a sense that a newer entity has entered into the equation and is helping throw things into greater metaphysical confusion. There's a big conflict of dynamics going on in there. If we could see it with our eyes, it might be kind of like a sumo wrestling match. Two heavy hitters trying to throw each other off balance, something like that. The new second entity has truly altered the dynamics, thrown things into a mess."

"Thanks for that observation Miss David. Can you possibly inform us how that second entity came to reside in this house?"

She turned back to glance at the mansion once again, looking at it high and low. Then she brought her gaze to rest solidly upon Hansel. "Not precisely, no, I can't tell you that. But I strongly suspect this one knows. So ask him." She pointed a crooked finger straight at Hansel, who shifted backward. How could he possibly drive this lady for two hours back to Branson now?

When they convened another family council, the first person hurt was Rosa. She'd always prided herself on being a fantastic cook; she'd always existed at the right elbow of Stella. Now, she'd taken over the family job of cook, but tonight nobody wanted to touch the smoked salmon salad she'd conjured up.

Two subjects weighed like anvil towers on everyone's mind: A missing dead body; a down-and-out ghost. For this family, two subjects like this might just have well rolled into their lives from some comic book.

Isabel had chosen this night to stand up and tell something for the first time.

"Like many of you, I secretly went into the old mansion. But I wasn't a kid. I should've known better. I took a guest with me and I've always felt badly about it. Gina Sater didn't know nothing about what she was getting into." Isabel paused. The family knew how she spoke in public. She could never go far without tears. "The fact is, she probably saved my life that day. That story we made up about my accident was a big lie. Burr Man done that to me. He liked to have killed me. Gina did something, I don't rightly know what as my eyes were so bloodied, to make him run away. In the end he ran off faster than a scalded dog."

Now Isabel looked at them all, right into their eyes. "If anybody can help us it might well be Sophie. She's got the same talents as her mother. If she promises what we want, especially promises not to try and make the light, I suggest we let her go in there and try to make Burr Man better. However that might be I do not know. But I bet she would know exactly what to do, to make things right by him."

Sophie took the call from Arkansas on her video phone in the apartment and transferred it at once to a large screen television. She was going to record this conversation with Henry. She wanted to study his every flit of eyes, every wrinkle of nose. He knew full well about Ruby's disappearance. It was Sophie's present curse that she dare not risk asking anything if she was ever to find out the truth. She understood the skill they possessed, as if by instinct, to obscure the truth, discard it, bury it in some convenient pit.

"The family's decided Sophie. Please come. I won't go into any special details on the phone. There are some promises you will most definitely have to make in our full view. If you can do it, well, then there's a story we'd like to tell. Most of it is...nigh unto unbelievable." His voice wavered, almost cracked. "Truth be told Sophie, this family is in need of you, really in need of you to come here now. I never thought I'd see the day. It...makes me...happy, but what's happened to us isn't a happy thing at all."

Sophie had been escorted directly from the Memphis airport by Hansel. He said almost nothing, barely looked her way. He took her straight to Uncle Jared's home. She sat down uncomfortably in a new wing of his log home. Everything sparkled in tones of leathery magenta, and she wondered about Uncle Jared's present preferences for abstract wall paintings. Hansel had wordlessly sauntered into the room where the family was already gathered. More arguing, more debate, but the heavy log walls easily muffled the words. Sometimes Henry's shrill tones rose to the top of the debate. Sophie shook her head. It was probably one last push by Uncle Glen to send her right back to Utica, permanently banished. And she felt the same way toward him. He'd always been dyslexic, moronic and rude, as long as she'd known him. In Uncle Glen's eyes, she was a family outcast, never to be given a true chance to prove herself.

She barely noticed the door ease open and there stood Henry. He took her into the den where the family sat in short sleeves before a roaring fire. On this cold March night they were all here, studying, watching the young Yankee transplant. Could she truly be family? Could she do what was needed to help them, whatever that might be?

"Maybe you are curious," began Jared, "as to why Henry has not been able to send you any money at all for the last six weeks."

"Yes, a little." Sophie's eyes met with Isabel's. They were always small, pig-like, but inside them perhaps the tiniest spark of hope that Sophie would win them over. "I suppose Burr Man comes and goes. Why should he come at all for strangers? He's always held his best grudge for family members, I've noticed."

Jared waved haughtily. "Now don't you concern yourself with any of that. That's not the reason business has fallen off a cliff."

Sophie feigned surprise. "Henry why hadn't you told me that?" She came up to Uncle Jared even though he stood half a head taller. "What do you want me to do to help you Uncle Jared?"

He turned to the group. She was unable to see his expression, but Henry visibly relaxed. Then as if on cue, he stood up and walked over to his daughter. "We must ask you one thing first and it has to be a solemn promise, made in view of this family. It's vitally important you keep this promise, Sophie."

"Ok." She said and also nodded her head. "I will hold to any vow I make. Now please tell me what is going on?"

Henry sat down and now Jared asked her to come over and sit down. She sat at the head of them all. Was she the only one who caught that irony? Jared reached over occasionally and dabbed his finger on the stripes of the pretty silk dress. "Our Burr Man has become afflicted. He's not the same at all. It has something to do with a terrible accident that happened during a tour. A customer, the one we asked you to check out, Ruby Keller, whose real name is Gellerman. She actually died that night. We are devastated and don't know what to do. Apparently, for some reason that's beyond us... Burr Man has taken her death in a very strange way. Maybe he's...upset?"

Amazingly, Sophie got to ask the question of the ages without impediment, without interruption, without the slightest hint of suspicion among them. "How did she die?"

Now Hansel arose. "I was hired to keep ghost-whisperers from coming in secretly and banishing Burr Man. It's happened in so many other places and the family didn't want it to happen here." Hansel took in the family's quick nods as assent to continue. "The problem was, I caught this lady Ruby right in the act. She didn't deny what she was about to try. She became aggressive toward me. But I know the martial arts; it's one reason I was hired. Ruby fought me. I had to defend myself. She meant business, meant to take me right out. One of my punches was a little off in the shadows. It killed her. I killed her. I'm so very sorry. It's caused the family so much grief. And now there's this strange business with Burr Man." His head turned down. He could go no further.

Sophie caught herself, dared not let a single tear drip. In fact, she'd known Ruby's spirit hovered over her bed sometimes when she tossed and turned, deep in dreams. Ruby had to be dead, she knew. But for her to die right here in Mountain Home, and Burr Man was not even responsible? She moved both hands toward her temples, and removed her eyes from everyone. So senseless!

"Ok, it's obvious what the first promise must be. So here I'll say to you all..." She did hesitate for a tiny moment, but there was nothing else to do but plow this field. "I promise not to tell anyone about Ruby Gellerman's death. I won't get the family into trouble with the law, if that's what you are worried about."

To that Jared smiled and sighed audibly. "You seem to know there are actually two promises involved. You are sharp Sophie. An astute young woman."

She became suddenly aware both her knees were not touching each other, and there was Uncle Glen, getting in a good stare, perhaps hopeful to see more than just her mid-knee skin. "The second promise now Uncle Jared."

"You're a ghost whisperer Sophie. We know that, but we don't know if you've practiced your talent any over the last seven years since you left Mountain Home. So we have to ask you first, if you came upon Burr Man, you must not under any conditions, make the light for him. If he chose to go this time, we would lose everything. Your family would lose it all."

"I promise not to do that if I see him Uncle Jared. I won't make the light."

Henry got up and hugged his daughter. It was as if he were welcoming her back into the family all over again. Isabel came over and grabbed Sophie, enfolding her into a big warm envelope of flesh and fat. Last to come over was Glen, "I'm counting on you Sophie. Don't let me down." He released her hand a second too long and Sophie shivered as his thick flesh coursed over her own.

On the drive to the mansion Henry briefed her on the family's needs this night: Find and confront Burr Man. Communicate with him. Release whatever spirit was ravaging him. Do not make the light door. Sophie heard the words of course, but she wondered if she could perform the role of obedient ghost whisperer. There were too many variables; the least of which was the question about why Ruby's spirit chose to hang around here, deliberately avoiding walking into the light. What massive chore did she find so important that she'd avoid what she knew was absolutely best for any spirit? Death to Ruby wasn't the end, it was a doorway. But she'd taken leave of that fact to stay here, to be stuck with Burr Man, perhaps for all time.

Henry shot a baleful glance her way just before they parked the car. The mansion loomed high in such a perfect darkness, a shadowy blot against an almost equally indigo line of tree tops. Sophie had paused to clear something from her eyes. Henry would be surprised if fear were tearing at her, getting the best of things. As long as he had known his daughter, she'd been the one as close to fearless as any of them. So much like her mother. He reached for Sophie's hand. Somehow he never wanted to let go of it ever again.

Propelled by the light from headlamps, the men followed closely behind Sophie Sater. She herself had declined any headlamp. All that light from theirs should be sufficient for the task. They were deep inside the giant casket of wood when Sophie felt the brush of wind against her cheeks. The breeze twisted quickly into a gale of wind, and Henry, Hansel and Jared cowered in terror, their headlamps askew spraying light everywhere, anywhere but straight ahead.

Hansel was the first one to make a whooping noise, a concoction between surprise and unexpected discovery. Henry's scream came out shrill, biting, and it curled over itself for many seconds. Sophie's eyes had been temporarily stabbed by slashing beams of light, but now she saw what had moved directly in front of them.

Burr Man was here. And he dragged a guest with him.

He presented the partly decayed body of Ruby Gellerman to them all. Her arms had curled across her chest from rigor mortis. The ripped jeans covered legs which were bent at grotesque angles below the knees. Burr Man had gripped a calf tightly enough so that when he flung the body it jarred the floor right at Hansel's feet. It landed with a thud and Hansel moaned and half swooned into Jared's surprised arms.

Sophie easily saw something else as the men scattered. She could only have hoped it would be here and exactly as in her dreams, it drifted down like a wisp, but one that had purpose. The entity pulsed lightly, its slender arc of light a distinct lavender ripple against the harsh darkness. She knew Burr Man's energy as a glaring pulsar, a negative cascade of doom. Contrasted against this gloom-Ruby's goodness. A base of energy that harbored her very own *After Death Spiritual Entity*. No doubt it was this great clashing of wills that was wrecking Burr Man's walkabouts, ruining his methods of garnering energy. Ruby wasn't about to leave him alone or let him off the hook. It wasn't her way, the way of a killer woman.

And now along had come Sophie to participate in what would be the final episode. Sophie suddenly realized why Ruby had stayed. She was waiting on Sophie.

Burr Man hovered, a soundless black soul watching the humans but mindful of the descending entity just behind him. Then a snarl and he snapped from his drowse. He surged forward. The three men had set themselves behind Sophie, as if she were a sturdy bulwark against evil, but Burr Man brushed past her with ease. The men could only say they got what they most wanted this night-the *old* Burr Man. He'd become his old self to suit this perfect moment. Blood spurted and sprayed from skin that was far too loose on the bones, and the blood vessels distended outward, superhighways for that foul, reddish liquid.

Sophie could not step forward, Burr Man was between her and the men. In another moment he'd be engorging himself on someone, much as he'd done those years ago with Isabel. Maybe this time, he wouldn't hold anything back. Sophie brought both arms forward and jerked them savagely into Burr Man's entity. "Enough!"

Instantly, Burr Man's bony arm came up high and he jammed it into Sophie's astonished face. She fell hard, directly on Ruby's protruding cheekbones. Burr Man moved to finish Sophie off, but the lavender light came upon him, fell directly his way and it illuminated a face that crucially despised anything heavenly. The pulsing black face contorted in what could only be pain.

Burr Man at once stepped away from his human prey. Suddenly he seemed agonized, confused, epileptic. His head swayed to and fro, and like a man with a vast migraine, Burr Man rested temples of fingers on the side of his throbbing head. He bellowed, wanted to leave but Ruby held him down. Then came a ripping sound, as a bed sheet shearing in half by some unseen hand.

The cleavage was sudden, dramatic, utterly unexpected. It was as if Burr Man had become a giant cocoon and some fault line opened up, cracking right down the middle. Something moved inside the cocoon, tried to step away, was restrained, stepped away again. It had two legs. It was human. A human man being stepped out. It pulsed in fits and starts, was mostly translucent. Its *After Death Spiritual Entity* was now freed from those years of freakish bondage. Sophie noted his shortness and she could not miss the pig-tail dangling, black hair long uncut. His flat round face looked straight at the lighted doorway, rippled in amber waves, inviting, comforting. He moved both hands across his chest, across the square blue shirt with bright red buttons and floated that way so softly, he could have been the wisp around a cloud.

Suddenly, another form walked out of the cracked black entity. Burr Man in eclipse folded over and moaned in clear agony as a second man bore himself away. This castaway was tall and thin and jutted his jaw line toward the watching humans with haughty dignity. Skeleton eyes only focused on one thing, the doorway for which he had yearned all these years.

After the freed spirits disappeared into the doorway, Sophie wondered why it did not close. And now a second thought filtered into her reasoning: How had she managed to open the amber doorway? She had not willed it into existence. How had it come on its own?

The answer came with stunning swiftness. There was no time for a single tear, no time to say goodbye.

Ruby's lavender well of consciousness drifted to the doorwell. For a fraction of a second, part of the bubbling, lacy wisp changed. Ruby's long, smiling face appeared. A hand came in front of it. It waved and moved in a certain direction, even as the face beamed its last earthly smile. When Ruby sailed away, the amber vent faltered, then wilted away completely.

Only Burr Man remained. The husk that was left of him.

It was then that Jared made a move. He stormed forward, his palms folded in an imploring fashion, "Stay with us Burr Man. Don't leave this way." But the great fissure that had opened up a pathway for the two trapped human spirits, could not heal itself. Some kind of great yellow pus began to ooze from the great wound. Burr Man's eyes sunk down, as if trying to see what kind of damage he'd incurred.

Jared stepped back yelping and holding his nose, a bare yard from the burning embers of the great, dying beast. Burr Man raised an arm, pointed toward Jared's astonished face. Then, like a light bulb whose filaments are finished, Burr Man winked out. In two flashes, he blinked off and on, and in a great whoosh, he flew away or simply disintegrated.

Henry came over at once and folded Sophie into his arms. Jared looked at the ceiling for many moments. Then he gave a loud sigh. He came and stood over Ruby's mangled body. "We'll take care of this at once, Sophie. The Sheriff has to know. No more hiding. We're ruined anyway."

⌘ ⌘ ⌘

At the final meeting, Glen again cursed her. "Damn you girl, you promised us all, before God Almighty, that you would not make the light. Now Burr Man is gone for good. He's left us high and dry. It's your fault." The finger almost touched her cheekbone.

"Burr Man never went into the light, family." Sophie shoved the trembling finger away from her face.

They all gave a huff and prolonged looks of astonishment lingered on Jared's uncomfortable face. He raised an arm. "I wanted Sophie to tell you this. She just did. Sorry if I misled you, but I had good intentions. What happened in the mansion was the most incredible thing I could ever hope to see. Nothing any church pastor could ever say about the hereafter could surpass…what I think…I know now. And as for Sophie, she was a trooper, as calm and steady as Patton. You all would have been proud of her."

Rosa stood up and spoke with voice crackling. "You mean Burr Man just left all on his own?

Sophie walked over and touched her aunt lightly on an arm. "Burr Man had no choice. Ruby had incredible power in her spiritual presence. Not only did she create the light, but she forced Burr Man to release his prisoners. Two men as spiritual entities walked free from their horrible prison. Family, Burr Man was a *demon*. A real true demonic being. But he had to leave when he lost the two disturbed spirits. Ruby forced his hand."

"And there's something else to make this evening most memorable. The family mystery is solved. We think we know what happened to Great- Grandpaw Bingham and the other two who were murdered."

Henry was in the know. He was eager to be heard, to be counted this night. "We all saw the two beings leave Burr Man's black cocoon. We pretty much know who they were, and once you know that, you can connect the dots."

"So do that for us brother. Kindly connect the dots so we can sleep contentedly tonight." Isabel smiled weakly. In fact, she was leaning so far forward only the tail end of her butt remained on the seat cushion.

"One of those entities that made up the Burr Man composite was one of the fellows who was murdered," Sophie said, taking over from Henry. "He was Benjamin, who was our great uncle. He was only twenty-one years old when he met his end. We matched him pretty easily from one of those ancient pictures on the wall in Bingham mansion."

"And we knew it was him from the huge hole in his head when he walked into the light. Somebody had taken a gun and almost blown his head off the night he was so brutally and suddenly killed. But we already knew that didn't we?"

Even Glen had nothing to say. He'd sat down, was staring hard first at Jared, then at Sophie.

"Who was the second person. Our Great- Grandpaw?"

Sophie looked around and Jared and Henry nodded for her to continue. "No, not at all. Surprisingly, the second entity that was trapped by the Burr Man demon was Great- Grandpaw's faithful Chinese butler."

Now Glen had cause to rouse to life. He snapped his fingers. "Wait a minute! That can't be. We all have seen those old photos of the murder scene. Three fellas are laying there face up, and there ain't no Chinese face among 'em." He shook his head for good effect.

Jared came back into the fray. "You are dead correct Glen, but nevertheless it was the Chinese butler we saw the other day. I checked some records and his name was Lo Chay. Lo Chay had been with our Great -Grandpaw for at least ten years. He did all manner of chores for the family who lived there. As we know, he'd completely disappeared after the murders and now we know why."

Rosa clapped her hands. "Because he himself was murdered."

Henry came over and draped an arm over Jared's shoulder. "But you know brother, I am wondering why his body was never found. That would've been four murders that night."

"Sounds like the work of the Macy family to me." Jared drawled the response out in typical Southern fashion. All eyes fastened back on his stout face. "That crazy feud lingered and lingered. Sometimes it burst forth with a fury. Something was going on, only God knows what, and it caused the Macys to get lathered up enough to sneak over here one night and do some executions."

Glen suddenly whirled, face bright with excitement. "My guess is that Lo Chay had betrayed our Great -Grandpaw. Maybe he wanted out, took the cash under the table for information about when the family would be especially vulnerable. They came in, executed the three they'd targeted and then double-crossed Lo Chay. Probably four bodies would arouse too much suspicion, and besides, if Lo Chay came up missing at that exact time, the dumb- as- mud Sheriff might go off on some wild goose chase and leave the Macys alone."

They all stared at Glen. That was the most sentences he'd logically strung together in many months, and the end result was entirely reasonable.

Sophie smiled toward Uncle Glen. "Your guess is probably very good. Just before Ruby completely sank into the light, she kind of turned her head in a strange direction, and pointed with her finger. More or less in the direction of that deep, dark ravine just behind the house. I've never walked there, but I heard there's some burrs and brambles the size of grapefruits. And how did Burr Man get his name? From such huge burrs that latched onto him. It could be, Uncle Glen, that Burr Man had always haunted a part of that ravine where there's a grave, the one the Chinese butler could have been dumped into by the Macys. When people came into the mansion, Burr Man showed up, so he could sap up precious energy that he needed. People's emotions were usually so negative, dark and intense, it became a habit for Burr Man. Go into the mansion when people were there. By good coincidence, along the way to the mansion, he couldn't help but get swamped by those big ole burrs all in the ravine. Because Burr Man was of a demonic essence, his metaphysical build bordered between substance and non-substance. As to the matter of that grave-maybe one of us can find it some day."

"And Burr Man won't be anywhere near there? Can you promise Sophie."

"No Aunt Rosa. I cannot promise. But I think he's gone for good."

The family broke into small conversations trying to digest it all. Sophie eased from the group and made her way to the door. She thought of Ruby's funeral and the irony of her body being buried in the family church cemetery. Jared had quietly agreed to let her have his very own burial plot. Henry was purchasing the grave stone. Sophie would impart the words on the granite. She hadn't yet figured out what they'd be.

How they'd all get past the Sheriff and the local District Attorney-well that was their challenge. Maybe their connections would be good enough to get off the hook. Blaming it on Burr Man might work-he was nowhere to be found anymore.

She shut the door as the family's voices rose eagerly, trying to recount what they'd just heard, as if repeating it over and over would somehow make it more true.

Sophie thought suddenly about her job at the library. How could she get anybody to possibly believe all this? They'd just say with a laugh, you've been reading too many mystery novels. Nobody's family *ever* has adventures like that.

They were far from perfect this bunch, but they were all she had. And Henry was her father. *Her* dad. He'd at last convinced her, and now maybe the weird, jagged edges of this family could dull just enough for a proper, if belated entrance for Sophie Sater.

Sophie might be leaving tomorrow, but when she passed a mirror and saw her own goofy smile, she knew she must at last be home.

THE END

What happens at the end of a long war where brothers and friends have been busy slaughtering each other? What's the aftermath of such an event? We also find that sometimes other spirits poke their noses around, perhaps curious or maybe ashamed about the stupid endeavors of living humans....

Fishville

Everyone in the small hamlet of Fishville knew a little something about Boyce Caldwell's plan. Boyce was not one to confide in people, but the village blacksmith had also fought in the Great War Between the States. Boyce's whispers to this fellow did not fall on deaf ears. Roy Whitlow also spread other types of news around: He was the first one to learn in Fishville hamlet that Robert E. Lee had given up his army to the butcher Sam Grant.

About a day later elements of the Yankee calvary dared to show their faces. On the main road to Jena they came gallivanting, and a hundred well fed horses pranced in front of any defiant and gaunt onlookers who risked coming outside. Nobody took the first potshot at the blue-clad men. If the war was really over, why die now?

Two days later, people began asking the obvious question: What about those two idiot Yankees Boyce Caldwell kept? Would he really execute them now?

Since Roy Whitlow knew, he quietly spread the word that this very afternoon was the time for what be an odd, if interesting spectacle. Boyce was going to pull off something at the Fishville swimming hole. Nobody would be swimming there in early May, but a few anglers might be goading the catfish at the old deep hole at the bend of Big Creek. That was where the kids had once begged their elders to place a wonderful old diving board and long, sturdy swing rope. In quieter times, Fishville swimming hole offered peace and repose to families and kids all through the hot summers of central Louisiana.

It was exactly two hours before sunset when Boyce made his appearance. The two Yankee prisoners shuffled along as best they could, encumbered with ropes around ankles, bound at the waist and half blind from rags over their faces.

When Boyce reached the high bluff where the Fishville diving board was planked, Boyce called out. "Halt!" The two hounds flanking Sergeant Gerald Tanner and Lieutenant Rob Battle sat down first. Weary from at least one mile of penguin waddling, the two prisoners came down to one knee and caught their breath.

Boyce turned thick yellow eyes on his prisoners and spat a heavy wad of sickly tobacco juice on the exposed toes of the one he'd come to hate the most.

Gerald Tanner lacked the energy to flick away the gob off the end of his foot. He couldn't move much anyway. Boyce had tied him up real fine for this little walk in the sunlight. Sergeant Tanner and his partner in misery Lieutenant Rob Battle, were bound at the waistlines for good measure. They'd mostly stayed at the edge of the piney woods since leaving the capture hut to keep too many stray, prying eyes from being too interested.

Lieutenant Rob Battle surveyed the early May afternoon. As the officer in charge, he'd done his best to cultivate some kind of relationship with his captor, this lunatic Southerner. Gerald Tanner, on the other hand, always told Boyce exactly what he thought of such brazen Southern trash. Now that the war was over, Gerald knew that Boyce could not keep them around. If not for a single stupid mistake trying to obey orders from the idiot Colonel in charge of Fort Buhlow, a goodly distance away near the Red River outside Pineville hamlet, they wouldn't be here now. The main issue as they had pleaded was that the landlubbers assigned to the skiff that day had no experience navigating on a rough and rising river. But the Colonel's minions had chopped down too many trees building the fort and getting through the cold winter. Now at least, maybe they could tow some free lumber floating down the river toward the bank's edge. So the Colonel gave the order and two men immediately paid the price when a giant root came gushing upward from a whirlpool eddy and swamped the skiff. Sergeant Tanner and Rob Battle found themselves unlikely sailors on that same stump of cypress, floating down the cold river, along with a menacing troop of water moccasins, who slithered and hissed barely an arm's length away from where the men had posted themselves.

Rob knew he had to say something right now at this very second. How could he just waddle without a fuss to his most certain death right here at this deep bend? Boyce had grown silent, but he was watching to see if they would try to do anything that might smack of resistance. From the corner of his eye, Rob saw the familiar smirk crease across Boyce's leathered jowls. Maybe talk over action.

"I don't suppose you'd loosen these bonds and let me take a dip." Rob found it necessary to look at his captor from an oblique angle. The old Southern soldier looked too much like the Devil himself for Rob to risk a head on stare. "I've got sweat caked up in layers I can't count. The war's finished you know. No need to keep us prisoners any longer."

Such begging only made Boyce bellow. "Take a dip you say? Yep, you'll be getting to do that right soon, but first let me shoo away these watchers."

Suddenly his voice boomed and it carried all down the hollow. "All my so-called friends can leave now. You don't want to be seeing what's gonna happen here. If the Yankees ever do ask you anything, you can say in truth, go to hell, I don't know what in hell you're talking about." For good measure

Boyce raised his good right arm and brought the pistol up high. A single '*kepow*'. Those present nodded. Caldwell wanted privacy now. He'd get it.

Old man Smoot glared at him for a moment. He was one of those men who regularly hauled big blue cat from a drop-off right under this diving board that this time of year was about 20 feet deep. "For once I believe you Boyce. I don't wanna be a witness to your craziness. Just don't leave a mess here. In a couple of weeks the kids'll be coming here for summer swimming."

Gerald Tanner was not a man who could hold back disdain from anyone he didn't respect. And this fellow Boyce Caldwell would always occupy the topmost pinnacle of any Most Hated Men's list for Tanner. "So this is where you're gonna kill us? You don't mind pollutin' this swimming hole with our blood one bit do ya? What a coward you are Caldwell."

Boyce stepped toward the Union Sergeant and put the tip of the saber's blade against the thin skin on his exposed abdomen. The pace of Tanner's breath suddenly accelerated as the saber tip sagged and expanded with each breath-laden exhalation. "You think you're a tough guy don't you Tanner? You don't know what tough is. Do you think you would've had the courage, the guts to go up that Harper's Ferry Mountain? I was there and don't think I saw you."

Sergeant Tanner set his best caustic gaze directly into the older man's steady gaze. "I guess this is the best time to tell you, your little game's up. You didn't lose your arm at Harper's Ferry. Maybe you was there, but no northern bullet took your arm off there. I know for a fact some little buckthorn tickled your arm and infection set in. When you couldn't fight no more they sent you back here. I guess you call this place home, but I'd call it living on the edge of hell."

Boyce gave a huff and removed the saber tip from Gerald's navel. But now his two curs picked up on their master's irritated vibrations. Jeremiah and Abram had been lolling at the feet of Rob Battle. But when Gerald Tanner finished his little speech, lathered as it was with hate and loathing, they sauntered over, eyes growling before the sound effected outward. Abram took his customary nip at Gerald's heavily scarred calf. The dogs had made a living this past year keeping that part of Sergeant Tanner's anatomy badly infected.

"You're definitely going first, Tanner. So get on with it. Go right over there and stand."

"Go where?"

"Right where that diving board is. Go waddle over there and stand like you're gonna take yourself a good dive."

"Should I lieutenant?"

"You've got no choice Gerald. Take it slow and easy. Don't fall off the bank."

With great care Gerald Tanner made it to the diving board. It was a fine board made from a pine plank and at least seven feet long. There was just enough spring in the wood so that a good diver could make a nice hop and hover briefly in the swamp-like air.

That fact hardly mattered to Gerald. With his wrists and ankles lashed together he'd do no better than sink like a stone. Even if he wasn't tied up, he had less than a chance of a rat against a fox. In upstate Indiana, he'd never once gone into water higher than his waistline.

Edging along carefully, he waddled along the bank and onto the pine diving board. Close to board's end, a shot rang out.

The rope lashes around his feet were smashed apart by a single bullet from Boyce's pistol. Gerald could not turn around on the board. Suddenly he realized he was slipping, his feet making small sliding movements on the pine board. And Gerald fell. He managed to land awkwardly on his butt, and he now straddled the diving board. Gerald gaped at the blood and flesh he'd landed on. When Boyce had blasted away the rope, the bullet also mangled flesh and bone. Gerald glanced down at the dark waters of Fishville swimming hole, and suddenly felt dizzy when he saw the first pint of his life's blood draining there.

Boyce was speaking, and Gerald heard the voice as if from a dream. "Go into those cool waters now Sergeant. Like a balm of Gilead, they will comfort you."

Rob Battle's muscles twitched and he lurched toward the crazy man. He launched his head toward where the fellow's sturdy chest was supposed to be, and came away with empty air, almost tumbling into the creek. The dogs were on him in that heartbeat, snarling and sending dog spit into his humiliated face. He slithered back onto a deck of level bank and watched when Gerald Tanner peeled over and went in feet first into the waters of Fishville swimming hole.

I am sinking, falling toward a murky brown bottom. Precious air explodes deep within my chest but I'm sinking and in only a few seconds I stand on the bottom, looking up through maybe fifteen feet of water. I'm not so cold. Then I see a fish, a big one swimming straight for my head. The catfish stops only inches away. It seems to be studying the stranger that invaded its realm. The current begins to steer me and I cannot fight it. Now I'm sideways to the bottom and the fish is still right there. I bounce off some underwater hill. The fish lets his eyes meet mine. I'm feeling warmth. Where does it come from?

The fish swims around me twice, flapping its fins as if in message. But I cannot grasp anything. All I can think of is fight upward, fight up to the top of this little hillock. Maybe there's something up there for me. Here at the bottom only death lurks and it's a matter of seconds.

Maybe I am clawing up the hill backward. I am a southern crayfish, frantic with motion, panic stricken beyond reason. The strange catfish swims up and places an eye directly against my own. I want to shriek, and wonder the odd thought, is this catfish really a shark? What other reason could its interest be in me, except for gnawing on my poor flesh? Now to my progress: Maybe I am actually clawing my way backward up that hill. Go up a hill! I'd taken orders just like that to heart before, against some of Boyce

Caldwell's minions. Orders come to take a hill-a soldier's sternest resolve! Charge! I make it through that day, but now any bravery I'd built up has puffed away like silken vapor.

Something hard grabs at me, digs painfully into the tender meat of shoulder. I somehow spin around, needing to see what it is. Now my thigh rams hard against what must be iron or steel. A barb burrows deep toward the bone. Such pain and astonishment! Air gushes from my open mouth. My last sight is to see, but not discern, what has killed me.

Boyce, that clever man- killer! He knew these currents, knew exactly how to set the trap. Any desperate fellow would have done exactly as I did to escape the deep water, fixed securely in these unholy bonds. And from my blundering I am in this thicket of hooks, set upon some kind of matrix of ropy lines. It's warm down here suddenly. And I roll over once and die even as my body flops about from the steadily rolling current.

"Sit down over here on this grassy patch, Lieutenant Battle. Make yourself at ease soldier."

Rob had not taken his eyes from the water. There was no hint of human life down there. It had been at least five minutes, and Tanner was nowhere. Rob fixed a sad gaze at the inhuman face of Boyce Caldwell.

This was indeed a pitiful scab of a man. That he'd been injured in the war between the North and the South was undeniable. But, in Rob's eyes, it wasn't the physical wounds that were the most severe. The interior flower that defined humanity, *that* bloom had died inside this man. The pain, rejection and humiliation that was his general lot in life, had all blended together to create a black oil that seemed to make malignant clots, perhaps invading as far as his soul.

While sitting long hours tied up against the iron pole between the pig stalls somewhere near the capture hut, sometimes Boyce would come over and rant for hours. He blamed the North for everything; his wife had died while he was out fighting. Even his dear mother was raped while he fought for the cause most sacred. But word had lately come that the man who'd saved him from becoming a teen age orphan in some nameless South Carolina town had died in a Yankee prison camp. That was when Boyce seemed to truly unravel.

Colonel John W. Henagan of South Carolina's Eighth Regiment did not make it through a brutal Ohio winter and in February his large heart finally failed him. He was buried near Johnston Isle Prison where he died. There would be no one to mourn his bones, nothing of him to return back to his precious South Carolina loam.

Rob eyed the increasing depth of shadows coming from the tall beech trees lining the creek. He'd do anything to keep away from death's doorstop. What kind of man would slaughter northern soldiers like this? But this fellow Boyce Caldwell's worst deviant traits had been provoked by this war between brothers. Rob cleared his throat and just said the first thing that came to his mind.

"As I told you before Mr. Caldwell, I'm sorry for everything that's happened to you. This war's just about taken the very soul out of this country. We've got to find a way to get our good hearts back. Killin' some more people sure ain't the answer."

Boyce Caldwell's weird, curious look bounced off Rob's sunburned face and Boyce let out a sound halfway between growl and laugh. "Ha! So now it's *Mr. Caldwell* is it? You must be angling toward me cutting you loose and letting you walk away. Is that it? Well, Mr. Boyce Caldwell may be sick, but he's in his right mind still."

Then his chest heaved and he worked hard to spit out a mass of smelly brown pus and blood. But some of it got stuck on his scruffy speckled beard. Rob had to turn his head when two blowflies came right up and began sucking up the parts of the pussy blood. Caldwell had no clue they were there. This disease that kept taking away Boyce day by day surely also contributed to draining out any remaining sparklets of humanity. He was dying and most likely he knew it.

"Most of what you are saying is true and makes sense, Lieutenant. I'm aware you think most Southern men are mere idiots, not much smarter than their slaves. I do understand when you say you personally are not responsible for all the bad things that's happened to me. But it was your General Sheridan that captured Col'nel Johnny Henagan over there close to Winchester. And it was your prison guards that didn't give him enough proper food and blankets this past winter. So your system has killed him. I owe my life to that man and his family. When I heard he was about dead, that was the last and final straw. I reckon I gotta kill you Lieutenant. Maybe if I think two dead Yankees might come close to equalin' the death of the good Colonel, I may be able to get some sleep in these last days of my life."

Suddenly Rob made the connection: "Did you happen to also serve under Colonel Henagan? Was the 8th South Carolina Regiment your outfit?"

Boyce made his head bob up and down one time.

"You just said you knew a lot about the battle that took Harper's Ferry. Lee sent Jackson over there to do that job. What was the 8th South Carolina regiment doing over that way? Weren't they under Longstreet in the 1st Corps?"

Boyce edged over to his prisoner. "Everybody knows about Lee's gamble. Somehow it must have passed you by. Yeah, Lee sent Jackson over to take Harper's Ferry and it was the first time we'd been directly under Stonewall. What an amazing man he was! I seen him once up close with those blue eyes blazing with hate. How that man hated you Yankees! He told us to clamber almost straight up a mountain that flanked Harper's Ferry, said the Yankees would never be suspecting such a dumb stunt. We did just that and when the Regimental Flag Bearer went down with a mortal wound, it was Colonel Henagan himself that picked up the flag and pleaded with us to go on. I tell ya, my legs were not hardly able to take one more step, but somehow I began to run toward the works the Yanks had thrown up. And do you know, Lieutenant, who picked up the flag when Colonel Henagan went down? It was me. And it was me who planted the flag into their works and a few hours later we owned the mountain. Our artillery poured it down on the city and they gave up."

"But you hurt your arm in this battle?"

"Sure did. It was in those works. The Yankees piled up everything they could find and threw it all together, logs, brambles, weeds and rocks. When I was scrambling around dodging bayonets, my arm jammed up into a big pile of brambles and some big thorns jabbed me good. Colonel Henagan had to go back to South Carolina for six months, and he almost didn't make it. While he was gone my arm swelled up like a red balloon. They cut it away and that's how I came to be back here so far from my unit. My wife's family was supposed to be here, but everybody was mad, dead or scattered. I was on my own."

For several moments it was two soldiers studying the truest metal of the other. Rob had suddenly become aware from listening that Boyce Caldwell was truly the consummate Southern opponent, the reason why the South had been able to hang on for so long. Despite his looks and the way he talked, Boyce was smart. But like all Southerners he was also wrong. Wrong to have fought in this war so savagely and lost an arm in the process. Wrong to have cultivated hate for so long. Wrong to have killed Sergeant Tanner just now.

Rob scoured his mind for something else to say, something that Boyce Caldwell could cling to for just a few more precious minutes. "I do regret, Mr. Caldwell, that you got the better of me. But if I may ask, what gave you the idea to trade for us with that fella who fished us out of the Red River?"

A gleam darted into those crusted foamy eyes, and Rob suspected he'd bored into a hopeful place. "You mean ole Hardy Mason? He's my dead wife's cousin. He owed me some money and couldn't pay me back and so got the idea of tradin' you two morons off. He suspected I couldn't do all the work on this farm all by myself with just one arm."

Boyce softly bellowed and jerked his head back in reflex. "I couldn't believe it when Hardy told me he was nursin' two half-drowned Yankee soldiers back to life because they fell into the Red River at flood time. I believe you told me before what you was doin' in the current, but tell me once more before you......go away."

Rob cleared his throat and watched as Jeremiah trotted over to his master for a little ear rub. "Yes, ah, it was because we needed some more firewood. Over at Fort Buhlow there weren't any good trees left. So our Colonel told me and Sergeant Tanner.., to get in the skiff and collect some of the debris the flood had brought in. Unfortunately, some big whirlpool caught the skiff and we were out toward the middle of the big, fast river when a tree just bobbed up and sunk us straightway. We tried to stay attached to that tree and got down to around Marksville. That's when the Mason fellow saw us and rescued us. Just in time I might add. We had just got bit by some water rattlers that wanted to own our piece of tree root."

"Ha, that's so funny. You'd a been better off just drownin'." He laughed heartily, as if Rob had just told a hilarious joke. Jeremiah seemed to understand because he cast two quick baleful glances in Rob's direction.

The lapse in talking came on too quickly. Rob's back ached from sitting up for so long with his legs stretched out in front. Some crickets in the reeds and grasses along the bank's edge began to chorus. Rob no longer felt the sun's warmth on his bare back. It must be going down below the tree line.

Boyce gave Jeremiah one last ear tug and then whispered, "Let's get this done."

In an instant, his gaze was fixed on Lieutenant Rob Battle. "Now it's your turn, Lieutenant. Whether or not you're a good and decent man can't concern me. Any day now your Yankee soldiers may be trooping by again and I can't have you with me. It's unfortunate for you. But you gotta go." Then his head dipped as if in finality, toward the Fishville diving board.

Rob tried to stand, realized both legs were numb and fell to one knee. Boyce seemed unfazed by the delay, but the two dogs took it as an affront, growling and standing up stiffly. Rob appraised Boyce one last time and saw how tightly he gripped his old saber. "Mr. Caldwell, I'd appreciate it if you gave me the fightin' chance you gave Sergeant Tanner. But without shooting off half my foot, if you please."

Boyce nodded and said, "Turn around." Rob felt the saber blade slash through the ropy anklet bonds. He spread his feet and considered one last desperate rush at his captor. Maybe if he made a good head butt, they'd both splash into the water and then, who could know what might happen? But the two mongrel curs had already read his thoughts. They were looking straight at him, as if some of his thoughts had somehow strayed into their minds. In fact, Boyce's two dogs were the primary reason there had been no successful escape from the farm. If Rob lived past this day he was certain that would be the hardest thing to explain to his superiors, his inability to outsmart two common, southern hounds.

He'd played pirate games around creeks in the depths of summer as a small kid. Somebody was always elected to 'walk the plank.' An old scarf went over some boy's eyes and while he tried to go across the log, the other kids threw mudballs. It was almost a relief to fall into the water in those days.

He stepped slowly toward the diving board.

There was no way to tell anything about what lay beneath the surface. He would have to guess the force of cold water might force the breath from him instantly. He inhaled extra large breaths.

Suddenly there was no more pine board. He'd come to its raw bare end. He bobbed slightly up and down just from the strength of his wildly beating heart. *Breathe Rob. Breathe some more. Can't get enough air. Breathe it in. Control yourself. This is just another battle to fight. We've won them all so far haven't we?*

He thought about humming some old church hymn. But he could not imagine God looking down from heaven and letting this go on. And talking to Boyce any more would be futile. In Boyce's mind this was it. The final ending was really here. The war was over! And Rob Battle had one last fight to get past, the one that confirmed he was fit to live, or his time to die was truly now.

Keep your wits Rob. Smart men can live. Breathe!

Suddenly a voice rang out in the growing gloom. It was Boyce Caldwell. He was speaking to Rob. "Maybe, Lieutenant, I'm more tired of death than I've let on. Or maybe it was the dream I had last night. I was close to the fiery pits. Could almost feel the heat baking my arms. I'm gonna die soon enough anyway. I s'pose I don't need your sorry memory weighin' me down more than I'm already weighed down. So I'm gonna watch you jump in, let you sink to the bottom, and then me and the dogs are gonna go home. I think you'll be just like your friend that just jumped in anyway."

Rob heard the words but could not understand. Maybe this was the first hint that ordinary human emotions like guilt and remorse could be torturing the man. He would watch Rob jump in and sink. But he wouldn't hang around after that? Rob couldn't digest the thought; it consumed too much energy and conflicted with the tiny thread of hope Rob clung to.

Rob took a single hop and his body extended skyward. He fought to keep his posture straight and went into the water toes bent downward.

Pressure on my ears! Will my head explode if I keep going down? Can't think straight. Oh no, my feet are digging into the muck. Yes, pull them out, scoot on the bottom with the current and go toward that little hillock. It's curving gradually upward and maybe getting past it gets you into water that's not so deep. That's it Rob. Good.

What's that fish doing? He's swimming around me. He's looking straight at me! Never known a fish to do such a thing! But wait. It's so much warmer than it should be. What's happening? Whose face is that in my mind? I cannot see the fish or the water anymore. Just a man with a kind face and his lips are moving. I see Colonel bars on his shoulders now. Can only see the collar, but he's a Southern officer for sure.

The man's lips make sounds I can follow with my brain but not my ears: "Boyce was wrong to do this to you. He will see in a few weeks when he dies and crosses over, that this kind of hate was something I never taught him. As for you Lieutenant Battle, it's not yet your time. Of course, if you let your air out, you'll be with me in just a few moments. But this fish that's working with me now is going to entangle his dorsal fin into in your wrist bonds. He'll carry you downstream where there is a sandbar and you can collect your wits."

Then the face vanished. Rob tried to remember the Colonel's features: A kind oval face, no beard or mustache, thin brown hair with a hint of gray.

The fish aligned himself properly and jammed its stout top fin directly into the ropes on Rob's wrists. As it began to swim, Rob's body flipped over. Then he saw it. Swaying in the gentle underwater current not quite halfway up the little underwater hill, hovered Sergeant Tanner's body. His mouth was agape, the face frozen in rapturous terror. Rob's fish savior detoured around this death zone. Rob discerned that such hooks were not placed here for fishing. Boyce did not have the gumption to just line up his Yankee prisoners and execute them outright. He had figured out a way to kill them, but out of sight, silently. No doubt he'd borrowed some of Hardy Mason's big catfish hooks and got some special lines for this job. Let them jump from the diving board! Mad from panic, anyone would claw his way up the underwater hillock. The hooks would latch into the flesh maybe in an arm, a leg, possibly the chest. Brilliant. Brutal. Deadly.

So this was the reason Boyce did not mind releasing the ropy ankle shackles. It would make it far easier to allow the prisoner think he had some chance to go up that little underwater hill. He wouldn't be looking for hooks, concentrating so much on keeping air in his lungs and making his feet dig hard in the muck for traction to go up to where beautiful air laced the world.

Rob forced himself to think of anything but air. And if this ordeal ends with my life intact, to whom or what would I say I owe my life? To this catfish towing me secretly downstream? How could it be explained to myself, much less to others, that apparently, the kind spirit of a Southern Colonel, one John W. Henagan, had come back to this wicked realm at this exact time. Was it because perhaps he'd been watching and fretting about the moral diminishment that had washed over someone he cared for, this depraved man sitting on the bank? So if the Colonel could not influence Boyce to avoid this deadly deed, then the least he could do was try and intervene and save a life? Mine? What kind of story was that? How crazy and unbelievable the turn of a life!

But no entity on earth or in heaven could do anything about Rob's lack of oxygen. He thought: Wouldn't it be the height of irony if he breathed in water now only a few moments away from safe harbor? Rob forced the image of Colonel Henagan deep into his mind; suppressing the fantastic desire to inhale was his sole mindless directive at this moment. Think about anything but air!

Just at that moment of blackness, when sheer weariness wins and the lungs make bellows for breathing air or water, it does not matter, when the muscles lack energy to do anything helpful, Rob's nose burrowed into sand.

He knew his eyes were closed and also knew his brain lacked the proper commands to make them open up. But he'd been deposited so that his face was pointed skyward, and from here Fishville's waters lapped against his half submerged form.

Time did what it willed. When Rob moved again, he rolled over and water splashed into his eyes. He opened them and the first thing he saw in the moonlight was an astonished raccoon. It had come over for a sniff, and now his body moved and the raccoon leaped backward, barking a warning.

Lieutenant Rob Battle arose and staggered downstream to a thickly wooded patch. He gradually worked his wrists from the ropy knot and he slow jogged down one thin moonlit trail and then to another. He knew the general way out. After a steady night of traveling toward the south, he would be close to his own.

Just then directly above, an owl flapped wings. It hooted loudly turning its head halfway around, the huge eyes focusing on the two-legged animal far too large to be food.

The owl had framed itself against the waxing moon. Just then Rob recalled the night his outfit had invited in an old Choctaw who'd been both a shaman and a chief. He spoke no English, but through the translator, told an interesting and fantastic story that night.

The Indian bore the name of Foreman, and from his native tongue he enthralled the soldiers parked around the campfire at Fort Buhlow just outside the town of Alexandria, Louisiana. Foreman had once been a chief and he claimed that he knew for certain that the spirits of the dead often worked with animals to effect good.

Foreman had been wounded in the deep woods as a youth. The wild boar he was trying to kill were now hunting him. He was leaned up against a stump resting when he saw the boars had silently and expertly surrounded him. Foreman could not have sprinted to the nearest tree. The troop of angry hogs would surely have nailed him. Suddenly there came a loud rustling in the bushes, and a black bear raised up on two legs. The bear turned and stared directly at Foreman and then it lumbered toward the alpha male. The hog waved its ivory daggers at the bear but quickly retreated. The boy limped away as the bear stood on two legs waving its paws toward the sky. When Foreman told his chief about his strange and awful day, the young Indian received interesting news: Your life is important. Your spirit guide intervened with the bear's cooperation, preventing your certain death this day.

Even recalling this, Rob's brain crackled at connecting the fantastic episode of the fish this afternoon with Foreman's bear. Western thought was nowhere near what the Native Americans knew as truth, and yet, he couldn't deny what had happened. How real *was* reality?

As Rob made good his escape, his fine-tuned mind hurled out different memories. More recent times of killing and slaughter rippled into the mind's eye, and he could not banish them. Once, he killed some Confederate soldier, and the pistol shot to the head sent blood and bone flying. There was the charge against the outmanned cannon outside fortress Vicksburg; Rob's astonishment welled up as he recalled the scarecrows called human beings inside Vicksburg City. Their eyes would roll up in their sockets when the Yankees offered them bread, and still, many starving people simply preferred to starve a little longer rather than acknowledge Yankee captors.

He fell to a knee, a few tears streaming down a cheek. In all this killing, he'd made it! Life belonged to him. He'd been delivered again, as if by miracle, from Boyce's evil clutch. Didn't this call for a quiet prayer, a 'thank you' to the God he knew as a child? He folded hands together, closed his eyes, but there was simply no prayer he could offer up. Pray now? How and to whom? Rob's reality now seemed so vastly altered from anything he'd ever known. He'd watched in sorrow and awe as his fellow men smashed skulls and had become beasts toward men who wore gray rags. The ragged grey men happily reciprocated. God watched all this? He made no effort to stop it?

Suddenly the owl moved its eyes upward and its head tilted upward as well. Rob saw nothing save starlight and moonlight. And so the owl sat looking up, staring as if wondering where the moonlight and starlight shone from.

So Rob looked up too. He kept his gaze on the sky, well past the short pine limbs and bough needles. Something came into his mind, at first a gentle thought that seemed ridiculous. It centered upon some notion that men were creatures both like babies and animals. Perfectly equidistant from both. Men truly didn't really know how to behave on this earth. If they killed savagely, they didn't know any better. If they prayed sweetly, they really didn't know how to pray. But whatever men did, it merely represented tiny fragments of what they did best, searching, incessantly questing. It was the odyssey that would never conclude, not in this life, or in any other.

Rob Battle smiled and got up from tender knees. He waved stupidly at the sky that seemed to want to give him answers to impossible questions. The owl was still there, watching with stout gaze, and when it hooted once, Rob rolled his eyes that way. Then he began to run.

THE END

****author's note**

Parts of this story are rooted in fact. Fishville was one of my first memories of swimming. My Dad literally pushed me and my brother off that diving board and we sunk like stones. Fortunately, he realized his error and he swam down and collected his two sons.

Colonel John W. Henagan was a great-uncle several times removed, who fought with Lee and Longstreet in most of the major engagements of the Civil War. He was captured late in the war, and died in prison as the war concluded. He was with the Eighth South Carolina Regiment, under General Kershaw. Indeed at the Battle of Harper's Ferry he was wounded in the manner depicted in the story. I drew most of my material from E.J. Dickert's book published after the Civil War. It's called *The History of Kershaw's Brigade.*

Key parts of the story of course, reflect the literary license granted to a writer so to create an original story.

Maybe you had a life filled with adventure when you were younger, and now an older person, your budget for high adventure has run out, Right? Maybe you could be very much wrong. It's so true that the errors of your past have a certain way of catching up with you at the strangest times. Is that a little bit what karma is? As for romance and paranormal stuff, such things have always eluded you. At least until now....

Coronado Casket Company

Alfred Cash was not one to agonize about the many ironies of his life. They did pass through his mind like ghosts from time to time. But Alf had never given himself over to a personal neurosis complex. He was a dweller in the here-and-now facet of base reality. He *was* thinking about one thing a great deal these days; what weird loop of fate had entrapped him now in its silky web?

Lately he'd had more than enough time to bemoan such things. His full-time job as a San Bruno taxi driver had dwindled. Now he could only practice the careful art of person hauling for no more than 20 hours every week. Some insane California rule had taken effect and if the other local taxi drivers knew much, they hadn't shared the news with Alfred.

Now sunk so woefully low, lower than a toad's stomach (his favorite Texan uncle would have lamented), Alf might easily have made hissing sounds whenever he passed by his bank. Certainly he found nothing amusing about his new ATM card's constant rejections. Alf's general insecurities only intensified when the thought struck him that he'd actually stuffed *his* old mattress with the last batch of that long-go-Thai laundered money. It was not the portent of a happy life as one approached those golden years of worry-less living.

Thus it was with some suspicion that Alf fielded the call from Lance Provine. Lance had a sly, special way of reminding Alf of his not-so-long-ago era of especially miserable failing. "Alf gotta minute? It's important."

Alf's grunt of indifference hardly deterred anything. "It's about Larson. You didn't happen to speak to him in these last couple days did you?"

Alf's ears perked halfway up. "I haven't seen Larson since..well..hmm…it would be just about two weeks ago."

"Oh well," came a snarky, annoyed voice, "That hardly helps me at all. Sorry I bothered you."

"Wait, hold on. Don't be so coy with me Lance. I know when you're up to something."

Now the voice barked with true exasperation. "I'm up to nothing Alf. It's just that Larson may have upped and done something…truly stupid."

Alf stopped thinking in circles and sat up properly in his favorite recliner. "Well, if it's trouble he's in, you just might want me around. I've been sniffing around the edge of trouble a lot longer than you."

"Ok, Alf. I'm here all alone. You might want to know about the last thing Lars told me just before he walked out the door last Tuesday morning. At the time, it didn't mean much. But now, after four days of hearing nothing from him, I *know* he's gone too far. You understand how he hated to complain about the pain he was in. I suspect it was building up to intolerable levels. It may have led to his…apparent lunacy."

Alf grunted. "We'll see about that Lance. Hang on while I fire up my taxi."

Alfred had known Larson Bell since both of them had slunk around in the halls of a suburban San Francisco high school. As a teen Lars had been tall and gawky. But he did have that long triangular face girls would love to have nuzzled if he'd dished out chances. It was with Alf doing most of the listening, that Lars came to concede a certain truth: Lars was gay. Even so, the gap hadn't been so wide that they couldn't remain friends. Lars had even helped Alf launder a bit of baht-into-dollars back in those heady days when he was deep into the con game.

It was only when Alf had left Thailand for good, informally banished by the tribe of crooks increasingly greasy with the mob that Alf knew Lars had taken up with Lance. Actually, they'd been business partners for the previous ten years. It was then that their antique business had boomed.

Alf accepted Lance's cup of green tea and sat it carefully down on its appointed coaster. He'd decided to just dive in, get straight to the point. It was the only way he knew. "What did he say, the very last thing that you mentioned on the phone?"

Lance sat bolt upright. Even now he was decked out in a fine light blue blazer and striped shirt. He was five years younger than Lars, but even at fifty-eight, his heavy shock of silver hair promoted him to an older age level.

"Lars said exactly this. 'I'm going to run a few errands. While I'm out I'm going to ask a few more questions to *Coronado Casket Company*. It may take a while', he said. 'I left my laptop on the writing counter. Don't turn it off.'

Alf tapped a couple of fingers on his square chin. He'd famously forgotten to shave and some of that thick gray stubble pinched at his finger tips. "There's a lot of stuff in what you just said. First, what could he have meant by asking Coronado Casket Company a few more questions? He was contemplating a traditional burial? Hadn't Lars always been more of a cremation man?

Lance nodded eagerly. "Exactly. Lars despised the pomp and ceremony of any ritual for the dead. To him, when you're gone, that's it. No point in drawing in others for any extra grief."

Alf leaned toward Lance. Both elbows propped themselves on the table. "Every kind of casket company I'm aware of just sells caskets. Most likely they'd deal with funeral homes straight out. Why would Lars be making contact with a casket company like this? It's damned bizarre."

Lance gently put down his tea cup. "I have no idea why. And there's that other part too-the part about his laptop."

"Why is that unusual? He didn't cart his laptop everywhere all the time did he?"

"Not really. It's just that he left it on. As if just for me. Like maybe he wanted me to check something there."

Alf's teeth clacked together. "So what did you find there?"

"Actually, I have not looked yet. I've been so sure he'd walk through these doors just about any second. I never poke around in his personal business, especially his precious computer." Lance flexed both eyes on Alf. "Why don't you do it? Now is a great time."

"Not now if you don't mind. We won't turn it off as we don't want password problems. I'll keep it properly charged up at my house. It's going to take hours of research Lance. I work better in my own environment."

He shuffled, crossing both legs. "I can respect that. So take it with you."

"And there's another thing you said Lance. You used the phrase 'more information.' Lars already had been there, knew a good bit. Yet he'd mentioned nothing to you about this casket company?

"Nothing at all. I would have recalled."

"And Lars had made the decision to go all out with his holistic therapy. No traditional doctor would back him on that. They all had urged him to go for some of the aggressive new treatments. But he feared he'd die anyway, and why plop down a hundred thousand grand and you're dead anyway?" It was easy for Alf to recollect his friend's passion against the big insurance companies. It was why his health policy was so inadequate. Perhaps, like Alf, Lars was gambling that he'd stay healthy enough until the age of 65 when Medicare would kick in. Then, the good ole U.S. government could look after his health.

"Yes. You were his best straight friend. He told you as much as he told me about his illness. He wanted his body to fight the cancer, but on a budget. He'd always been so cheap with himself, and yet so generous to me."

Alf fixed a stare into the sallow, placid face of Lance Provine. "We have to consider suicide. Did he leave any clues to you that he might be considering it?"

"What? Suicide? Absolutely not. He loathed such cowards. He despised firearms and he freaked out at high places. It was one reason he never owned a car. He could never have driven across the Golden Gate Bridge. For a self-professed tough guy, he has a core of cookie dough."

"Ok, so we are left to assume his cancer was wreaking havoc on his pain management. What he had were pills that probably wouldn't make a flea fart. I called his doctors quackos, told him so to his face. Yet he kept going back to them and took their prescribed remedies faithfully. It's a fair assumption to believe Lars must really have been in some pain."

Alf arose and pointed towards Lars' private study. "Show me exactly where his computer is and let's keep the power cord attached. I'm anxious to find out some clue he must have left for you."

"What about your taxi job? Shouldn't you be out making money?"

Alf laughed easily enough even though he hurt inside. "I'm not the money making demon I once was Lance. Guess I have to accept it."

Alfred noticed Lance stick out an appreciative hand too late. Alf had already turned his body, and had both hands firmly on the laptop. Maybe Alf might never be friends with Lance but they did share one link: Larson Bell had been a fixture in their lives for a long time. And his smile was missed.

It was a week later after Alf returned the laptop, when Lance Provine called him on the phone. He was shrieking about a cop theme: *"Idiots*! Is that all we have for police in this town? A bunch of clowns and town hall idiots?"

"Hold the noise down and take it from the top." Alf was already in his taxi, backing down the narrow alley drive that led to his apartment.

"As you know I'd already reported Lars as missing. And now another slew of new detectives stops by here. They tell me over and over again, could you have made a mistake Mr. Provine? There is no Coronado Casket Company in this town or in any California city. Could you have misheard?"

"From all the clatter you're making now, I'd guess you insulted our boys in blue."

"You bet I did. I told them I already had that information. Any baby googler could know Coronado Casket Company does not exist. So the cops basically told me they'd put him on the missing persons list, but there was no evidence of a crime." Lance barely recovered his breath. "And the last part was just incredible."

"What last part?"

The fat cop winked at me and said right in front of the others, "And you'd better not be involved with your lover's disappearance you lovely old cock-sucker. I'd hate to think what they'd do with you in the pen."

Alf halfheartedly braked in the alley. "So where does that leave you."

"You mean where does it leave *us*, Alfred Cash. From now on you are the only person I trust on this case."

Alf's ears perked. "Case? Didn't know *we* had a case Lance."

"I'm officially putting you on retainer plus expenses. What you dug out of Lars' computer impressed me a lot. I need to get to the bottom of this. And yes, I have compelling financial reasons pushing me as well. Lars and I had built an impressive portfolio. Unless he's declared dead, I may never get my hands on that money. It's the better part of my nest egg. Without it, I cannot retire."

Alfred fired up the taxi. His present route was becoming more defined by the second. "How much am I worth?"

"You get five thousand right away. When you return from interviewing Miss Iris Cather, I'll spot you two thousand more for your growing list of expenses."

Alf's eyes puzzled over. "Don't recall seeing that name, Iris Cather, in any emails or computer entries. Where'd you get it?"

"A phone text message. It came on Lars' other phone, the one he uses when he travels. He must have met her somewhere. And at last we have an idea someone else in this world knows a tiny bit about Coronado Casket Company."

Now Alf full well knew the direction he was going. "So this lady mentioned them?"

Lance's voice shifted down. "Not exactly, but here is the main question in her text message: '… did you ever check more about *ccc*?' What else could it be Alf?"

"I'm on the way Lance." For once it felt great to be passing by paying customers. They could jump around and point all they wanted, because today he was spurning every cheapskate that waved an arm.

They sat at the now familiar problem solving table. Alf knew Lance better now, so when he inquired about ditching the green tea that tasted like yucca cacti for sweet lemonade, Lance only grimaced a little. The sourness from Lance's homemade lemonade recipe punched a hole into the minute of silence Alf needed to tease out some crucial fact that lurked in this pool of information.

"So we think there's a good chance those three 'cs' in her text message might be a reference to Coronado Casket Company. It very well might be true. But I think Lars knew them by their actual name."

"Which was?" By now Lance had grown use to Alf's penchant for metaphoric melodrama when he hung statements out on a line.

"Look here. You admitted this entry looked strange. $45,000. Paid to someone you thought was initialed KCC. And two weeks later another $30,000 to the same KCC. $75,000 total. It appears to me as if this is payment rendered for services, not for purchasing antiques for the business."

Lance mulled the statement and spoke with little conviction. "It wasn't terribly unusual for Lars to purchase antiques from his personal account. But this amount is very excessive. I tend to agree with you. He'd clear that kind of money with me first. And he never talked about buying new and expensive things since the melanoma appeared."

"But you have no idea who this KCC is? If it's a person or not?"

His head barely made it back and forth. "What are you implying Alf?"

Alf's voice picked up speed. "What I am implying, in fact clearly suggesting, is that Miss Cather's 'ccc' and Lars' 'KCC' are one and the same entity. Miss Cather only heard about them in someone's speaking; but Lars knew of them from perhaps seeing the name on letterhead or in actual company brochure material. Maybe he last saw it on some kind of contract he signed with them.

"That's interesting," said Lance. "But at this time it's only speculation. I cannot imagine Lars signing any contract that pertained to his…death, unless he told me first."

Alf plunged on. "It means that Lars was further along with making a highly personal decision than you ever dreamed. He'd paid them in two separate installments, and since he's gone, we can infer that was the total amount for services rendered."

"What kind of services?" Lance adopted a bland face that matched his voice. At least he wasn't into arguing.

Alf shrugged. He hated to say, 'don't know' this early on. So he said nothing at all.

"One of these days I'm going to definitely sit down with a tall Bloody Mary and get you to tell me how an obviously smart, sharp, maybe even talented fellow evolved into a clever con artist in another country, and now has morphed again into the return of Sam Spade." Then Lance Provine dipped his head in Alf's direction. It was the highest sign of respect Alf had yet received from Lance.

Alf smiled at the gracious display. "And Sam Spade will guide you through the incredible details soon enough. But first, it's on to see Miss Iris Cather. Since you are Lars' companion and you saw the message on his phone, please do phone her and tell her she's getting a visit."

“What if she mentions Coronado Casket Company?”

“Then Lance, tell her that’s why we’re coming. We’re interested in what they do. Like our Lars, we desire more facts, the most information possible.” He bolted away before Lance asked another question.

⌘ ⌘ ⌘

Iris Cather adjusted her heavy spectacles when the taxi came slowly up her smooth shell drive. As soon as Alf emerged, she was right there, hands upon indignant hips. “I have my own car. Just because I don’t drive it these days is no reason for you to come all the way out here and insult me.”

That introduced Miss Iris Cather. Alf prided himself on meeting so many different kinds of people in his travels. But right away, after this one session, he already would know enough about Iris Cather to put her in a loft of her own.

She absolutely insisted that both of them partake of her favorite cocktail, one that she alone drank exclusively in this world. Alf sat there full of content even before the alcohol spun its magic. The really crazy thing was that he felt like a true detective. He was so confident he could spin through any conundrum, latch together clues with flawless inference. He had no idea where this confidence had sprung from. But as he watched Iris Cather take her precious ethers, blend and shake them together to create the concoction best suited to pass a heady afternoon, he leaned back further in his chair on the deck. Waves crashed hard on the Pacific shoreline. He wondered how long it would take to get used to such a perfect rumbling of sound.

Presently, Miss Iris Cather presented a Rocky Road Martini. Her glass clanked from his and she slurped eagerly. Alf would be careful to corner old demons today. He had an important job to do that had to be far more important than ripping through the agony of another drunk spell.

“There’s a man who’s an expert on Coronado Casket Company. His name is Storm Berg. He’s been in our travel club for quite some time. He’s a real talker when he gets drunk. Acts like he knows everything about souls, reincarnation, astral planes and stuff like that.”

Alf wrote more carefully on his note pad. He put three question marks right next to his first true lead, this fellow she’d called Storm Berg. “I take it that Mr. Berg is some kind of New Age devotee?”

“Hey I don’t know Mr. Cash. I happened to be sitting at his table when that topic arose. We were in Saipan. It must have been six months ago. Larson came right over from another table and joined in. Somewhere in the middle of talk about *soul wandering* and *After Death Spiritual Entities*, Storm mentioned Coronado Casket Company.”

“Do you recall Lars’ reaction when that came up?”

"No, but I recall my own reaction. I got up and left the table. It was getting too heavy for me. I'm not into spiritual mumbo-jumbo. Even less now in my old age. I'm pretty sure I have a spirit of some kind. It's going to walk into some kind of light eventually. It could be heaven but who knows? No big freakin' deal."

"Where might this fellow Storm Berg be from and what might he do for a living?"

Iris looked at Alf askance, as if he'd suddenly done a flip. "We don't talk about stuff like that in our travels. Most of us are traveling to escape something in our ordinary lives. We hardly want to bring it up in the middle of a new fantasy. That's what each trip actually represents Mr. Cash. A way for us to renew our penchants for fantasy."

Alf was sorry to hear it. "What did you know of Larson? You'd known him a good long time from your joint travels from trips sponsored by the Sierra Travel Club?"

Iris poured another martini into the glass from the mother lode, the tall pitcher placed right in the middle of the table. "I knew him well enough not to bed him."

"But he was gay. He never let you in on it?"

Iris guffawed. Now she sounded like a macaque, one that saw the harpy eagle coming in plenty of time. "Hey my friend. His dick is like most of them. It could slice into my cute cupcake or some guy's pecan pie with equal ease."

The sudden imagery jolted Alf from a slumping posture. "I guess he could've been Bi." It ended up hardly a mumble.

"I don't know if he was or not. I never gave him the chance to prove it. I had just turned 65 when he asked to bed me. I know what blueballs are and he was afflicted. But I'm too sweet for all that now, don't you think Mr. Cash?"

Alf glanced at the wrinkled face, the heavy black rims. Were those the eyes of a dancing leprechaun? "Yes Iris, let's cut out that kind of risk- taking at our age."

"I don't recall exactly telling you my age young man."

"No and it hardly matters. I really dig your approach to life Iris." Alf couldn't help it, the talk just spilled out. He'd never seen an older woman anything like Iris.

She lifted again for yet another toast. "And I dig yours baby. I really do."

The special combination of a perfect day at this Monterrey beachhead, along with the spirits of the afternoon, must have given Sam Spade a valuable edge. It was the last moment, in fact just after Alf had slammed his car door, he shot a final question at Iris. She was right at the window, looking at everything the interior of the taxi had to offer. "Iris, why was it you sent the question to Lars at all, the one asking if he'd gained more information about CCC?"

Now Iris had good reason to poke her entire head through the window. "Because I got a weird message from Storm Berg in email. He asked me to reconsider about CCC. So naturally I wondered about Lars."

Alf whistled. Very nice Iris! Now the day would be complete if the cops didn't stop him on the way back to San Bruno. The way the Coast Highway curved, Alf's slow driving might not attract the first bluecoat. That was certainly the plan, unless he dared stay here overnight. But the taxi quickly roared to life.

❈ ❈ ❈

The idea came from Lance and Alf posed no objections. Of course, there would have to be a few whopper lies told on the initial application to Sierra Travel Club, but who really checked? All they cared about was the bank-to-bank transfer that proved one thing-this customer has the right stuff.

In fact, Alf was more than a little surprised Lance would part with $5,000 so easily. Alf would never have paid that kind of money just to join a club. There'd surely be more to fork over later. But first Alf's boys had some hacking to do.

If Alf believed they had turned the first corner, had some key facts lined up, his employer thought otherwise. Alf heard the first hints of desperation uttered by Lance. But Alf forced himself to simply listen, let the man vent. He'd calm down sooner or later.

"Ok Lance, I do get it and I share your relative frustration. The best googlers I hired cold not find two licks and a hoot about a Coronado Casket Company, with a "C" or a "K". It's been a month and Lars is still this mysterious missing man. It hurts us both. I get that. But we have made good progress on Strohmberg. As I said his name is Reynaldoh Strohmberg. We can thank my hackers for that bit of crucial information. He uses Storm Berg on his trips. So he seems to be hiding something right there. We are waiting for him to book his next trip with Sierra Travel Club, and I'll be there, only a little drunk, asking him about the afterlife."

Lance's eyes almost crossed. "What if you're wrong? What if the little old lady already blew our cover?"

Alf waved at thin air: "Don't worry about Iris. She's no admirer of Strohmberg. She's not interested in what Coronado Casket Company is hawking."

"Still, I'm worried about her. I want you to go back there. Have another little chat. Tell her to keep quiet about Lars."

Ten objections had already lined themselves up in Alf's mouth, but when his actual brain took control, he merely nodded an ok. "Sure you're the boss. I'll do whatever you want Lance. Let's give Miss Iris another call."

She received her guest warmly. Alf noted the well coiffed hair. Some stray wrinkles on her jutting cheek bones seemed to have vanished. Her silk dress made whishing sounds in the stiff Pacific breezes.

They quickly got into the round of Rocky Road martinis. "Can you taste the light chocolate essence Alfred, but there's that tart bang coming right behind, the one that really wallops you by the third drink?"

Iris had once again answered her own question and Alf sipped his drink like an exhausted hummingbird. The story came out much too quickly. "So Iris, that's the tale about why I'm here, about why Lance Provine is upset." Alf was quietly upset with his timing. It wasn't even sunset yet.

"Hey, Alfred, he has a right to be upset. His lover and companion, hell let's say his husband, has vanished off the face of the earth. And it's all because of this outfit, Coronado Casket Company."

"How do you know it's Coronado with a "C"?

"What else would it be? This is California. Coronado the explorer was Spanish and he would've spit out tar balls to have known of so much placer gold up this way."

"But I think it's really got a "K" instead of a "C". Lars apparently had seen some company material, brochures, maybe even a contract. They probably use a "K."

"Well I'll be." She grabbed her glass again. "You know," she said studying Alf's face yet again, "Not only do you think a bit like Sam Spade. You even resemble him just a bit."

He smiled. What else was there to do? He felt good here; his brain seemed to mine ample volumes of dopamine in this special Pacific Beach enclave.

"No kidding Alfred. I really did know him. Almost."

"Him?"

"Bogey. Humphrey Bogart. My family made its fortune back in the days when Hollywood was run by the moguls of the business. My father had weaseled himself in as one of the top accountants for Mr. Warner. I was a teenager and some handsome fellow walked up to me outside a Hollywood set. I was delivering a sandwich to my dad who was always incredibly cheap. It was *Bogey* himself who stood right there and lit up a cigar, just like in the movies. He looked me over real good but never said a word."

Alfred studied Iris for a long moment. It took several moments for his brain to mine every scrap of data about Bogart. Nothing came together that would fit this conversation. "That's great Iris. Just great."

"Think nothing of it. Hope you like fresh crab stew. Tonight when the tide is lowest we'll scamper out and collect us some big ones. My breakfast recipe is the best I've ever tasted."

It wasn't until well past a spectacular sunrise that Alf brought up Lars again. It would take a little time to register that Alf had managed to glide into the life of a minor Hollywood heiress. He hadn't bedded with her last night, but then again, he didn't have to. After they'd caught a bucketful of crabs somewhere past midnight, they watched old movies and shelled the unlucky creatures that were too slow to dart away. Iris didn't tolerate hard, tasteless pieces of shell in her soup. So there was no time for any bedtime tom foolery, even if Alf had been so inclined. He began to wonder about that-if he ever *could* be up to the task.

Over morning coffee as the stew boiled and puffed, he asked: "When do you think Storm Berg might be planning another trip?"

"Next week." She'd just adjusted a claw to better fit the boiling pot, and in an eye blink had altered a cheery morning.

Alf blinked and the word, "Great!" spilled from his mouth. He added, "How can you know about such a thing Iris?"

"He loves to watch the half naked girls play volleyball. He did his share of sideline ogling in Saipan, and I recall in Fiji about three years ago. Next week is the national championship in Clearwater Beach, Florida."

"You are sure he's going?"

"No not sure. Just a gut feeling. You check it out yourself. I'm staying put here. I hate Florida."

It took another day, but Alf's master hackers chopped into Reynaldoh Strohmberg's PDA to conclude that he was indeed going to Clearwater Beach, Florida. But he hadn't scheduled it through the auspices of Sierra Travel Club. No wonder they'd missed it. Alf had chosen to leave Iris' best guess out when he'd reported back to Lance. Alf had to get credit for something. He'd spent the better part of two days there.

At the last moment, a cancellation in Stromhberg's hotel opened up an expensive room. On the plane flight to Florida, Alf acquainted himself with the nuances of women's volleyball. No point in blowing the case for too much ignorance. Just how much he'd be able to say to the man was impossible to predict. Alf had been a great con man once but all of it was behind the scenes. Now, he had to rise up to the big stage.

The opening night party made Alfred Cash pine for days gone by. The fire in those days always flamed up when the money poured from his pocket and the girls danced in his lustful face. Which part of him was going wrong the fastest? Stromhberg on the other hand, plunged headfirst into his element.

He was decked in full tuxedo, his tight red cumberbun stretched lightly across a lithe, straight abdomen. The most attractive and daring of the young women found themselves at his knees, looking up and laughing hilariously. Stromhberg had discovered a pair of stilts and had begun walking around like a deranged mantis. The younger women who'd seen him flash heavy cash, hung close by, but most people simply moved aside when he came near.

"You go get 'em Storm. Make 'em come right up to ya!"

Alf whirled. She'd come up right behind him, had already taught the bartender how to make a Rocky Road martini. She had one in her hand, and two in reserve. He hadn't seen a whit of anyone over sixty in this crowd, and yet, here she was.

"Here take this Alf." Now she had one in reserve.

"Iris! What in all of hell? You said you hated Florida!"

"Yes, it's true!" She hooted the word *trooooo*. But I like my two men who've come to Florida. That would be you and him."

Alf stepped aside and gave a deep sip. A tottering man was falling slowly his way. Stromhberg crumpled from the stilts onto the chest of one of the beauties who'd come quickly over. Nice landing, thought Alf.

Stromhberg had heard and now he spied Iris. She embraced him heartily, and friends rejoined again. "Hey Storm. Why didn't you tell me you were coming here? You're not trying to avoid me are you?"

Alf had moved back, stepped away. He flipped his Ray Bans over. Why chance talking now? Iris could do more for Alf than he could do for himself at this moment.

"Of course not my dear Iris. But with so many lovely young women at my beck and call, I certainly do not want to provoke your jealousy. You do follow?" The man joked. But he was not humorous. And what was this jab at sounding like a Limey? Alf knew he hailed from New Mexico. Stromhberg's fake airs poked out to Alf like fangs on a goldfish. But maybe a few of the young beauties wouldn't care.

She lowered her voice, glanced around. "I have changed my mind about one thing. I found out not long ago that my diabetes has become so severe that not even injections will help much. I'm looking at multiple organ failure within a year, two at most. It's the most horrible thing. I don't want to suffer like that."

Stromhberg raised his arms, and his brows furrowed. "Iris! Why did you wait until now to tell me? This is most serious. I'd want to talk about this great change in your plans. But not here."

She waved him off. "Thanks for your concern Storm, but I'm not in great pain yet. However, I am looking ahead. I may want to know more about the Coronado Casket Company's ideas. Do you think they could help someone like myself?"

Stromhberg grasped both her elbows. "Yes! Yes, without a shadow of doubt. Not for a cure you understand. But for terminal patients who have the greatest amounts of foresight, patience and curiosity, what we do is simply incredible."

She nodded, still unsmiling. "And by the way, is that Coronado with a "K" or a "C"?"

Alf never heard the response. His head was turned the other way, better to let Iris bring her Gina Davis performance to a ringing conclusion. But Strohmberg had clearly uttered the' we' word. He must be involved with Larson Bell's disappearance. Coronado Casket Company had fleshy parts after all.

A bright February sun glinted away from their bronze skins. Alf had seen so much gorgeous flesh, so many outlandish jumping jams, it was almost a relief to break away in early afternoon. Stromhberg stayed. He had the perfect chair to ogle the perfect woman. She was from UCLA, more than six feet tall, and her preferred bottom cloth, hardly more than a thong, clearly revealed half moon pulsing buttocks, especially when she leaped. Alf didn't wish to take another glance at those breasts. They made him swoon.

He knocked once on Iris' door and there she stood. They sat on the balcony. She'd been up only an hour, was still nursing a strong cup of coffee.

"Iris, to be blunt, who invited you into this missing person case?"

Suddenly she removed those thick black glasses. For the first time Alf saw eyes as green as fresh prairie grass, and they flickered playfully. "Didn't know I needed permission. And besides, without me, where would you really be now? The truth from you Alf, where would you be without me?"

He still couldn't stare into her face. "You have already sent my self-esteem crashing back to earth Iris. So, I'm gonna make a crazy guess and assume you went to bed with him last night?"

"You assume correctly Alf. But what do you think happened?"

She fiddled with her glasses, thought better of it, and let those green eyes dance all over Alf's befuddled face a few more seconds. She watched Alf mutter sounds that never became words and he squirmed like some worm stuck on a hook. "Ok to answer my own question, he never got on top. I don't do that these days. We tried to play around a little on our sides. But I've never seen a more repressed man than Storm. He'd never make it with those beauties he loves to ogle. They'd laugh him back under his covers."

Alf's hands came up as if in self-defense. "I don't care about all that Iris. I'm sure you can handle yourself very well in the bedroom." Now Alf leaned forward, his own brown eyes gleaming. "What facts did he happen to let loose while under your spell?"

She swigged hard on the coffee and leaned back in the chair. Alf noted that the lines on her face were heavier after she woke up and her brownish hair took on a more silver tone. But the lively eyes- they always stayed the same.

"For $75,000 Storm can lead me to his business associate. It's this man whose name is Driggers, that handles the contract. Storm is really only a kind of front man, a marketer."

"Aha, great work Iris!" Alf fumbled for his notepad and felt foolish as she watched him jot the lead down in a scribble he'd be lucky to decipher a minute from now.

"He told you how to reach Driggers?"

For several moments she dallied, running her fingers through her hair or mumbling at the crease lines on her long cotton dress. "I'd best not contact Driggers."

"Why not?"

"Once you do that, you are admitting you have a terminal condition, and I do not."

Now Alf picked up his own cup of java. "You didn't have to go that far Iris. Never wish upon yourself a death sentence, even if you have a good reason."

She made a clucking sound between her teeth. "Oh I am a diabetic. But it's so mild I don't even have to take medicine. If I ever stopped drinking, it'd probably go away on its own."

"So Driggers must be the one who takes a close look at the medical papers a prospective client gives him. If the condition truly is terminal, people can go to the next step?"

Now their eyes met. He didn't blink and simply allowed her green gaze to enfold the lively intelligence his own eyes possessed. "So why the hell bother with Coronado Casket Company in the first place. Nobody in their right mind would be paying $75,000 for a casket from an underground outfit like this."

Iris arose and leaned on a balcony rail. The view of the sea-blue of the Gulf and the light breeze belied the stark subject at hand. "Alf, it's not so simple. Coronado Casket Company attracts those most ardent believers in the New Age mumbo-jumbo you and I reject. Storm told me this for the first time last night, that his company is the only one in the world that possesses a device that can draw out a soul from a dying person, and hold it still. It cannot just dissolve into the ether. And thus," Iris paused to search for the correct words- "And thus, you can meet your soul, let it talk to you, learn from it. It's the last thing you see before you die. And there's the information that is recorded as proof of your experience. It's given over to your designated beneficiary."

Alf gathered it all in and focused on one small part of Iris' incredible discourse. "Device? You said they'd invented a device that…holds a dying person's soul in place? What device was that again?"

She blinked as if not trusting her own words. "It's a casket. Their special casket. The one designed by Coronado Casket Company."

"A casket can do this?" Alf scratched at the place on the top of his head where there was a large bump. He shook his head while the first peal of thunder destroyed the illusion of a perfect Florida afternoon.

⁂

Lance Provine had always been good at working the problem at hand. And this one, although emotional in nature, required the same dictum. If he plunged even harder into his antiques business, Lars' face would not pop up so much. If the day was busy enough, the picky customers annoying enough, he'd make it back to the townhouse dragging his tired body up the steps, and simply collapse into his favorite chair.

The second step was dealing with a stony silence. Lance never cared for television. The few movies he appreciated he'd watched at least 100 times, and he knew every pause, every utterance the actors would make. He drank alcohol cautiously. The one thing he felt giddy about was throwing his heart and soul in Lars Bell's direction. If Lars was yin, Lance was yang. If Lars was alpha, Lance was zeta. Two opposing forces, exactly opposite. Now Lance had all the time in the world to think about it. Lars magnified a side of Lance that was always diminutive on its own. Lars magnified a stillborn masculine robustness that existed in Lance only in whispers. The fact was overwhelming now-he needed the big, surly guy. He wished he were here right now. Lance would happily invite his long-legged lover to sit right here, cracking bone on knee. If it hurt a little-so what? And a hug would be nice right about now.

When he swished the whiskey sour with a straw, he noticed his phone's vibration. "It's Trick. You gave me a thousand bucks last week, remember?"

"Yeah sure I do. I gave you one simple task, Mr. Master Googler. You better have achieved it."

The voice on the other side coughed nervously. "It's like this Mr. Provine. There does exist a Karando Casket Company in North Dakota. But they specialize in making baby caskets. Is your friend a midget?"

Lance easily delivered venom. "You, Mr. Trick are as dumb as the cops who can't do anything for me in this simple matter. So you tell me, as they did, a Koronado Casket Company does not exist? I know damn well it does exist. Tell me something new, sir."

"Not in this country Mr. Provine. You aren't in possession of facts you didn't reveal are you sir? Always tell me everything you know, don't short me on information. It's a waste of money."

"You were a waste of money Trick." Lance folded the phone's outer casing softly. He wasn't going to lose his temper tonight. Indeed, it now seemed Lance had no choice but to go with Alf's lead, as bizarre as it was. But somebody had to front the man the outlandish sum of $75,000. Not only that, but medical papers had to be forged. Did Lance want to solve the mystery that badly? He closed his eyes and tried to rub away the *drub-drub* feeling at the top of his brows that told him another headache was on the way.

For two weeks Alf savagely drove his taxi. He went past the twenty hour limit. So they could sue him. It was his taxi, wasn't it? One of the better decisions Alf had made back in his money-laundering days, was to buy a car, call it a taxi business. He never dreamed he'd be the one actually driving it to survive.

Lance's stony silence gave cause for worry. It was quite possible that Lance didn't have that kind of money to spare. It was equally plausible that if Alf met Driggers, but got in over his depth, he just might not return to tell the story. In a bad ending, there might be zero justice for both Alf and Lars.

He told himself it was because there was absolutely no other person in the world to talk to about this mystery. And besides, Iris seemed to love his midnight phone calls.

Need to see you right away!

Maybe he was surprised, maybe not. But once again, it would take Iris Cather to dynamite the heavy inertia this matter so easily attracted. When it came to this lady, Alf had swallowed his pride so many times, his neck was one big goiter. Maybe she was like medicine, take it enough times and it's not so bad.

By later morning the next day he was there. This time she set two chairs right on the sand so close to the water, it lapped at their toes. There was no wind, no clouds. The yellow sun and blue sea informed Alf that Nature held its tight grip on everything that was truly beautiful.

"I've got to ask you something personal. I may have an answer to the big problem of the hour."

Alf nodded, quietly said, "Ok, I'll tell you. Go on."

"May I assume you hold some kind of life insurance policy?"

"Yes, I do."

"How much is it?"

"It's for exactly 100,000 grand ole dollars. But it's the term kind, and it expires when I hit 65.

"So two more years are left before..." As her voice trailed off, Iris' hand cupped over her sagging, white chin. "Actually, that'll do. It's a nice coincidence. And we could use a break."

Alf waved both arms at the sky. "Naturally I am unable to put two plus two together. So you have me wrapped up Iris, once again."

She laughed. She guffawed so hard, one leg poked down into the sand enough to send her body spilling sideways. She landed on an elbow and a knee in the soft sand. She hadn't stopped laughing and Alf had already forgotten what was so funny.

"You big dummy! It's the $75,000 we need to pay Driggers. And it's the $25,000 I need to pay a doctor to forge something that documents a terminal medical condition. $100,000 total!"

All Alf could manage was a stern look straight into her dancing eyes.

Iris simply lay back in the sand, reaching for her Ray-bans to counter the daunting beams of mid-day. "You don't think I'd be risking my own money do you? If you didn't come back, at least I'd eventually have my money back from your insurance if you made me beneficiary."

"You're forgetting a major point Iris." Suddenly Alf got right down there, was suddenly reclining next to Iris. She looked sideways at him. If her eyes were curious, Alf could not tell. "What if I *came* back? What if I returned from wherever the hell Koronado Casket Company does business, not only hale and hearty, but with full information about them and about what really happened to Lars? You'd still be out the $100,000. They certainly won't be giving out refunds."

She chuckled again, this time with a lighter touch. "I made no mistake Sam Spade. I didn't forget anything as you just accused me. It's you who are leaving something out of the equation. If you come back, it's true I'm out of 100,000 grand. But what have I received in the deal?"

Alf's mouth released the strangely entrapped word. "*Me*?"

Iris tapped him on a sand speckled cheekbone. "Good answer!"

Their lips moved closer but a sea gull began to squawk feverishly, and hovering wings made little vortices of sand. Together, not quite entwined, both giggled away any tension. At this close range she could fiddle endlessly with his lucky gold necklace. She was an old girl, thought Alf. Maybe even *his* old girl.

⁂

Lance was appalled that Iris Cather treated this like some board game. "It's nuts, Alf. A hundred things could go wrong."

Alf shrugged at the tired formal man who'd just plopped himself into his favorite townhouse chair. Alf glanced around for the remote control. Since Lars was effectively no longer living here, the big screen television rarely was turned on. "It's all taken care of Lance, so don't worry. It's my hide on the line not yours."

Lance's brows arched. "Indeed correct. My hide is far too valuable to risk being ditched forever into a New Mexico uranium mine."

"With luck, not only will Willie Griddle return with his hide, but he'll know precisely what fate befell our own dear Larson Bell. Who can tell, there's a long shot he's still alive, but is somehow concealed or hiding. I'd risk my life to know this mystery Lance."

Lance clasped both hands together. "You believe your Iris Cather has capably created this Willie Griddle character. And you believe that his condition is convincingly terminal." Lance shifted and thrust one leg over another. "And most of all, you are sure you can become this guy and ole Willie can get the full Koronado Casket Company treatment."

Alf tapped all ten fingers on a nearby plastic coaster. "I hope so Lance."

Lance leaned forward. He touched Alf's knee. "Is that good enough, mere hope? How would I explain to the cops *your* disappearance?"

"I admit I have not done all my homework yet Lance, but once I go over it all again with Iris, I'll feel much better."

"Have you become lovers?" Lance wasn't smiling, his round white lips made a grim smacking sound.

"No, it's just business. She's like a pirate, has that flamboyance. She's plenty gritty, but too old for me. Don't worry. I'm approaching this problem as pure business."

Lance gave a limp wave on one hand. "Then begone! Get an answer for us. And above all, don't get yourself killed." Then they shook hands. Alf couldn't help but smile for a tiny moment because Lance held his hand much too long, and pumped up and down a bit too hard.

⁂

Iris moved them into the study where a nice fire crackled. A cool front had plastered the coast with its foggy tendrils and the drizzle felt cold on Alf's shoulders when he got out of his taxi.

Iris presented a cup of hot tea flavored with a dollop of honey. For once, Alf appreciated her serious tone. He'd flicked through pages of information in the yellow folder. "I'll have this memorized by tomorrow afternoon. So you got me in? Just on your good recommendation?"

She nodded. "But if truth be told, I got the idea that Storm, or Stromhberg, was disappointed I'd changed my mind. I had to tell him I was holding off in hopes that some of this new fangled gene therapy might become available for me. It was then that I told him about you, Willie."

He understood the test, tried not to blink at the mention of his new name. "And I see here that poor ole Willie is expected to die in as little as three weeks. He has a double aneurysm condition."

"Yes, Dr. Millie Morgan knew of this from some previous case a partner had presided over, and pulled the data from those old files. No doubt she appreciated the 25K for all that hard work. Double aneuryisms that don't kill you first are very rare Alf. In your case, your aortic valve is paper thin, bulging out like a balloon ready to pop. Even worse, you have the exact condition in the other big artery. This is your abdominal aneurysm. Maybe it's congenital, an inherited defect."

"And they won't check it there, at Koronado Casket Company?"

"Why should they? We have those x-rays right in the file. Dr. Millie has forwarded the same data to them already. Everything nicely done, we hope. It's just like Willie Griddle knows he's about to die. And so he figures, he may as well have a little chat with his very own soul before he departs this world."

Alf noted the time, just about ten. "Why don't I stay right here and get in about two hours of studying. You go on about your business, don't worry with me."

Iris stood up and Alf noticed for the first time she was in khaki short pants. Alf could not help but marvel how Iris' legs could have both avoided wrinkles and saggy spots after more than seventy years of wear and tear. The one real thing that gave away the cruel ruse of getting old lay in that craggy wrinkled face. If only that were not the case.

Alf was getting used to his seat, and to the fire. But Iris silently padded back into the room. She'd printed something out and thrust it into Alf's face. He read it silently, unsure of where he should go with this news.

"They want me to come after all. They apparently want me to recommend you to them in person." She grabbed her cold tea cup and fingered the edges nervously.

"I'm pretty sure the flight to Santa Fe is booked." She took a swipe at the paper as if the fault came from it.

"That's hardly the point. You'll get to the airport first and they'll whisk you off to where Driggers is. When I get there, they'll whisk me away. We may end up in the same room, probably with Driggers there."

"You don't have to come Iris. Why shouldn't you simply decline?"

Iris removed the thick black glasses. Alf now suspected why she wore such unstylish eyeglasses from some long ago eon. It was her way of making a ruse work even better. Now the green eyes bored into him. He could only endure it for a moment. "If I'm not there, who will cover that flaccid ass of yours?"

Suddenly Alf knew he was ready to play the game again, even if it had to be her way. "How do you know it's flaccid?"

She shook her head sadly but the eyes glowed. "Can't say for sure. Want me to prove it?" Alf gave her his hand. She took it and palm on palm they walked slowly into another part of the house.

Iris waited calmly at San Francisco International with her nervous companion. Alf had gone through the file at least five times. He felt he knew a great deal about Willie Griddle's terminal medical condition. But try as he might, Alf could not force himself to try and understand how it *felt* to be certain life would shortly flee your body. In that, Alf knew he would be most unconvincing. But how far would Driggers go? Very rapidly this man, Driggers, was being conjured up as a monster in Alf's active imagination.

He had no faith, but it happened. Just before he boarded the flight to Santa Fe, she got her boarding pass. Now at least, they could face the music together.

Stromhberg spied Iris Cather right away. This time he looked like a proper New Mexican citizen with heavy denim blue jeans, a corduroy shirt, and something that looked like a cowboy hat. "Iris, thanks for coming on such short notice. And Willie, how do you feel? This air today is very dry."

The Land Rover easily absorbed the three people and two short suitcases. Stromhberg spoke in quick, gentle tones as he drove into the countryside. He'd never actually said where the main office was. After forty-five minutes Stromhberg turned off the main highway onto a gravel lane that quickly turned into a road of dust. The main office was truly in the middle of nowhere. The lucky guess Alf had imparted to Lance about the abandoned uranium mine suddenly didn't seem so funny.

Stromhberg stopped driving. Curiously, they parked right in front of some large hill. A few mountains were in the distance, but this hill poked out of level ground in a strange, unexpected manner. Right there in front of them was a large steel door.

He moved his head in that direction. "Come on let's go." When he took a firm hold of Iris' arm, Alf noticed the grave look of determination that had suddenly appeared. Alf slowed his walk, but the distance was short. Just before Iris and Stromhberg were there, the door opened. Alf heard the clicking sound. Someone had pressed a button to let them in. He glanced around for the camera that must surely be watching, but there was no time.

Surprisingly, Stromhberg elaborated. "This used to be a uranium mine. I owned it and the U.S. government leased it when they knew we actually had uranium ore here. For ten years it paid its way, but eventually the engineers left it alone. It reverted back to me and so we had to figure out a way to make it pay again. Not an easy job. About then I met Lin Ten Feathers. You are about to meet him yourself."

Alf would have liked to digest that Indian name, placed it properly into this odd file that was generally labeled Coronado Casket Company, but there was an open door, and they were shunted there. Then the door closed and Stromhberg was gone.

Someone had been standing beside an old desk, in a room that held no redeeming features. He strode over to the two guests. "Welcome to Koronado Casket Company. I'm Ten Feathers. You can call me Driggers."

Something about Driggers seriously disoriented Alf. Was it the tilt of names that so ferociously clashed? Most likely it lay in the face. Driggers was a tall, slender fellow, but his face looked like it had been pinned on. The chin draped too low, almost falling into his neck. Driggers possessed lips that were thin as razors, and yet those brows presided over his eyes like parts of blackbird wings. Two brown eyes bored like laser tag teams, dragging out any reluctant energy the two visitors may have reserved for themselves.

"I would offer you a chair but there is barely a chair for me to sit in. I'm not often in this room."

"I trust," said Iris cautiously, "it's not your habit to let your paying customers come here first. Not much of a good first impression waiting for them here."

"No," Driggers chuckled. "This is more of a problem solving room. And we have a big one, don't we people?"

Alf risked a glance to his partner. She just stared right back at Driggers. Alf hoped the thick black glasses would come in handy just now. If they ever had to fall back on a ruse it would be now. "Go on about that Mr. Ten Feathers. You mentioned some kind of problem."

"Let's start with you Iris. You told Reynaldho about a specific medical condition. You said you feared a bad case of diabetes was about to run completely amok, rendering your body in great pain. Are we correct that you said such a thing?"

Alf knew she'd plow ahead, even if Driggers had the trap already set up. She nodded, glancing for a bare moment at Alf. He stood helpless. Nothing could help her now.

"As a control to make sure we are attracting the right kind of customers, it's very easy for us to conduct a fast, low cost check on what we're verbally told. Reynaldho did his job, getting that information to me, before you'd changed your tune about our services. I can tell you plainly Iris, you have no such condition like severe diabetes."

"How can you be sure?" The eyes were already turning downward.

"The meds you take, the meds your doctors prescribe. Oh yes, it's easy enough to tap into the proper places. Personal data is cheap in these times. But I guess you must not have known that." Driggers presided over the verbal lashing in a gentle way, as only his soft but firm voice could have done. "So you lied to us right away. But what was your motive to take the chance? And I've wondered why Reynaldho told you so much in your little bedroom escapade. It was a bit too much for my comfort, and thus you are here along with Alfred Cash. His story is quite different from yours Iris, and I can only guess he thought he could play his old con game with us. Do you know his story Iris? Mr. Cash has been quite the adventurer."

"Yes, so what?" She must have been getting tired of being on the back side of every jab Driggers was making.

"Of course we quickly found out that Mr. Alfred Cash is healthy as a stallion. And the more we dug, the harder we chuckled. For how many years Mr. Cash, sixteen or seventeen, you were an expatriate type who lived in Thailand. You were an English instructor of a sort. Your clients were teens who already must have known a little English, but it was your job to improve their English, at least to a point where they could more easily lead unsuspecting tourists into disaster. Your kids joined them whenever they got into certain taxis at the airport, right Mr. Cash? They'd sit next to an English speaking tourist and work up a mild conversation. Somehow the taxi gets off course, the driver stomps away, and leaves the con artist waif and the buffaloed tourist alone. Along comes the thug calvary and the tourist is stranded in some rice paddy, no money, no ID. What a game you played then Mr. Cash! The man in the background, but just as guilty!"

Alf felt the cold glare of Iris. He fumbled with a defense, "What does my past have to do with anything now?" Alf fought against the strong urge to ask '*How*?' It would only make matters worse to know exactly *how* anybody could discover his past sins. He would have been greatly impressed with the thoroughness at which they made background checks, if the situation were less acute.

Ten Feathers didn't flinch. "Not much at all. I'm relating that story to you to reinforce the fact that we full well know you also have no medical condition, and your terminal condition has been forged. And pretty crudely I'd say. Someone took you to the cleaners on these medical documents."

"Are you some kind of a doctor?" asked Iris.

"Not of Western medicine. But I am a full bore Indian shaman of the Arapaho tribe. What few are left of us. I know a lot about spirits, more than you could ever guess."

"So the casket thing is a foil, a ruse for customers. There's nothing special about them after all. It's your chanting mumbo-jumbo that does the trick."

Driggers stepped two paces closer in Iris' direction. "No, the caskets are special. They are custom-made and the maker is dead. We don't know how to duplicate them. We only have two, but it's been enough."

"What's in the wood?" Alf wasn't enjoying the session, but buying time seemed like the best plan.

"It's not only what's in the wood, it's what's between the wood planks. There's some kind of a blend of minerals like gold, platinum, uranium and rare clays. Along with special, careful steps we've also incorporated, spiritual awareness is accelerated. Recall that our client is a dying person. This greatly speeds his spiritual awareness on its own. The soul is expectant, hopeful that it can leave that dying husk. At some point, maybe in a few hours perhaps in a day, the soul draws itself away from its host. But it can't just leave. It's trapped as well. It's the only way on earth a living human can meet face-to-face with his very own soul."

"So a person can stay in his own casket, perfectly alive and aware, for many days. And his soul has no choice but to be right there. Bizarre." Iris made a whistling noise.

"Days without food and water," Alf added. "What a way to go."

"Not so," Driggers moved his eyes slowly back and forth. Something about them caused Alf to stare. It was as if Driggers' eyes were dark magnets, and the natural human impulse to look away was somehow reversed. "They have access to all the food, water and air they need. When their last breath has been taken, we know at once. The casket is opened. The spirit departs. A cremation is done."

Alf breathed once and the exhale caught Iris' attention. "Mr. Driggers, all this is borderline wonderful for those people who want your service. But as you are so aware, Iris and I have been merely curious. We've broken no laws trying to satisfy our curiosity. And there is something I have not told you. One of your last paying customers was a friend of mine. Larson Bell. I guess you just informed me of his fate."

Driggers made a huffing sound. "I can't discuss anything about his case with you. His beneficiary will eventually receive both his ashes and the CD that recorded his conversations with his soul entity while they were trapped in our casket."

"When is eventually?"

"After he's legally been declared dead by the state of California plus a few more months for good measure."

"That could be quite some time. How about a little closure on this matter? Mr. Lance Provine would appreciate it."

Driggers shrugged. "It can't be any faster. We must reduce our exposure and liability as much as possible. It's the very reason we are such an underground operation."

Iris shifted her gaze toward the door. "All this is pretty amazing Mr. Driggers. I suppose you want to extract a promise from us not to ever tell anybody." She raised her right hand. "I solemnly swear to keep all this a secret. I'll carry it with me to my grave. I promise."

Alf marveled at Iris' capacity to continually go for the big bamboozle. She even had her hand on the door knob, although her eyes were fixed upon the twisted half smile forming on Driggers' bronze-red features.

He made a half wave. "No that cannot be the plan Iris. It's our policy not to allow people to walk out our doors with a great deal of information. At this stage, you are not even a believer."

She shook her head vigorously. "Oh no, Mr. Driggers! You have convinced me. Has he convinced you Alf?"

Alf went for the truth. "Yes, I suppose I am a believer now Mr. Driggers."

Driggers walked up to Iris and gently removed her hand from the knob. "When you are truly a believer in our service, maybe you can go then. But not before." Then he was gone. Iris jiggled the knob for good measure, but the big steel door was shut tight.

"I guess he's gone to prepare something. Looks like we're gonna become true believers today, Alf."

"Yes," he said softly. "Either that, or we'll die trying."

After a passing of hours, it was Stromhberg who unlocked the door.

"Nice of you to join us Storm. Now, where's the lady's room?"

"Both of you follow me."

They quickly came upon an elevator and went in the curious direction of down. More turns in some dimly lit hallway and two rooms adjoined. There's a place to take care of personal business. Do it all now is my advice. In the casket, there's no way to get that kind of relief." He pointed to a chair. "And take your clothes off and put these light togas on. I will come back in thirty minutes."

"What about Driggers? Will we see him again?"

"Not likely. He's already begun his chant."

Iris glanced at Alf and all he did was return his own baffled stare. "Why's he doing that?"

"For two reasons. One is for your soul to withdraw itself quickly. You two aren't exactly dying, so he has to make a special kind of prayer." He turned to go, but Iris caught his arm.

"The other reason for the chanting. You said there were two of them."

Stromhberg kept a serious face. "To keep the Others away. When a soul becomes exposed like yours soon will be, it's very vulnerable to being taken in…by….the really dark entities that exist in places like this. Ten Feathers is a shaman, I'm sure he told you. There's all kinds of spirits out there. Let's hope he keeps the worst ones away, while you're deep into the experience."

They felt ridiculous in the togas. Both had modestly chosen to keep their underwear in place. When Stromhberg came back he took their hands and like a school dame leading her charges to the principal's den, they marched down dark hallways. The hallway suddenly ended. It simply dropped away, and beneath the cliff screamed a suffocating darkness. Blackness of a kind that ruffled Alf's spinal hairs to full arousal. You fall here and maybe your atoms cleave to mantle rock.

Then a slight rumble and two caskets descended from somewhere above. Slowly they came down until they dangled invitingly. Stromhberg opened each top carefully. Nothing creaked. The caskets were of metal and wood. There were no encrusted jewels anywhere, and for a $75,000 rental, Alf wondered where the gold and platinum was that Driggers had mentioned.

"After you step in and lie down, I will adjust your water sippers. You can also feast on strawberry yogurt with the other sipper. It's not a great deal, but good enough. A special form of oxygen is pumped in. With good luck, your souls can be coaxed out quickly and you can meet them."

"I meant to ask you this earlier Storm, but never got the chance. Is there going to be a double murder here today? We die in the caskets and our bodies just dumped down there. Nobody would ever know."

Stromhberg laughed and an eerie echo reverberated from the deep pit over which they were apparently to be suspended. "We don't kill people Iris. But you know a lot about our operation. It's best you become a believer precisely because you know too much. It's mostly my fault you know. I told you far too much when we lay together that night. So now….we must try and make a bad situation…better."

Stromhberg made a simple motion-get in now. Alf never felt closer to his own cowardice. He was fairly amazed he just simply hadn't bolted. But of course there were reasons. Iris didn't seem fazed. Where was this woman's fear? If she kept hers at bay, shouldn't he as well?

They agreed to simply get in at the same moment. Ok Alf, step in. Alright, now lie down. What else was there to do? At once, Stromhberg jammed the top down. He rammed something and a low bank of lights hummed. Air rippled in. Two sippers came down. He could indeed drink water and take in suckles of yogurt if he wanted. But no thanks.

Something about this place. It was a fuzzy place for time. Time seemed to form like a circle or a hula-hoop. Alf's fuzzy vision reported to his brain the hoop had begun turning faster and faster. Alf noted his body rising up, as if levitating an inch above the silky bedding. Thoughts began to form in the loop, and the loops divided like a picture of the way atoms were supposed to look in some ancient school book.

Alf's mind had become one big dream. He was free to enter a door, become a part of this or that haze. In each door he floated into, the *feeling* was different. Sometimes it was joy that catapulted him. He was turning over and over, like a ham bone on rotisserie. But he was only embroiled with happiness. He was certain he lay there smiling, maybe even laughing at something he could not explain. In other areas, he became *awe-struck* as he watched something unfold. What was it-space? Planets? A display of how the universe came to be? What was his brain doing with all this?

Suddenly a photo shot embedded itself in his vision, and he couldn't let it go. A wolf sat on a crag high up on some mountain. It howled and gazed up. The stars came out. One star came down. It zoomed down like a wild, hard comet. It struck the wolf. Now the wolf morphed into something golden, elongated, wispy. A fog enveloped something that seemed to have a head and four legs, but no real body.

Then something real puffed into view. The wolf had to be imagination, but this thing right in front of his astonished eyeballs, had human essence. Alf couldn't know a name for it. But it was *himself.* Not in any form he could ever have known. The face looking down at him from the casket's upper space was *Alf.* The human Alf managed to wiggle his arms and get both hands to thoroughly rub both eyes. He blinked again. It was still there, just watching in a bored way.

Alf did not speak with words. Somehow his mind knew how to take charge.

"What's your name?"

"Just call me 'S'." The wispy man thought back.

"Does that mean *soul*?

"Could be. You figure it out." Alf wished it would coalesce even more. It was eerie to see through his own half transparent face.

"Do you want to talk to me now?"

"No," said S. "I want to leave. But something is keeping me here. Some human creation. Did you do this?"

"No. It's not me." Alf closed his eyes, could view S equally well now with mind or vision.

"You aren't supposed to keep me penned like this. It's not right. Wait!" S suddenly turned on his back. Alf saw the back of his head, and a much younger head it was. It was the time of his pony-tail! That would make him around 28 years old!

"Something is out there! Just beyond this strange wall of mud and wood. I can see its eyes. Very dark. Terrible things. It must not enter here."

"Ok," Alf replied. "We won't let it come inside. Does it have a form?"

"No, it's energy, but it's letting me see its eyes. It could kill us both. It wants to."

Alf felt little sweat beads forming on his forehead. He could barely get his arms raised to swipe at them. "Let's concentrate together. Keep it out."

"Them!" S almost shrieked the thought. "There's more than one. They're massing. They will figure out a way to get in."

Alf forced his logical mind to come forward. Wasn't it up to Driggers, or Ten Feathers to stop such a thing from happening? Alf's mind dipped into the waxing irony. Ten Feathers could go either way. He could pray hard to protect Alf and S. Or he could do what perhaps he intended to do all along: Cause the extermination of the meddling Alfred Cash.

For many minutes S said nothing. Alf saw it more distinctly than ever, a head connected to a body. It hovered a bare few inches from Alf's own nose. S preferred to face up and the pony tail dangled almost dipping into Alf's chin. When S at last turned to face Alf, it posed an astonishing question.

"They say they won't enter here if you, Alf, tell them what they'd like to know."

"What do they want to know? I'll tell them!"

S seemed to turn its eyes up reflectively. "Something about your past Alf. How come you never said you were sorry?"

He snapped both lips together. More beads of sweat on the forehead. "Sorry to who?"

"To them." S's hands waved in a half moon. "To all those people you offended when you were that clever crook. These dark entities that have assembled wish to know why you have not told anyone you were sorry for helping to steal their money. You helped promote fear, Alf. And you did it for a long time. Such a thing attracts their attention."

Alf forced his logical mind up from some abyss. When this happened, S became a bare fog, as if he'd evaporated from existence. Alf knew he hadn't moved. It was Alf's feeble spiritual awareness that was to blame. But the biggest problem at hand had presented itself. As Alf paused, unable to respond, he felt S's growing unease.

"They're coming much closer Alf. Do something!"

He had to divide his mind up in order to even consider such a question. Why? Why indeed! He'd never felt the need to tell anyone he was sorry for being a bad man. It was just a fact. Sure, he could admit the great money he'd made had temporarily corrupted him. The girls he could have anytime, this too was part of his corruption. He hadn't cared about humanity in that time. He only cared about himself.

"One is coming in right now. He's fighting hard to come in with us! Do something Alf. No time!"

"I'm so *sorry*!" The words came bellowing out, as if blown by a steamy force of will that engaged itself like a big rig lurching to life in the middle of winter. "To every citizen I affronted, I am sorry. I would give you back every cent if I could."

Suddenly S was frozen. It didn't move, perhaps could not any longer. "But you *can* Alf. I'll help you. I'll show you how to make it right." Whose voice was that?

A deepening essence had moved in, held Alf's wide open eyes spellbound. Suddenly he plunged down. He knew where he was, in a casket. The casket itself was in a cave. He was suspended by cables over a deep ravine of icy darkness. Something had come up from there, hadn't it? It was right here, right now. Speaking to him. This entity that had come inside the casket had immobilized S. Whatever it was did not reveal itself, spoke with its own voice that fairly rocked Alf's own brain, which had rallied itself to highest alert status.

"Yes, yes. Please show me how to do that. Let me out of here and then show me." Alf spoke with actual words now and his eyes searched in vain for something to talk to.

Alf searched for a face, for eyes. There was only the voice. It didn't seem inherently evil. If it were so evil, why was it interested in Alf rectifying long ago wrongs?

Then a quiet laugh. "But when you start to truly make it right, you know you'll have to leave Iris. Maybe for a few years. She may not make it without you."

"Then I'll bring her with me. Can she come with me?"

Another quiet laugh. "That's up to her Alf. It's her choice or not."

Alf felt his eyes close tight. Had he done that? His mind began spinning, spinning. He dreamed he was an electron, a part of some eternal atom, going nowhere, and yet was everywhere at the same moment. He could see everything now as his mind totally relaxed. S came back to live inside Alf's body. The entity departed. Alf dreamed a jumble of dreams and then heard the loud click of sound.

When his eyes opened, Stromhberg gazed at him. The casket was open. Iris was there too. She reached in, touched his face. He grappled with her sweet, gnarly hand.

Alf arose unsteadily. They stumbled back in the changing room, yanking off their togas, oblivious of near nakedness. They met with Driggers for only a minute. His hair was still matted with sweat. The eyes were drawn out, every stitch of facial skin flashed with taught brightness. "Now you understand, both of you." Driggers tried to smile. "And Alf, I believe some entity extracted a promise from you. You must keep your promise that you made."

Alf nodded. "Would that entity have been attached to *you*? It was you Ten Feathers. Wasn't it?"

Ten Feathers' head neither moved up or down, but his eyes connected with some new level of understanding Alf had now acquired. Alf thought hard, like he never had before. What kind of man was this Driggers fellow, this Ten Feathers character? A demon? A monster? Did Alf now comprehend the answer to that? Perhaps… an angel?

On the plane ride back to San Francisco, Alf held tightly onto Iris' hand. Sometimes she placed her head upon his shoulder. Neither spoke actual words.

But just before they landed, Alf directed a thought her way, and her head arched, eyes bolted straight into his own. *Will you come with me Iris? Will you help me keep that promise I made? I can't do it without you.*

No earthly sounds passed between them. Iris just smiled. Alf kissed her on one of those wrinkled, craggy cheeks. It was getting time. Time to get on with the next part of their lives-wherever that might lead.

THE END

Writing fiction that discusses religious figures is a delicate undertaking under the best of conditions. How does one keep one's opinion completely out of the picture? At the heart of this historical fiction piece is my interpretation of the facts. And I am backed up by some of the most respected Bible historians of our time. I did hundreds of hours of research to be confident of my factual projections. It's mostly all in the New Testament reading. Go there and check. It may do you good.

John the Triangulator

First off, I must tell any reader who ventures here, it is only by virtue of the unique project I had been assigned (and had been hugely successful with, but you must know that already) that I write at all. I am not a natural writer of fiction, although historical fiction like this is a suitable venue for me since I've already explored so many fascinating and interesting details creating the software behind the virtual reality experience.

Indeed, I am the main guy behind the explosive interest in the virtual reality experience called *John the Triangulator*. When virtual reality parlor rooms began to explode all over the planet, developers had need of a huge amount of material. Not just any material, good, original material, and soon thereafter, great, original material. Once the public, so bored with movie sequels of every variety, and untantalized by book reading, found their appetite for actually experiencing things, demand soared past the stratosphere. Now developers could at last place that most sensitive of subjects, a treatment of how characters in the major religions may have had their own unique beginnings, onto the world stage.

The result at first was mayhem, distrust, disbelief followed in short order by torrid blogger talk that endangered many a server. Buddha got the first treatment. Most of the world community felt the unique initial effort was thoughtful and realistic. Many people expressed great surprise at the depth of their own visceral feelings as they participated in the Buddha's historical and cultural milieu of that time in rural India. Fortunately, Buddhists are by nature not too prone to the worst styles of confrontation, and thus, *Buddha, the Beginnings*, suffered no unusual boycotts or provoked mass riots. Hundreds of millions of people have since enjoyed living part of the long departed Buddha's life right along with him.

Subsequently, I played a minor role in the design of *Mohammed in the Caves*. The part of my designing was showing how Khadijah urged her husband to plow on, to believe in himself. It was Khadijah who convinced Mohammed that he was not losing his mind. Some people claimed that it was this part of the virtual reality experience that allowed millions of Muslims to ignore the *fatwah* demanded by the fundamentalist Islamists. So once again, the new experience we were creating avoided a fantastic and bloody meltdown.

Thus it was that I became the point man, the executive producer in control of character development, of a new project, one that took my days and nights away from me for the better part of three years. To say I was totally consumed would be a vast understatement. The more the research boys placed material in front of me that showed so clearly how John the Baptizer was a real person, in a real time, and how he well must have known and spoken often to Yeshua ben Yosef, later to be known as Jesus the Messiah, the more I realized the importance of creating the most amazing experience possible. I was utterly absorbed in making the experience of John the Triangulator the most moving and vivid encounter of a lifetime.

And so my most energetic dreams became reality. Peoples across the world from every faith deigned to praise the four hour experience. They came out from the virtual reality parlors of the world, drained, exhilarated, babbling with pure strangers, curious to dive into the historical material themselves, to see just how much creative license I had taken making this so real and vivid, a rare must see event in the mundane life of the ordinary person.

Since I was the chief designer of The Triangulator Project, the historical fiction piece for readers was a natural corollary and so it fell into its own logical place. I enjoyed being the sole writer as I declined time and time again, the services of a ghost writer. In fact, the writing was almost fun. I had already placed myself back in the times of John the Baptizer from the software project. Writing allowed my imagination to paddle around in that ancient past in a totally different way.

In fact, I have added only a few wrinkles of difference. Mostly, these center around the fact that reading is a different kind of experience from virtual reality, where participants become convinced they are really touching things, hearing things, smelling things, watching events unroll to eventually become part of a realigned belief system.

I hope you will agree with me that I have managed to make a book that does for readers what virtual reality did for action seekers; to allow John to spring to life with all the cast that originally came with him. I'm so certain that's all he would really ask for if he could.

⌘ ⌘ ⌘

John stood before his father Zecharias, castigated but still defiant that he had done nothing wrong. It had taken barely two days for news to filter in from the backwoods into the heart of the Temple where Zecharias performed his duties as a priest from Aaron's lineage. Some fellow had found Zecharias and tugged anxiously at his belt.

"Yes," Zecharias had said. "What do you want with me?"

This Jew had dark features, a sign he worked the land. "I want to tell you," he said in Hebrew, "that we are proud of the braveness your son displayed. You must be pleased with him."

Zecharias at once stopped, and put down the knife he'd been sharpening. His eyes scanned once more this fellow who knew some fact about Yohanan, a new fact that had somehow escaped Zecharias. "So you think my son's act was brave. Tell me why."

The small, dark man had eyes that darted here and there, even as his voice cratered into Zecharias' eager ears. "John saved that shepherd's life for sure. About the newborn lamb, I cannot say. I got no news of the lamb. And the rogue lion is one less problem to trouble us. All thanks to John. Bless you sir."

He backed away slowly, signifying he appreciated Zecharias' position in the Jerusalem Temple. Zecharias nodded politely and turned away. His heart began to race. John had ventured into the heart of the rugged hill country again, in defiance of his father's command. He sighed loudly enough so that a fellow priest came over and patted his back. Zecharias managed to say something, but it sounded silly and useless. "It's not easy being a father, is it Levi? And you have five sons. I cannot imagine such a thing. My own Yohanon, a single son, is befuddling to his mother and I, so that we are constantly on edge. We know so little about raising an energetic and stubborn lad like this."

Levi smiled. "You'll catch on old friend. Or else die trying."

Thus it was with zero anticipation that Zecharias came upon John. Zecharias had been home for one full day, having taken leave of his Temple duties for a short time, and had said nothing. Yohanon easily avoided him even though the house bordering the hill country was not large. In the evening, he'd gathered his full thoughts, talked it over privately with Elizabeth and was ready to deliver his verdict.

They stepped outside. Underneath the huge old olive tree John squatted. His eyes never came up to meet his father's. Instead John found a stick, had begun to draw an elaborate triangle in the sand. On each leg was a single Hebrew letter. When John finished, when he was ready, he stood and his eyes collided with his father's.

"For a twelve year old boy, you have the deepest saddest eyes I have ever beheld." Zecharias always told his son this when there was trouble coming.

"It's because I make you sad and I cannot please you Father. You must have heard about what I did to that lion. I do not wish to be patted on the back for the good deed by anyone."

"You killed one of God's great creatures. Even if he used to feast on the blood of sheep and lambs." Zecharias wanted to reach out, give his son reassurance. But he held back. He dared not inquire just now exactly how John had pulled the incredible feat off. "Not many lions left around here, but that rogue was a bad one."

John's eyes lifted and brightened a shade. "So you are not so angry about that?"

Zecharias shook his head. "Not that exactly. But it's your disobedience to me that frightens me. If I say to you clearly, 'Do not do that, avoid it', what do I see? You always go and do precisely what I say not to do! For that, I am troubled."

"We know in the stories of old about David, that neither giants nor lions caused him fear. He's my hero coming from all those stories you told me as a child. I revere David and all the glory he brought to Israel. May we regain that glory, Father!"

Zecharias mumbled something and brought a hand to touch the bottom of his chin. Something about this boy stood out, blazed like a comet. Already he'd persuaded Zecharias to delay punishment for disobedience. And delay usually meant all was forgotten. John had never really even tried to wiggle out of it. Such a persuader and only at the cusp of accountability!

Zecharias stepped forward, put two hands on the boy's shoulders. "What David did was God's design. Israel had cried out for a leader for a long time. God delivered giants and lions into David's hands for a good reason. From thenceforth, Israel could spring forth. But you…it's a different time altogether. Do not deign to be David. There was only one for all time."

John was looking down, staring at the meter long triangle he'd drawn in the sand. Zecharias saw it, knew his son's habits all too well, and was almost eager to hear the connection.

John pointed with a long stick. "This straight arm of the triangle represents our lives now. We are born at a certain beginning time, and we go through life, and it ends at a specific time. God is with us all the time we live, so let me also draw this arrow, coming from the outside, the influence of God. Just as he was with David, Father, he's with us. You can at least agree to that? *Aleph*."

Zecharias fought back tears. It was not often that a senior temple priest was lectured to by a twelve-year-old boy!

"Now to the second leg represented by our letter *chet*. *Chet* signifies the great importance of our deeds and words while we live. The finite length of the bottom line of the triangle signifies the words and deeds are truly limited. Thus they need to count. They must be a testimony to a holy life, as well as move and motivate the people to follow God's will. To that, can you assent, Father?'

Zecharias used the back of his hand to brush away a single, flowing tear that meandered across a ruddy cheek. "And the third part of the triangle, my son. You have the letter *samech* there. What does it signify to you?"

John paused. He looked up. A songbird had posted itself in a low branch, had suddenly stopped singing. It cocked its head back and forth, was looking directly at John's fervent gaze. John reached into a pocket, withdrew bits of bread crust. He held out a hand. The sparrow flew into his palm, pecking and clicking happily. It dipped its head once when all the bread was gone and flew away.

Zecharias observed the departure and turned to smile at his son.

"You may not know I've watched you do this before. I've studied you as I hid right over there. Imagine a father sneaking around like that to try and understand how his own dear son's mind actually works."

John nodded. He stood to a height almost up to his father's chin. No doubt he'd grow to be a sturdy man with an impressive brain to match. And who could know what else, Zecharias thought.

"Actually father, it's not so difficult to understand my mind. It works in accordance with the third letter of that triangle, the one right at our feet."

"Do go on John." Zecharias watched closely as John bent low stooping, as if studying the lines in the dirt he'd so assiduously drawn.

"This is the final line, the connecting line. It represents all the people in our nation. It represents what God wants to do with us. And you already know that. He wants to make Israel, Judah, Galilee even, the focus of the nations. And thus, the third line is the one most associated with conflict. To get there won't be easy. We won't become the focus of the nations with Rome on our back. And yet we are not powerful enough to cast off the heavy yoke. Yeshua has told me many times about the humiliation he felt as he trekked with his father Yosef from Nazareth to Sepphoris in those days when the roadsides were filled with the rotting corpses of the followers of Judas the Galilean who led the great revolt. Those poor zealots were crucified mercilessly and without regret."

"So your third line, of *samech*, shows us we aren't just living our lives for ourselves. Whether we like it or not, we are participants in some vast play."

"And those who are most worthy are the ones who will play a role in the kingdom to come. I refer to the kingdom that God must establish right in our midst. Not in heaven, that would do no good for the justice of the nations. But his kingdom is bound to come right here! It will be right in the heart of the Holy City, even in the Temple where you work for the good of the righteous."

"You have thought all this out son? To whom have you been speaking" You are far too young for such thoughts."

John smiled, laughing softly. "During our holy events, I can leave these confines. During Passover and Feast of the Tabernacles, Yeshua and I have already managed to get our views across to certain priests who are always gathered in the outer circle of the Temples. Thus, they are not too offended when we offer up our views. We began to do it when we were just ten. They're almost used to us showing up."

Zecharias nodded approvingly. Yeshua was a distant cousin of Elizabeth and of the line of David. He was gifted with a beautiful mind, very much like John. But Yeshua's job was destined as a *tekton*. Even if his father Yosef had been a supervisor of laborers, the training of learning how to make foundations for buildings was as backbreaking and strenuous as anything imaginable. It would most likely be Yeshua's curse to bear for a lifetime.

"I've been hearing that young Yeshua has talents that go way beyond his job calling. Hanina ben Dosa told me so himself. He's met with Yeshua. He can see the energy aura the boy possesses. He's going to be an amazing healer someday, if he can find the time."

"Indeed father," said John. "I say the same thing myself."

⁂

Broken yokes were costly to fix, but most owners of yoked oxen preferred to pay for repair over a new one. For the ambitious cart owner, Yeshua labored for at least a week, doing practically nothing else, so that the new yoke might be made precisely to order. At this time, thankfully, Yeshua's job was repair, re-work, replace.

Every morning at dawn, as Yeshua sank to his knees in grateful prayer to the God he felt so close to, he always mentioned Clophas and Zecharias. For it was those two men who'd surely saved him from the backbreaking, thankless tasks tektons were expected to perform. Technically, Yeshua realized he was still a *tekton*, but thanks to Clophas, he was able to branch out into a more highly classed specialty.

Clophas had become his father since Yosef died when Yeshua was small. Mary had born no other children to Josef, and it was a poorly kept secret in tiny Nazareth village that in actual fact, someone else was Yeshua's real dad. Therefore there was a need for a Levirate Marriage, in accordance with Jewish law, so that the true line of Yosef might continue. Clophas was perfectly handy, having lost both his wife and first child in a terrible breech birth. So Mary and Clophas would become man and wife, have their own large brood, and in general, be happy enough in the crowded hovel they called home.

Clophas and Josef had both learned how to be *tektons* from their father. But Clophas was a *tekton* with a twist. He'd managed to branch out from the hard, hot labor involved with making foundations and walls for buildings. Clophas had gradually become accomplished in the delicate art of yoke-making.

From early on, Yeshua had impressed Clophas with his deftness in woodworking. Before he was fourteen he'd crafted his very first yoke. The step-father Clophas was continually amazed by Yeshua, and not solely because he was such a quick learner and willing student.

Secondly, it was natural for Yeshua to include in his morning prayers, a tribute to Zecharias. It was he who had prevailed upon the Sanhedrin to allow Yeshua to be the primary person they'd call on and recommend when a team of oxen broke a yoke, hauling in the huge rock slabs that eventually formed the beautiful columns, floors and walls of the nearly built Temple. Herod himself had of course, commissioned the original construction all those years ago, and now, at last completion was on the horizon.

To be eligible for this position, Yeshua had to live in Jerusalem at least some of the time. It was fortunate that he made friends easily and with an alliance with a young priest named Yohanon ben Lazr, Yeshua shared the house the young priest had been given by his father.

On a certain day, Joseph from a place called Arimathea not too far from Jerusalem, visited Zecharias as he prepared to depart the Temple. This would be no ordinary departure. Zecharias was turning fifty years of age. Other, younger men would be taking his place. Zecharias' duty extending from Aaron would be finished.

They talked of the old days but whispered when discussion turned toward the horrible events of recent times. "Rome has proven it is nothing more than a collection of savages. Sure, we can use more water in Jerusalem. But for the maniac savage Pilate to upend our sacred treasury to find his precious money to finish the giant stone path for water, well it shows we must be at the end of days."

Joseph looked around. His heavily beaked nose twitched nervously. "I lost more than a few friends when our people had that legitimate demonstration. Who could have known that Pilate would place his killers among us that day, stabbing with their daggers from concealed robes? And to teach us a lesson? For what? For venting our frustration at being led by such a disgusting rogue as he? We are determined to get Rome's ear on this atrocity! Pilate will surely pay this time."

Suddenly a trio of Roman soldiers turned the corner. Their arms were not at the ready, in fact one of them had just told a joke and the other two were puffy with laughter. There was little doubt any of them knew even a whiff of Aramaic, but why take a chance? "To change the subject," said Zecharias, "We had three teams of oxen to break yokes coming down the big hill by the western gate this morning. Yes I said coming down. I wonder if that's a sign from our God he's about to get busy doing you-know-what?" Joseph smiled, did not take the bait. "So that would mean young Yeshua has been a busy man today. I'm sure you heard what he did just last week when that top stone fell on the poor mason potting his next batch of mortar." Joseph gazed at the many lines that had formed on his friends face. In the last few years Zecharias had began to look like a true grandfather. But he needn't worry about grandchildren with Yohanon going off with the white robed ones. He had really made the vows of a *nazirite*. Who knows what he resembled now? His full beard would no doubt be at its peak, and with so much wild, curly hair, he must resemble a true desert ascetic by now. Joseph probably would never recognize him.

"Let me ask you my friend, what are the Temple priests' positions on such a miraculous thing being done in our very midst?"

Zecharias let both hands run down the center of his smooth linen vest. He doubted if they'd ever call him back again after he retired. "The priests made a special offering of incense and slayed a tender young lamb. I myself was nearby and when I heard the commotion. I managed to peer through the crowd to see Yeshua bending over the crumpled worker while people tried to shove the giant stone from his torso. After they'd done that, neither Yeshua nor the hurt man moved for five minutes.

Yeshua was draped over the man like some kind of human cloth. When Yeshua finished whispering in the man's ear, they both just stood up. The man swayed back and forth, not quite losing his balance, and appeared astonished at his good fate, as whoops of prayer filled the air. In a few seconds Yeshua was gone, leaving the healed worker the task of explaining how he felt so good, considering a two ton stone had just effectively squashed his guts out."

"And this is not the first time my ears have picked up deeds of the young man. He is of the line of David, you know."

"He is. He's a second cousin of my wife. And Yohanon and he are good friends as well. They speak as much as they can."

"I must go, but before I do, please inform me of Yohanon's next step. Surely he'll not segregate himself for his entire life in the secretive company of the white robed ones."

Zecharias' hands flew high into the air. "With John, only our Lord God knows." Then his eyes suddenly twinkled. "But I've prayed earnestly John will step forth in these times of our greatest needs."

⁂

John intended to keep his vows as a *nazirite*. Nothing in the world, not even the scent of a good woman, could lure him away from the strange bond of kinship he felt toward his god. But as to the white robed ones, when the tenure of his final probation with them was due, he had determined that he would just walk away. In his last conversation with Levi ben Anias, John had become fully convinced the famed Teacher of Righteousness, a man most adored by this band of highly motivated Jews, was not the long awaited Messiah. Levi had argued that he was. John contended otherwise.

"Levi, the holy texts give us a clear calendar that counts down to the final generation. This Holy Teacher lived askew. His timing was off to be the Messiah. At any rate, Israel did not know him. Only men of our persuasion knew him. How can you keep claiming he was the Messiah, but improperly cut off too soon?"

Levi would nod gravely, as they all did. These desert believers were endowed with great politeness. They always gave John his due respect. But soon enough, they would be right back on target as if John had presented no convincing facts. That was the basic problem here at this compound. John had learned so much. The white robed ones had definitely rounded out his spiritual education in the Holy texts, plus some. But it was maddening to be around them.

He snapped his fingers in the silent room as he squatted against mud walls that managed to stay cool so close to the greatest lowland area of earth around the Dead Sea. "That's it summed up perfectly," he said to himself. "These people do not take action. It's really that they themselves do not think, not even for one second, that any person should rise up in Israel and say things about these times. It's more they believe that if they simply segregate themselves from evil and hypocritical men,

God will think that's enough. Such passive actions will prove they are of the elect, and thus they will be rewarded when God does plant his kingdom upon this earth."

John paused for a long time. He closed his eyes for many moments. He wanted to feel the fire inside, the fire that God planted there. But today, there was nothing, no sign. So John asked the obvious question, the one that was a nagging blister on his mind; he simply asked himself out loud: "So do you Yohanon ben Zecharias, do you think it's possible to sit back passively and do and say nothing at all? How would you reply to these questions?"

He waited for the answer to come and when it did, John smiled and wondered what they would say when he told them the news. He would be departing earlier than anyone expected.

⁂

The visitor to Zsuba cave bent low and stepped carefully down the tiered steps. A few well placed torches provided just enough light for Tsivah ben Hussah to see the stocky hairy man shuffle in from somewhere in the back, and seconds later a powerful stare bored itself into Tsivah's eyes. The distinct aroma of a desert ascetic drifted into Tsivah's nostrils.

"So you are the one who has come from Herod Antipas' castle. I was wondering if you would really come at all." John made no move for further greeting. Anyone and anything of Herod reeked of suspicion. John half expected this visitor to draw out the dagger from his belt.

"Yes, but I come on my own behalf. Herod Antipas did not send me. In fact," chuckled Tsivah, "if he knew I were here with all his other problems, he'd probably be most unhappy."

John moved two steps forward and motioned to a small stone bench at Tsivah's elbow. "Sit down then. I might welcome you as an inquiring Jew. But as a spy for Herod, I would dismiss you without regret."

Tsivah looked around as John's eyes prodded every available fact from Herod's assistant's face. Tsivah noted there wasn't much here, but maybe this was only the anteroom. There must be more interesting things further back, however far the cave stretched on this downhill slope.

"What would you ask of me?" John reached over to grab a torch and now both men's faces were fully illuminated.

"I ask of you nothing, nothing at all. I simply wanted to meet you."

"Not to size me up?" Now it was John's turn for his rough face to bear the tiniest of smiles.

"No, not really. But as you must know, there is talk among some people you've baptized. Your work out here in the *arevah*, your strange habits as a devoted *nazirite*, your message of doom in the impending judgment to come, is causing some people to say you must be Elijah returned to his people."

John shook his head swiftly and so decisively that flakes of cave dust sailed off in two directions. "I'm not Elijah. Never said I was. It's crazy talk not coming from me. Have no fear of that."

Tsivah puffed out two strong breaths. "I'm happy to hear that. For if you purported to be Elijah, then you'd qualify as a prophet. That's something we haven't had in hundreds of years. And for one to pop up now, with the whole population on edge, well, it wouldn't be such a good thing for peace."

"But I do consider myself as a messenger. How would that affect the peace you talk about?"

Tsivah shuffled closer to John. It was impressive how the man's eyes appeared to burn, as if tiny flames were embalmed there permanently. "Why should you be a messenger, Yohanon?"

He turned to look at a far wall and spoke so softly, Tsivah turned both ears hard in the speaker's direction. "You are a good Jew, Tsivah. I can sense it. You want to do right, do the best thing for God and your fellows. So you must know that according to the holy texts, we are in the countdown of the final generation before God returns and sets his kingdom down upon this earth. You do believe this don't you?"

Tsivah cleared his throat and brought both hands toward his face in the most thoughtful gesture he could manage. "Because I work for Herod Antipas I must be careful in my words. Sometimes even stone walls seem to speak to the man. Herod thinks like his father. In his heart he feels it is he who should receive first consideration for that title-The King of the Jews-if that's where you're going with this line of reasoning." John nodded and Tsivah continued. "But I know God would not tolerate Herod's massive and unpliable ego. So if not Herod Antipas... then who?"

John arose and began to pace. "God's messiah must be of the line of David. And the learned ones speak of a priest by his side. This priest would be of the lineage of Aaron. So, two, not one must arise and be counted. These two will mostly implement God's design."

"And you will be one of these two men?"

For many seconds John said nothing. "If it be in God's holy will, then I will step forward as a true servant for this task. It's one reason why I house myself here, and make a few proclamations now and then. I must be worthy. We all must be worthy of what God will demand of us."

Tsivah nodded. It was easy to admire this man. But what was the line between admiration and ardent zealousness? Herod Antipas was a man who would not catch that fine distinction.

"I do ask one thing of you my friend. If you can deliver it for me, I would be most grateful." John bowed his head suddenly.

"Tell me, what is your wish Yohanon?"

"Keep Herod Antipas off my back, away from me. Soon, I will move from here. What I do at the Jordan will be in keeping with many of the things I just told you. And my complete message, as a pure and humble messenger, will be heard. Your job is to insure Herod Antipas does not take it the wrong way, does not misunderstand. He doesn't need to interfere."

"You ask virtually the impossible Yohanon. I am not that close to the king. Keep your eyes and ears open is my advice to you. And don't go…too far in what you say."

The two men moved out of the cave. Tsivah heard all too clearly the last thing Yohanon said: "What will pour from my mouth I cannot say now. But it will be the words our God himself would want said, as if from a messenger. That I can promise."

⁂

During the long winter months, more and more people filtered silently to John's cave. He happily, continually ran low on the small plaster vases the newly baptized person shattered after they'd removed their foot from the stone basin. This aspect of the ritual resembled in part a kind of *mazultah*. Just as a newly married man crushed the stone wine cup, signifying the new and eternal bonds just created, those baptized in John's unique style, crushed the small plaster jug. They were uttering more than just mere words. The simple action meant they would give double effort to perform God's justice on earth and keep the Torah.

John never understood the odd habit he'd quickly developed with all the pieces of plaster on the cave floor. He never bothered to sweep up the growing mess. Of course, he had no broom to perform that task, and the litter reminded him that impressive numbers of Jews knew of his mission here in the middle of nowhere.

This was the exact moment Yeshua chose to show up. Even though in the cave's rear, where the water flowed in a continual, natural tiny waterfall, John's sharp ears detected the gentle swish of long cotton robes descending the front stairsteps. He closed his eyes hoping it was Yeshua.

"It's about time you came my cousin." He turned suddenly, even before the figure of the man had registered on his brain.

Yeshua bowed, then galloped over to John and grasped both hands. Yeshua stood half a head taller than John, but John was a thicker man. "Is it against your rules as *a nazirite* never to bathe? You have plenty of water to wash away the weeks of grime that must coat your skin."

John smiled broadly. After more than ten months Yeshua greets John with an insult! But it had to be well meant. Sometimes John's odor even offended himself. "Outside. Let us go outside and sit under my favorite shade tree. I'll grab a few locust cakes and we can eat too."

John sauntered up the steps and was half shocked to be greeted by the light of a full moon. Even so, they sat down against the cool bark of the ancient olive tree. "No shade required, forgive my concentration Yeshua. But do watch out for scorpions. This is the time they scurry around at full speed."

"Are you still going forward with your general idea?" Yeshua had quickly made the half silent prayer of thanks for the food, and then taken on the great issue at hand.

John gobbled down two locust cakes before replying. "Yes. I have to say this testing phase was a success. The people came and gladly took the baptism. But in the River Jordan, I won't be doing foot immersions. Their whole body goes under. It's far more dramatic. It's something they will always remember. And so will the onlookers."

Yeshua nodded. "I regret to say that I myself will not come that far south to receive baptism from you. It took some time for me to organize things to get here this time. I'm not in Jerusalem any longer. Clophas has died. My mother needs support from me. My brothers are doing what they can as well. We dare not let our mother and sisters go hungry."

"I understand brother. But I have good news for you if that is your concern. I will begin the mission in the southern confines of the River Jordan, and many from Jerusalem will stream out to hear my message and take baptism. But I fully intend to move upstream. By the fall season I expect to be at Aenon, near Salim. It's at the great crossroads as you know. The people who will be heading to the fall festivals in Jerusalem will cross the river right there. It should be convenient for you as well."

Yeshua's eyes shone as sprinklets of moonlight bounced off them. "Yes, I can manage that. I'll be there, one of your many devotees."

John's voice came on softly, only a little higher than a whisper. "I'd hoped you would aspire to be a little more than that."

Yeshua brought his head down. His long braided hair flowed thick, a brownish-black cascade that made it to his long, visible collar bones. He flicked two fingers toward the slightly beaked nose and brushed away a trio of gnats. "I also tested out a theory, more or less. The result was comical, not the intended thing I'd hoped for."

John moved both feet under his slightly stooped form. He arched his neck toward Yeshua's face. "Tell me about this test. You did it in Jerusalem?"

"No, in our tiny synagogue in Nazareth. A discussion turned toward the expected Messiah, as predicted in the Book of Isaiah. I myself read the passage. After reading it, I paused for a moment then continued with this very question. I said, looking all of them squarely in the eyes. "Could not the Messiah spring from our very village, our Nazareth, where twigs of David's seed cluster and prosper?"

John barely concealed his excitement. "You said that, in those very words?"

Yeshua nodded sadly. "It was the village butcher who first responded. Imagine being put in your place by a slayer of animals. This butcher shouted for all to hear; "And do you suppose Yeshua ben Yosef, that you yourself might be up to this exalted task, to be the Messiah for all of Israel?"

John shot to his feet. "He mocked you! You allowed this?"

"Sit down John. It gets worse. The local priest himself then walked over and put his hands sadly on my shoulders. He said: 'No one can be the Messiah right now, Yeshua. That's what I think. Israel is not ready, is not purified, is too divided.'

John shot to his feet again. His breath came in heaves and bursts. "That's insanity and coming from a priest! If I were there I would have said to his face, 'if not now, when? There is no later. The holy texts we revere tell us God is coming within this very generation, to make his kingdom, and Israel itself will lead the nations."

Yeshua sighed. "It's a good thing then, that you were not there. The people are on guard against false messiahs all over Galilee. It has gotten us into so much trouble before with the Romans. They come in and pillage however they please, as if collecting the taxes is not outrageous enough."

John leaned against the olive bark. It was rough, but cool now. A shooting star beamed hard, flashing against the silver tone of the moon.

"Lastly the silversmith chimed in. We were still sitting in a tight circle in the temple and he said, "We have to keep out the rabble rousers Yeshua. Maybe you've been away too long from Galilee. But we are quite prepared to accompany any false messiah who gets too loud, right over the face of that cliff, just across the hill there. We won't even try and cover his bones."

John stamped his feet on the ground, like a young bull that's had enough."Ok, come, I'm tired of this report, so much bad news for one night. Let's go inside and prepare for sleep. You may use the only sleeping cloth I possess, as it sometimes can be cool in the cave." John grinned as he laid an arm affectionately across Yeshua's strong right shoulder. "And yes, this night I will wash well. No grime to stink up the precious air you breath as my cherished guest."

When Yeshua awoke John had just finished laying a small towel on the cave floor and placing down three squarish locust cakes. He scooped water from the tiny pool, and Yeshua enjoyed the refreshing splash of aquifer water. His throat must still be parched from the heavy pace he'd put himself under the day before.

"When do the people begin to show up?" Yeshua sat cross-legged across from John.

"By about mid-morning three or four should be here. I should like for you to observe, and then to perform a few baptisms of your own."

Yeshua reached for one of the hard cakes, blessed it, and stared at John as if in deep thought. "No, sorry, I have to take leave quickly. My family was upset enough that I took time off to trek all the way here to see you. James, my younger brother, is not so adept at handling the wood for yokes. Customers will run from us if he is in charge for too long, I'm afraid."

John grunted and Yeshua noted how much noise was generated in eating these cakes John made himself, from whatever was available out here in the *arevah.*

"John, it's not so far to Ein Kareem. Surely your mother would greet you with open arms and make you meals that could ensure a little fat on your bones. Do you not miss her?"

John tugged nonchalantly at the salt and pepper hair of his sideburns. The hairy beard didn't yet have silver parts. "Aye, most certainly. But in my vows as a *nazirite*, I cannot take my mother's help. I must do all on my own."

Yeshua stood suddenly and John caught the signal of departure. "Let me accompany you for a distance. I want to show you something."

They walked past the large olive tree, already offering morning shade, and two pairs of bare feet stirred up tiny whirls of ancient red clay. John led Yeshua toward a patch of fine red sand, and they stood there for a moment as a cloud passed over the early, hot sun. John picked up a long stick and began drawing in the sand.

He drew a large triangle. On one side he placed a circle which bisected the baseline. Just outside the other two lines he placed two simple signs, a positive and a negative symbol.

Yeshua bent low and lovingly placed his finger over every line, every symbol, retracing them. "You are a great thinker John. But what does this signify?"

"It's both simple and complex, Yeshua. This simple pictogram represents what God has indwelled in my heart since I was a boy. That's the easy part. Here's the complex part. See this circle, the one bisecting the base line of the triangle?"

"Of course, it's right in front of me."

"The circle is there because it represents the perfectness of God's plans. Did you learn that the Greeks know the concept behind circles? That no matter how large or small the circle, the miraculous number that truly describes them is the same, no matter what?"

"Yes, I know that number. It's 3.146."

John shot an amazed look toward his cousin. "Where did you pick that up? You can read Greek?"

"No, but some friends I made in Jerusalem taught me lots about the Greeks. I can even speak a little Greek."

John slapped Yeshua on a shoulder. "Good! There is no sin in being an erudite, well informed Jew. And for your future mission, having a broad background won't hurt."

Yeshua cocked his head. His eyes stared intently at the energetic dynamo right beside him.

"So back to this." John pointed at the negative symbol. This represents me. In God's big picture, I myself will always be a servant. This line represents my servitude, as the priest at the right hand of the Messiah who is to come. The Messiah of whom God will install as chief prime minister in the new kingdom. This is not the first you have heard of the good news, is it Yeshua?"

"No, not at all. I've said something like this many times to anyone who will listen. But is Israel ready for this message?"

John ignored the question. He was staring intently at the final line, at the great connecting line of the hypotenuse of the triangle he'd created in the red sand. "You need to know what this positive symbol signifies, Yeshua. Most urgently you need to know."

"So tell me, but I think I already understand."

"I know you do." John smiled and laughed. He reached out by instinct to touch his cousin's hard, muscled forearm. "God's always talked to you, just as he has to me. Only with you, he's had a harder time. You've always been a stubborn, hard-headed one, and that yoke business hasn't helped matters."

Yeshua stood up. He put the back of a hand across his forehead to wipe off the droplets of sweat. "I don't know about this John. I have my doubts."

John drew very close, as if to whisper a secret only he knew of. "Then how to account for your gift. No one in Israel is like you, and few have ever been like you. This gift of healing…it captures the public's imagination like no words anyone could utter. You don't have to be a great orator Yeshua. Let the words speak from your actions. You'll learn what to say when you need the words to flow."

Yeshua bent down again, ran his fingers across the triangle line coated by the positive sign. "Why did you make the symbol positive for me and negative for you?"

"That's the central core of my entire argument, and a good question! Here's why: From the line of David will spring forth our Messiah. The people interpret that to be someone who has God's ear, is powerful and capable, and who can administrate in a political sense. Messiah is equated with kingship. That would be you Yeshua. You demand and deserve the positive symbol. As for me, I am the priest by your side, descended from Aaron, wise in the ways of the Lord. A helpmate in every way as God implements his kingdom on this earth-through us!"

Yeshua's eyes did not blaze, instead turned into beads of sadness. "So this triangle represents God's ultimate plan. Everything inside the triangle is all he stands for, and all we stand for. It's how the new world will be once he returns on the clouds of glory."

"You know much, Yeshua. God can take action through a man like you."

Someone shuffled dirt uncomfortably with his sandals. John and Yeshua turned suddenly, and there stood Tsivah ben Hussah. He'd been watching and listening for how long?

Yeshua leaned toward John and whispered. "I'll tell you my final decision when you baptize me in the fall. May God be with you my cousin."

John turned to greet his visitor, but Tsivah's eyes had never left the other man. John's visitor had a glow around him, a light blue aura, that left Tsivah speechless. Was it the early morning sun playing tricks on his eyes? After what he'd just heard, somehow he doubted that.

John took Tsivah's arm and they turned toward the shade to talk.

THE END

Lawyers will always be themselves, being as heartless as they need to be. But what happens when an equally maligned client combines with his attorney to use an incredible new age device to help get his final wishes across? What's the result to a common, mild mannered fellow who wouldn't harm a flea?

"Let me out!"

Warning! This is flash fiction! Your attention span disorder will love this story.

The entire family was now assembled, having slipped toward Atlanta through the gorgeous Georgia countryside. While brothers and sisters eyed one another warily, lawyer Harry Mason and several paralegals kept going in and out of the conference room, whispering continuously, as if the secrets about to unfold were too momentous to contemplate.

There was only one thing that could bring such a fractious group together like this: Grayson Fratshire, the oldest brother, a brassy, bossy man, rude to both women and children, the Storage King of Tifton, had departed earth without taking his money. So now they were all in the outer conference room, leaning forward on tightly cushioned chairs, all thoughts feasting on the very real chance Grayson would be forced to be extremely kind to them today.

As the general confusion subsided, Harry Mason managed to wave his staff from the room. For the first time, he eyed the family in one sweeping glance, these mostly blessed heirs of Grayson Fratshire.

Mr. Mason nodded and unceremoniously began the attendance roll call. In silly fashion Cathy said happily, "Here I am." Camilla smiled shyly being sure to hide the large golden tooth that had become her main incisor. Landel's grunt of, "Right here," identified the youngest Fratshire. Corey jabbed at a layer of air. "I'm present Mr. Mason."

Lawyer Mason dutifully acknowledged their presence with a pasty smile that revealed uneven, moly dimples. "You all are obligated to watch something on that screen there. Some of the strangest images you will ever behold will come from that machine right there. This little gizmo flashes a kind of movie." He paused to clear his throat and search for the best words. "Your brother had his thoughts *imagined* while he was failing. Before the worst of the Alzheimers kicked in, he'd begun to do this." Harry gave the family adequate time to digest the strange information.

"How does it work?" Corey rose efficiently to the lawyer's bait.

"Ah yes, indeed, how does it work? That was the main reason I had to have my entire staff plus half the staff next door here; you saw us scrambling around as you assembled. We've never used or seen this little high tech tool before. But your brother Grayson loved to dabble with technology. He found out about this, and it's a very important component of the will review today." Lawyer Mason stood straight and shook his head gravely. "What you will see will both astonish and reveal some aspects of your brother, that perhaps, you had been unaware of. This set of images, or movie, came straight from your very own brother's mind, even as the Alzheimer's was progressing. In the disease's last phase, he stopped the –ah- movie. But it was sufficiently finished for our purposes."

This revelation of uncertainty made every Grayson sibling glance simultaneously at one another. The family had done the obligatory rituals, had seen Grayson in the days when he was lucid. They'd visited him from time to time at the Hospice Center, sent him cards. He never hinted he might surprise them too much at the will review.

Lawyer Mason clapped and the lights dimmed. He touched an icon on a projector-like machine, and a simple plot played out on the screen, so much like an old black-and-white movie, Corey assumed Grayson had chosen this unusual means to grant to his siblings the fortune he'd made in his lifetime of hard work. Did Lawyer Mason just say all this had come straight from Grayson's own mind? Corey must have missed this development. From his many hours watching Discovery Channel, Corey had no clue this had been invented.

In this odd movie scene, Grayson occupied some kind of small room. He paced about, pushing up at the ceiling which flexed without breaking. He began to pound on those walls. Exactly as in some ancient soundless black and white movie, his lips moved making no sound at all. Was he screaming?

Now the walls were drawing in, like some box folding back on itself. As Grayson realized this, he plopped himself in the center and continued to say something.

"Uh-excuse me sir," Corey said. "Why doesn't this movie have sound? It's awful enough to watch my brother grovel around like this. He wants to say something, but he can't."

"Grayson wanted you to think a bit, to study what he must be saying. He's silent on purpose. Can you tell what he's saying by reading his lips?"

Corey surely did. "He's screaming: 'Let me out! Let me out."

"Oh my God, look now!" Something had excited Landel. He huffed like a small black bear and scooted forward.

Dark spikes suddenly sprouted from inner walls. Grayson still wanted to pound, but now his jabbing fists half impaled themselves. He stared in disbelief at the blood flowing like black ink from his wounds. Now Grayson's bushy silver hair became speckled with dark spots, the blood that rapidly dried up in this bizarre movie Grayson had *imagined.*

"Poor Brother! How could he endure such nightmares!" Cathy asked anyone who'd listen.

"These were not true dreams. Recall I just told you he *imagined* them on purpose. They were the story of his mind in that they fit in with his final wishes. You will-ah-soon sadly see, this directly has to do with our distribution of monies today, from this very hour in fact." Harry grunted to himself. This group pretty much was not curious at all about why Grayson had done this. They must not have known their own brother had once been a monster of a geek, worshipping very much at the altar of high technology.

"Hey, looky here!" Camilla almost laughed. "What's Corey doing in Grayson's movie?"

Corey's pig-like face gushed red. It was him, exactly him. He'd just walked right up there, like some lunatic actor. What was he doing here? Could it be he was put here by those thoughts *imagined* by his brother, possibly to save the day, to somehow rescue his brother from this terrible predicament? Suddenly, the first sounds of the movie, Corey's own basso rumble: "Let me in! Let me in!"

Grayson knew the voice, reached out even as the walls and spikes closed in. The family's eyes could have popped from their sockets when Grayson's tears streamed down both cheeks. The family had talked about this many times before. Nobody could ever recall Grayson crying. Not even when he was a kid, when he'd run through the fire to escape their burning trailer house. He was put up in the hospital for weeks, but he never cried, at least never in front of people.

He could not sit up now. He braced himself with both hands, slipping a bit in the small pool of blood that had poured from his injuries as he continued to jab at the spiky wall. But Corey was here now. The family watched transfixed as a pure drama of life and death played out. Corey had bobbed his way around the entire diminishing room and suddenly rammed it. It gave way to his great bulk, a wall caving in easily. He was in the room and reached out to his brother to pull him from this hellish creation of his own design.

But something, everything morphed. It happened in the course of a blinking eyelid. Not only did Grayson Fratshire simply vanish from sight, but the room itself changed dimensions back to the original shape before it had begun to shrink. And the spikes were gone.

What was this? There was no door so he rammed the walls from every possible angle. "Let me out! Let me out!" But those walls as before flexed but never broke. They all watched with eyes glued to the animated action figure Corey had become. Their brother wailed and wallowed, bouncing his ample form from one axis to the other like some sorry cartoon beast. Corey himself was now as trapped as the poor beavers he used to molest when he was younger.

For many long moments Corey expended himself there. At last he plopped down upon the virtual floor, his chest soaked in sweat. He breathed hard, sucking in liters of virtual air. Canny eyes slowly began to bend their gaze, more eyeballs now aimed at the flesh-and-blood Corey than toward the screen concoction. It was Landel who coughed boldly and then sputtered, "Looks to me like Brother wants to tell you something today. Maybe he has some bad news for you Corey." He gazed stonily in Corey's darting eyes. "We all know he never liked you."

The lawyer clapped twice, and shouted, "Lights!" The movie was finished. He paced lightly around the rich Persian rug. "It has nothing to do with liking or not liking Corey. It has everything to do with how Grayson wanted the money in the will distributed."

If this were a courtroom summation, the lawyer had them. They inhaled his words the way lice feast on blood. "Now you know the reason Grayson insisted on DNA samples from each of you. From these samples, Grayson's worst suspicions were absolutely confirmed." He frowned and brought two fingers toward his nose. "Ah-one among you is so unfortunate. There is no doubt that one of you will soon fall into Grayson's condition. Therefore we know, and must tell one of you today that you have in common the gene sequence that initiates…Early Onset Alzheimer's. The identical gene sequence that killed your brother."

Each family member blew out great bubbles of air. The two girls almost fainted in their seats. But Landel had already begun to smile even has Lawyer Mason tried to wrap this odd afternoon up. "Family, listen to me. Grayson had about ten million dollars. He wants to withhold distribution for one year, so nobody gets anything just yet. After that, you will get a one-third share. Notice I said… one-third share." The Lawyer had turned away from where Corey sat.

Camilla interrupted, could not restrain herself "It goes to three of us? But there's four kids."

Landel slapped his knee. He gave a strange hoot. Understanding had dawned. His dead brother had a strange way of getting the message across, it had worked well today. Gratefully, Harry allowed Landel to have his say. Let a family member make the fateful pronouncement. Grayson's fees weren't sufficient for many tricky speeches like this. Already it looked as if Corey would completely break down. Landel stood and gestured freely. "Grayson already knew Corey would get Early Onset Alzheimer's, just like he did. So Corey gets cut out of the money. Right Mr. Attorney?" Landel barked out that he'd just solved the puzzle. He'd become a gleeful man, eager to share today his unrevealed genius.

Lawyer Mason shook his head sadly. "Indeed Landel. Grayson has fully excluded Corey from this distribution. From the movie, Grayson wanted you to grasp his feelings, his way of thinking about this tender subject. If he'd just put the terms into a will document, he feared the effect of how much he'd thought about this would never come out. He was never much of a word guy, as you all know."

They moved their gaze away from Lawyer Mason and everything fell on Corey's baffled face. Now, he was nothing more than a lost and angry baboon; his disturbed form was on full display for all to see. He wanted to swat them, mangle those smug grins of amusement from their faces. But he only sat dope-like, unmoving in this ridiculous chair. "What did I do that was… so bad to Gray? I don't understand." He'd managed to say something, but it was worse than pitiful, hardly the way a man who has been immensely offended should behave.

Lawyer Mason managed to shuffle over, place a hand on Corey's shoulder. "In truth of fact, he never told me why he chose to exclude you from the big money. I suspect he was simply being practical. Corey, you will die early, all too soon. But your siblings, well, they may live a long life, the one you will be denied. Why give good money to a dead cause? That was probably his way of thinking about this."

He was left to wrestle with blank despair. Anger on a cosmic scale slashed across his mind. He cupped both palms over his eyes, and large tears filled the cup. Lawyer Mason pulled out his handkerchief to place over the salty mess, then realized silk would never absorb anything like this. He picked up the handkerchief and watched as they all sauntered away. Corey's withered cries moved not a one. No one dared even place a tender hand on his outsized shoulders. As the door shut, light hoops of delight yapped from both sisters.

Lawyer Mason almost wondered aloud how he'd allowed this, to be the last one out that door. He muttered something. "He could have been kinder to you I suppose. But it was not his way to mollycoddle anyone. He was a rough Marine at heart. He only believed in tough love for everyone, even family. Of course, it's gonna be awful for you. You've lost your brother to a gruesome death. From what I see today, the rest of your family is leaving you on your own. You will soon lose..."

Corey waved madly in his direction, and the not- to- polite shove at Lawyer Mason's backside easily propelled him in the proper direction. When Corey looked up again the only people in the room were the staff. They had already removed the special screen on the wall, and placed the machine that had just wrecked Corey's life, back in its box. They moved silently around Corey until the last person in the room gave a light moan in Corey's direction and manually flipped out the lights.

Corey didn't move, couldn't get up. He would just stay here and die. What was that flicker in his head just now anyway? He was wilting away already. He wanted it done.

THE END

We hear a lot of stories about the sperm of men. Sometimes they don't do the job, it's true. But what happens if a true crisis grips the world, and at first men's sperm are blamed? It takes some sleuthing, but two attractive figures emerge, young twin brother and sister scientists, to set the record straight. It's not the sperm of men, but the ova of women that are creating the problem. Now how do we solve the crisis when it's only Mother Nature doing her thing? When the Red Queen dances, we can watch in wonderment. But it's much harder to take action...

Sxperm Scell

In Bess Lee's family, aspects of human reproduction were not a part of after dinner discussion. Not once. Not ever. Her mother and father knew for certain that she would pick up this information soon enough. They knew as well about her moral compass. It was set to true north. She was a fantastic daughter in every way.

And now it was a point of some embarrassment to her that at the age of 32, the world recognized her and fraternal twin brother K.R., as miniature *Einsteins* in the important arena of sexual biology. Both Bess and K.R. full well knew they'd been very lucky to have been in an ideal position to make their original hypothesis about worldwide birth rate declines. After heavy scrutiny from their peers, it was enormously comforting to know the twins seemed to be correct.

In medicine, people of the world had come to expect a curving exponential line upward for progress and gain. It was most evident in the arena of human longevity. Since the costs of therapeutic cloning and other measures were costly, only the rich tended to benefit. This left the vast majority out in the cold, living only to the normal and expected age. Societal divisions in this era cut across those gaping lines of wealth and age.

Into this social jambalaya came Bloomberg's ideas which apparently revealed to the world why it was harder than ever to conceive a child. His charts and simple graph made enough sense. Even though he used questionable data, people tended to believe what he proposed and for one good reason: Having unprotected sex more and more often led to no pregnancy for the woman. It had been so much easier for grandparents than it was now to begin a family. Scientists were hard pressed to falsify Bloomberg's strange tales about human sperm cells. It would take some time to falsify. But along had come the twins' discovery derived from superior scientific sleuthing.

Bloomberg had invented the most colorful labels that caught the common man's fancy: *Befuddled sperm, More befuddled sperm, Most befuddled sperm.* Most of North American males had the distinction of possessing sperm that seemed to barely do the job. And why were the spermal gametes of North African men only demoted to "*Befuddled*"? Bloomberg could not say why. In the middle of the pack *More Befuddled* sperm took in most of Southern and Central Asia. Bloomberg offered no realistic answer as to why this was so. But there was nothing else for a questioning world to latch onto.

The Lee twins surmised the exact opposite. It wasn't necessarily the 'fault' of sperm at all. The eggs women regularly shed once a moth seemed to be performing shenanigans that nobody could ever have predicted. The Lees tied it to the behavior of the *Dance of the Red Queen*. So for the first time in history, concepts of genetic evolution were on the lips of men and women from every nation.

The world at first breathed a deep sigh of relief. Bess and K.R. were stunned to receive a personal invitation from the President of the United States for a formal dinner in their honor. So relieved were American leaders that Simon Bloomberg was wrong after all. American, North American and Mexican sperm were in no way inferior to sperm anywhere in the world. The correlation between *Most Befuddled Sperm* and the men of most of North America could at last be dropped.

The Lees became heroic figures overnight.

Because of them, their parent company, *Samsung Biometrics International*, had easily jostled into full partnership with the Center for Disease Control to get a firmer grasp on this matter of why human egg cells were firing off such strange signals in the Fallopian tubes of women. Everyone supposed the obvious-if we can identify the problem a cure is possible. Such a supposition rang to the very core of modern scientific belief. It was what science was ultimately there for-to come to the aid of humans when they most needed it. While people on the street could let the word 'cure' roll off their mouth with ease, for K.R. no such a thing existed.

Bess knew K.R. was nearby, had that familiar feeling of his presence as twins are prone to do. She reached for her phone and as she spoke the text formed on the screen. At the touch screen she finished and dashed it off into cyberspace.

K.R. was by her side before she had blinked three times. "Brother, a word with you." He smiled and made one of his silly bows. These days K.R. was always happy, always upbeat. Bess contrasted this with her innermost attitude toward fame. Even though she could not frame the words, her enthusiasm hardly matched her fraternal twin's exuberance. What was missing in her life? She could not pinpoint it exactly.

"We did hire the personal manager, the fellow King Frampton. But now he tells me he's already totally swamped with work, and he himself requires a staff. Who will pay for these expenses?"

Ki Roh Lee brought a hand toward his chin and tugged a few times at the small but already pointed goatee he'd been cultivating. "Well, Bess, the CEO of the parent company told me himself that we could have whatever we wanted if it promoted the discovery. So I'll tell accounting it's ok for King Frampton to have his staff. Do I need to ask you why he considers himself so 'swamped'?"

Bess tapped four fingers on the table. "He said people are already wanting to know why we haven't developed a cure for the problem."

K.R. shook his head. "I sure don't get it sister. Is the world that stupid? Don't they realize how lucky we were in the first place to be able to so clearly falsify Bloomberg? That took us four years of constant work, we had to dream up highly specialized software, and acquire the cooperation of nations. And now, we can just snap our fingers and understand why the *Dance of the Red Queen* has turned this way?" He shook his head again.

Bess moved the chair aside and stood. At her full height she only reached to K.R.'s chin. They both had a slender, gracile build, but K.R. had always been taller, handsomely taller she thought. "Dr. Margie Herger has been promoted to be our contact person at the CDC. I'm sure you remember her; she was the lead speaker at that seminar those years ago that introduced us to the variability of human sperm for the first time."

"Right! Of course you'd remember the seminar. Your face stayed red the whole time, except for once. When Dr. Herger likened sperm cells to three kinds of little men, you burst out laughing right in the middle of her lecture." K.R.'s brown eyes danced at the recollection.

Bess smiled, maybe for the first time that day. "Yes I did and for good reason. Who'd ever have suspected that sperm really come in three varieties? What was that first type she alluded to? The speed guys, young and brash, thinking only of getting to the female's egg. Margie's second kind of sperm represented men who were killers; so it was the first time I'd ever heard of *killer sperm*."

"And the third variety of little men were the sperm who were more elderly, content to sit in their rocking chairs blocking the channels in the cervical mucus." K.R. fiddled with his phone then stuck it absently in a front pocket of his lab coat.

Now she laughed again, just as she had at the seminar. "And for what reason do the little old men block the cervical channels? Just in case some other guy's sperm are deposited. Oh my how men have evolved!"

K.R. detected someone shouting his name in another room, but spun suddenly around. "Oh, we did get a message from Dr. Herger. I just read the text message. She'd like for one of us to drop by next week. Send a message to her secretary, ok?"

"So I'm the one who will drop by? Got it K.R."

He whirled away again, and Bess immediately set out concentrating into what she saw in the picture the electron microscope revealed. What was really going on in the bodies of human females these days? Why would they send siren calls out that baffled sperm? She paused and then looked again, as if she'd missed something the first time.

The twins' mother lived in Seattle and her habits of communicating with her precious, brilliant children were as sharp as her cutting wit and formidable intelligence. She expected them to be ready for holographic communication at nine p.m. each and every Friday night.

Bess activated the speaker unit as the form flickered and gained substance. The partly transparent hologram had the amazing quality of looking around the room. "I don't see K.R. Bess. Where is he?"

"He's finishing dinner, just right around the corner. How are you mom?"

Jade Lee's virtual eyes stared lovingly at Bess, who had crossed her legs in that sweet, feminine way she had, sitting on the leather sofa in the living room of their apartment. "I'm fine Bess, but I continue to be amazed at the jealousy my friends display. Is it because my son and daughter are young and famous worldwide celebrities?"

Bess shook her head. "Unlike K.R., I'm not sure sudden fame agrees with me. We've been lucky coming along when we did."

"Nonsense!" Jade almost barked aloud. "You and K.R. made your own hypothesis, put in the work, even designed your own specialized software. Ah-I see K.R. has joined us."

He sat down near Bess on the sectional. Playfully, he flicked an apple seed toward his mother's glowing, tangible form that grew up out of the hologram box. She never detected the seed go right through. K.R. smiled playfully in his sister's direction.

"Son, it's great to see you will give me your full attention this time."

"Right mom, no disruptions, no calls, I've arranged it. We have our own personal organizer, King Frampton. He takes care of every detail we ask him to." K.R. placed the half-eaten apple on the lamp table. "So mom, has the press continued to hound you?"

Jade smiled and cackled. "As the official writer and biographer of my son and daughter's life story, I'd say yes, I am being hounded. But it's a happy kind of hounding."

Jade reached for a sheaf of papers, half bound together. K.R. groaned and Bess slapped him lightly on his wrist. Again, they'd have to endure Jade's rough draft of the book that still had no name. Jade had predicted it was sure to be a world-wide best seller.

Jade flipped absently past the childhood pictures, stories from young adulthood, tales of their med school experience. "I have most of the picture groups pretty well organized. I have this part of the draft written. That takes me up to the present time which, for obvious reasons, I have not written yet. May I ask you some questions, children, to prepare my mind for what may be the toughest part of the writing for me?"

"Ok mom, ask away." K.R. seemed happy to not have to comment any more on the photographs and commentary from his teens, a time he admitted was a rough patch.

Jade glanced toward her notes and cleared her throat. K.R. knew full well this was her first venture into true science writing, and if his mother was a first-rate journalist, it was not in this field. "First of all, please briefly summarizes to me how exactly you falsified Professor Simon Bloomberg's hypothesis, of his three classes of so- called Befuddled Sperm."

K.R. gave a knowing look toward his sister. It was his way of turning over this part of the conversation to her. "Mom, Bloomberg oversimplified matters, but he had enough evidence to seem very convincing. He was half showman, half scientist, if truth be told. When the world erupted over the controversy he'd created about the *'Most' Befuddled Sperm* belonging largely to North and Central American men, he took advantage of the situation it seemed, to become more famous and more rich."

Jade acknowledged understanding with a wave of her hand into thin air. "Yes, I know that background Bess, but how exactly did you falsify him?"

Bess got up and walked from side to side, a habit she'd always criticized her brother about when he was concentrating in some important lecture or seminar. "K.R. and I simply did not believe sperm could be divided into three neat groups that corresponded curiously with the geographical map. It made no sense. We could see no mechanism for it. So while everyone else was examining sperm all over the world, we began to look at the egg, to see if we could find any interesting clues that might be affecting sperm."

"So that's when you first detected the anomaly in the chemical signal the egg sends out to any sperm that might be around?"

"Yes. We were the first ones to turn the chemical signal the egg releases into a tonal modulation. The fact that the tonal modulation starts out very near the piano key of Middle C helped simplify matters to people."

"But the tone does not stay at Middle C. Is that the anomaly?"

K.R. almost butted in as Bess stared his way, hands on hips. "We simply do not know if what we just discovered is an anomaly or not. We have nothing to compare it to."

"You're talking about when the egg 'screams' as you put it." Jade jotted notes as she spoke. She had only recently learned shorthand, a skill she found to be necessary as she gathered the huge body of facts necessary for the book.

"Yeah, mom. That scream is the entire basis of our hypothesis. It just so happens that the chemical signal given off by the eggs of women everywhere, correspond and dovetail with Simon Bloomberg's Befuddled Sperm. That is, the more Befuddled the sperm seem to be, the greater the frequency in a female population of a tonal modulation that spikes at close to High C. Eggs for these women send out what is probably a normal chemical signal that excites the sperm to action. This happens for about five minutes. Then suddenly, for about five minutes, the signal shoots way up, what we show as the 'scream'. At that point the sperm behave oddly, especially the killer sperm, which normally do not seek the egg."

"What are the killer sperm actually doing?"

"Killer sperm have these caps on their heads that have toxins. And they also have a little spike or horn on their head that they can flex outward. It's here when the egg's signal changes. And curiously, it's here where the carnage commences. Many of the killers suddenly turn on their brothers. It doesn't take many to clog up the space. Thus few viable sperm can get to the egg before it dies one day later."

Jade's holographic form hardly moved. She was staring at the couch, at the space directly between the twins. "But you also contend that where the females live that possess on average, a more consistent scream signal, the sperm can't do their job. And where the females reside where the scream signal is still lagging, the sperm can more effectively swim up to the egg."

Bess said, "By George mom, I think you've got it! The graph we put out paralleled Bloomberg's almost exactly, but we showed it was the signal from the egg directly affecting sperm which only made them appear Befuddled. In fact, sperm should consider themselves free from being charged with any degree of Befuddlement. They still know what to do."

K.R. cut in. "And it seems to have nothing to do with race or region. We full well know as you do that so many people in the U.S. have been quite angry and almost raging over the idea that the sperm of North African Muslim men seemed to be the healthiest in the world, so much better than North America's Befuddled class of Sperm. But it was never so. People have offered us their thanks so many times, I can't count them, that we were correct and Bloomberg was wrong."

Jade's image suddenly crackled and wrinkled. It folded halfway up on itself, then came upright again. "Your signal's going away mom. Might be another solar storm. They've been messing up our signals at work too."

Jade could only wave goodbye. Bess reached down to turn off the receiver unit, then turned to ask K.R. something. But he'd already left and when Bess saw the shadow of his bedroom door close, she knew her brother had already shut down for the day.

Bess came into the office of Dr. Margie Herger with a Cappucino in each hand. Margie had asked Bess to pick hers up on the secretary's desk, who'd ducked away at the last moment.

Margie could not get off the phone in time and thus only grunted in a smiling way as Bess sat down. Bess's eyes milled around the office. Margie obviously had barely had time to get settled in, and yet already, mounds of papers and print-outs covered a u-shaped area of tables in the center of the room. Bess was not sure of Margie's official title, but the Ph.D degree conferred upon her by MIT hung gloriously on a panel just above her cluttered desk.

When at last Dr. Herger released the image of the man she'd been speaking to, she stood and gave a hearty double-fisted pump of greeting to her guest. "Ah, Bess Lee. I'm so happy to meet the only person who ever found my description of sperm as men, truly hilarious!"

"I'm sorry you remember that. It was quite some time ago." Bess smiled and wondered where the worry lines had gone on Dr. Herger's well lined face. Bess had read how therapeutic cloning had been perfected to change the faces of patients back to the appearances of an earlier age. Margie seemed to be one of those clients.

"Well, at least you and K.R. have let us get past Dr. Bloomberg's craziness. So...we have a problem with the eggs from us ladies. It appears the sperm of our men folk have been exonerated."

"It does appear that way Dr. Herger. And I'm sure you called me here to coordinate efforts that lead to the question of why this is so."

"You guess correctly. I'm going to put something up on the screen right there. It's a computer micrograph taken from a scanning electron microscope." Margie touched a screen and Bess saw the mid-piece from a human male's sperm cell. It was attached normally to the head and flagellum. Some curious specks in the midsection seemed to stand out.

Margie pointed her laser pen and counted pieces, "One, two, three, four... all the way to sixteen. Bess, what would you say those flecks of materials are?"

"Well, Dr. Herger, since K.R. and I have been focusing all our attention on eggs, not on sperm, I would hope it would be you to inform me what they are."

"Surely. They are tiny pieces of iron. The same iron you'd see anywhere in a human body such as in hemoglobin. Do you notice where these pieces of iron are situated?"

Bess could tell that easily enough. "They are either touching or almost touching the mitochondria. Is that unusual Dr. Herger?"

"It might be, Bess, very possibly. Here is a micrograph taken by an old electron microscope, back in the 1980's. Notice where the iron flecks are and how many there are."

"Hmm...I count only seven and it's obvious they are some distance from the mitochondria in this picture. 1980 you said? That puts some 70 years of distance between what we see now and the way they were then. Of course, I'd guess we don't have many samples to go by, just this one?"

"We have exactly 12 samples to go by. It's not much. But the average number of flecks of iron in the spermal mid-piece averages 9. And on average they are exactly 1.2 micrometers distance from the mitochondria. Thus they can have no effect on the mitochondria from that distance. Would you agree with that?"

Bess caught the connection at once. "You think this may be a clue as to why sperm are reacting to a changing signal from the egg?" Understanding dawned suddenly and she let out a quiet, "Wow!"

Dr. Herger smiled. "Evidence of the actual Dance. The mystical, fantastic and ever changing *Dance of the Red Queen*. The male makes a move, the female responds. Or else maybe it's the opposite. We can't know just yet, can we?"

"Would you please get your people to relay all this pertinent information over to us, Dr. Herger. I'm sure I won't tell K.R. until he can take a look himself."

After three months of constantly attempting to balance speaking engagements with his passion for research, K.R. at last gave the thumbs down signal to King Frampton. "I can't do this any more. It's not just explaining things over and over, it's the missed lab time. I have a hunch I want to examine, but it's gonna take some time to set up."

King Frampton munched absently on a chip and then rubbed excess salt on the front of his plaid shirt. "Does the same go for Bess?"

"You can speak to her yourself, but my guess is most certainly yes."

King had no problem with what his boss said. "I'll take care of everything as usual. You just tell me what you want."

Over the next weeks K.R. lived in the lab with Bess close by. There was indeed no way to know how much the iron flecks in sperm had changed over time, but there was a way to know if the iron somehow acted as a receiver unit for the chemical signal given off by human eggs as they were shed from the ovary. If only K.R. could put together all the clues in front of him. But again, K.R. received the usual major interruption.

The man who ruled over *Samsung Biometrics International* had required no appointment, and now he stood erect on the stage of the Primary Teleconference Room. K.R. knew something about the home office in Seoul. He'd spent a month there off and on over the last five years. Bill Kim had often sought him out, seemed to enjoy speaking with K.R. who was very much Mr. Kim's junior. Bill Kim was not a man smitten with cultural traditions, K.R. had surmised. He was the big boss, a CEO who had been both a researcher and a doctor in his rise to power.

"K.R. and Bess.! It's wonderful to see you and I appreciate your speaking to me in light of your busy schedule. I understand what you are working on, and it's hugely important as we continue our cooperation with the Center for Disease Control. But we have a fantastic innovation in our BioMechanical Division, and I'd like to see you use it to further simplify the theories you've expounded. I'm sure the world will be both sufficiently electrified." Bill Kim smiled, the way someone would who held at least three aces in his hand.

Bess put her hand on K.R.'s shoulder and whispered, "This may be good."

"We shall see Sister. We shall see."

K.R. and Bess did not have to fully understand how *SpermCam* worked. But in their characteristically thorough way, in a few weeks they had dissected it minutely. Truly, as Bill Kim had said, it was a fantastic merger between nano and bio technology. *SpermCam* incorporated most of a living sperm cell with precisely those aspects of biotechnology that allowed it to do its remarkable job.

K.R. still did not know exactly how he felt about being one of the main actors in the drama Bill Kim had concocted. For Bess's part she made certain every detail would work as advertised. If not, they all stood to be humiliated in front of the entire world. After all, the twins were research scientists, not entertainers. But how many decades ago had those lines turned fuzzy?

Jade scarcely could contain her excitement. "Only two more days my daughter. I hope you are getting all the sleep you need." Jade paused and let her eyes scan every centimeter of her daughter. "You are so beautiful. That is only important because I know what the world will be thinking when they meet you for the first time."

Bess sighed and made her eyes roll. In fact, she knew full well of her desirability. Her oval face had that fine regal nose, something her mother was fond of saying was a leftover remnant of the kingly nobility present in their family tree. Bess's eyes, brown and almond shaped, held the allure of someone blessed with acute intelligence. Indeed, from childhood Bess had known of her astonishing IQ. Both she and K.R. had qualified for MENSA since age 12. Inside her beautifully coiffed mind, the neurons fired up endlessly and worked in full cooperative fashion.

Bess held every physical feature common to any Korean woman who fancies herself beautiful. Bess often slapped her hips as she dressed, half admiring the shapely flair that could attract men if she so desired. One day, she mused. When the time is right.

"K.R. cannot be here tonight?" Since it was Friday, Jade had hoped against hope she'd get to see her son one last time, before she too, turned her holographic receptor unit on to gather the signals from the incredible scene that was soon to unfold from an Atlanta studio.

"No mom, I'm barely here myself. We have a few technical problems that have come up at the last second. You know K.R.-he wants to be absolutely certain everything works."

"What is it that he's worried about?"

"It's going to be a live ovulation. A woman is going to actually secrete an egg at a precise time. We will have *SpermCam* exactly where it needs to be positioned. We have to inject the sperm army, and on their own they have to go up toward the oviduct. It has to be perfectly natural, no tampering by any of us."

"So what's the problem Bess?" Jade had been letting her hair grow out. Now it came in nice waves well past her shoulders.

"We have to be able to translate the chemical signal the egg will give off into the modular tone. As you know, that will be Middle C. But since there is no egg at this time, we have to simulate, and that leads to miscalculations. It could be a disaster. There may be no sound at all. This worries K.R. to no end."

"So...do you think this egg will do as predicted? For five minutes send out its chemical signal that will translate into Middle C, and then....suddenly.... *scream.* It's the scream that is critical, right daughter? When that happens the sperm begin to run amok. Without that drama, that picture, the world only gets a hard boiled egg when you expect it to enjoy a full blown omelet."

Bess smiled and pulled away the pony tail. Her thick black hair spilled onto her back as Jade looked on approvingly. "You do have a way with words. And that's exactly right mom. So if your kids fall flat on their faces, would you please look the other way.?"

Bill Kim had flown in from Seoul, had worn his characteristic ten thousand dollar suit. "This is our incredible moment K.R. The world watches and it will understand so much better. I know we all have had our moments in trying to explain the conundrum the Red Queen Theory brings on. But tonight...a picture is worth far more than a thousand words." K.R. shook his hand firmly. Inside, no one would possibly know the depth of his own fear.

It was as if Louis Pasteur, in his time, would use flash cards to demonstrate the amazing and historic experiment of germ theory to a querulous world. At its heart it was simple. But so much could go wrong.

In a holographic beaming, there wasn't that much stage light required. The amazing machines that transformed live people into holograms seemed mostly like big square boxes, posted in key spots on the studio floor and above. The technicians assured K.R. and Bess that the thousands of tiny laser beams would be mostly invisible to them. They posed no harm. Their function, of course, served to be the precipitator for beams that became holograms in the receptor units of people everywhere.

The announcer suddenly stood there and began talking. First, he explained this was a live event. The woman whose body would provide the expected battleground would remain anonymous, as would the name of the man.

SpermCam, however, the announcer proudly noted, was the product of *Samsung Biometrics International.* It was created especially for this occasion, "to instruct the world in a highly visual way about the challenges involved in understanding today's complex situation in reproductive biology."

Bess wondered how long it had taken for writers to figure out that one line. In one stroke of genius they had laid open the problem without having to use the flash words, 'sex', 'evolution', 'crisis', or Red Queen Theory.

Now both K.R. and Bess walked to the narrow green line they'd been told to toe. Walking around and pacing could not be allowed. When they spoke, to keep things functional, they were required to be still, keeping eyes focused only on the screen right in front of them which told them everything going on. The camera operators were not humans as in the old days, but merely robotic arms that manipulated the holographic uploaders within very defined parameters.

"In fifteen seconds a woman will ovulate. We will all see the egg squirt out from the ovary exactly as they do each month with every fertile woman in the world." K.R's first lines to the world came out as if he had only breathed them out.

SpermCam provided the amazing view. It sat unmoving, a few centimeters away from the target area. Then, a quivering of the ovary and the fingers that dangled from it. With a quiet rush, something bobbed out from a reddened wall, almost like a baby coming out from its mother. But it was not one egg, but two!

K.R.'s mind spun hard, quickly cracking the numbers. Two eggs! Twice the modulation they'd estimated. Could the software handle it? Hadn't he warned the technicians this very thing could happen? He trusted they'd listened to him.

Bess took over, her voice perfectly free of worry. "We were not counting on two eggs ladies and gentlemen. But this can happen. It's nature. Now, we are going to let the modulation software do its job. A chemical signal in itself makes no sound. Both eggs have just begun to release chemicals that convert to ions in the oviduct's fluid, which is slightly acidic. The chemical signal is slightly alkaline. This can create a tiny electrical ripple which we can turn into sound. It's amazingly close to Middle C on the piano. Are we going to get two Middle C's?"

On perfect cue came the answer. The handpicked audience just beyond the invisible glass wall, erupted in sounds of amazement. An audio box had morphed into the screen just below the live picture from *SpermCam*. Cleverly, the graphics unit had pasted piano keys right up against the actual modular tone created by the two eggs. Middle C.

K.R. released his own gasp of relief. "Now for five minutes this sound will emanate down the oviduct. It's probably already been detected by the sperm in what we call the waiting room. The waiting room is that natural area about five centimeters from where the oviduct and womb intersect. Here naturally occur two important kinds of sperm: *Egg getters* and *Killers*. The *Egg getters* are there for obvious reasons; it's their job to proceed swiftly to where the egg is and one of them will be the victor in fertilizing it. The killers are there to keep away any other man's sperm from fertilizing the egg. How long ago Killer sperm evolved is anybody's guess. They are as old as the hills, present in the species of other lesser animals as well."

Bess knew the scene would switch to another *SpermCam*. It had been positioned in the midst of the *Egg-getters* and the *Killers*. Ten long seconds passed before tails began to shiver. Suddenly, an explosion of movement! Like pure bred sprinters both *Killers* and *Egg getters* exploded off the mark. Lithe, slender tails swirled the fluid so much, that *SpermCam* temporarily only recorded trails of bubbles, as from popping champagne in the tiny camera embedded in its head.

Beneath the picture the picture of the sound presented itself. At first the audio signal dimmed and ebbed. It was impossible to know if this was the norm, or simply a technical glitch. This anxiety, thankfully, only lasted a few moments, and twin tones sang their incredible harmony out to an astonished world. Bess felt her heartbeat race as she never had. She reached down to feel K.R.'s own sweaty palm trying to grasp her fingers.

"Yes! We have two notes maintained. As you can see on the chart, both are identical and equal in strength. Amazingly, they hit right on Middle C. We have no idea why this is so, or even if it means anything at all. While we are listening, we can all see how the sperm are quite orderly, flowing up the oviduct toward the two eggs. Both kinds of sperm are wiggling their flagella in swirls of figure-8s. But the truest function of the *Killers* is merely to accompany the *Egg getters*. Think of what bodyguards might do, and you have a good picture of their purpose. Now, our technicians are going to do something interesting; they will give the *Killer Sperm* red heads, and the *Egg getters* get blue heads. The 'scream' that huge upward spike which can approach High C, is due shortly. The nice tone of Middle C will be suddenly and awkwardly altered. We'd like to know the reason why. It's at the very heart of the problem in the way modern day eggs and sperm are dancing with one another. It's part of our theory that concerns what is called, *The Dance of the Red Queen*.

When the moment came, perhaps it was the actual seminal moment for the world to fully comprehend in the most visual of ways, exactly what the *Dance of the Red Queen* meant. It was, in fact, a double shriek. Two notes just shy of High C. Bess watched in amazement as more than one person in the audience covered their ears. If the note seemed unnatural, unexpected, to human ears, how was it when the sperm 'heard' the sound?

Most of the reds suddenly whipped and turned at close to ninety degree angles at the scream signal. Their heads invariably tangled with the whipping tails of the blues, who themselves paused at the unexpected 'sound.' From the heads of the reds tiny axes suddenly protruded. The axes contrasted sharply with the color of the gray heads from whence they had sprouted. The axes wore a tone of magenta, as if to presage their bloody purpose. These *Killer Sperm* also wore caps. This allowed a sperm army to engage in chemical warfare. Nature had designed these cells to root out and destroy any sperm from another man. But now the *Killers* worked at cross purposes from days past. The world saw this very event unfold, one tiny battle inside one woman that was almost a direct replay of every battle going on inside the bodies of fertile women anywhere who wanted a baby.

The reds whipped their tails frantically, but they were entangled with the blues. The blues were being dragged along almost the way one dragonfly does with another when it is mating. When the reds collided with the walls of the oviduct, most of the reds let go of their chemical loads. Confused red heads with wildly whipping tails reacted with anything they collided with. Like Medieval mace wielders, the axe's sharp head severed hundreds of tails of the *Egg getters* and lacerated tiny wounds in the thin walls of the oviduct. The walls of the oviduct instantly swelled and reddened, as if billions of white blood calls had already been primed to action at the apparent invasion of Self.

Something caught K.R. completely off guard. There was the actual sound of battle coming from this oviduct. Sounds of war wrapped in special effects. There were no human sounds, no screams, moans or cries of terror. Instead, what caught the ear was a din of mechanical grating, of spermal heads being speared, and the noise a spear might make puncturing its target. Sounds of hard collisions, as red and blue headed sperm, wound together at their tails, hit the oviduct wall hard. The sound came out rather much like a car wreck without the squealing of tires. K.R. had no idea why they'd want to add this dimension to the science on display. It seemed like Hollywood hucksterism, and unfit for this serious venue. But he could do absolutely nothing but go along.

The *scream* only lasted five minutes. Then it modulated back to Middle C before it dwindled to nothing. The eggs themselves had barely moved. Nothing apparent to the human eye had proceeded from their frothy, white membranes. But to the sperm trying to get there, those five minutes had been traumatic, deadly, utterly confusing. No wonder Bloomberg had invented the term, *Befuddled Sperm.*

Again, the audience gasped. A gaggle of *Killer*s snaked along the oviduct wall. When they caught up with some Blues, they killed them too. Why was this happening *after* the sound had come back down to Middle C? K.R.'s jaw dropped. Surely Bess had noticed as well. It was the first time he'd ever seen such behavior. And if was consistent, would the model they were working so hard on have to be scrapped?

The egg was now in sight, but it was only a target for the red-headed *killer sperm*. No Blues were left. Six of them swam lazily up to the egg and around it, but none made the effort to penetrate. *Killer sperm* were the rage these days. More questions were asked of them than anything else. They seemed to be out of place, completely illogical entities. Yet their purpose shone clearly for the world this night. They were not programmed to fertilize-only to kill.

K.R. barely caught his own breath. "What you have just seen ladies and gentleman of the world, is the problem we all face. For some reason, eggs are changing their signals right before our own astonished eyes and ears. The sperm are not yet programmed for this change. The *scream* coming from the egg directly affects Killer Sperm, of which there are far more present than Egg getters. Killer sperm are relics from an ancient time, when there was far more sexual competition over females than exist in our own time. Men evolved this way, like it or not. The Killers will probably adjust with time. It's the way of the *Red Queen*. But what we are going to do in the meantime, while the adjustment is being made? And… well, who knows how we *shall* adjust?"

With that dramatic flourish, the program ended. Bess flicked her eyes. Is this how they wanted it to conclude? With K.R.'s somber question on the minds of almost everyone in the world? What was going to become of their privacy now?

It was only due to King Frampton's expertise that they were mostly able to stay in the lab the next two months. Many times Bess rolled her eyes in total amazement at the celebrity status they'd attained. For two straight weeks, a different driver in a different car picked them up in the lowest level underground parking level at their apartment complex and whisked them to work. There, secured and ensconced in a powerful safety net, all was well. But the moment they needed to go outside, the papparazi awaited.

For a scheduled meeting with Dr. Margie Herger at the CDC only six blocks away, a helicopter had zeroed in on the bullseye high atop the main building of *Samsung Biometrics International.* Media had gotten wind of the meeting and sniffing around, had determined its importance.

They were guided to their destination in the internal maze of the Center for Disease Control by two chaps who clearly did not work for the CDC. K.R. had lined up the first question for Dr. Herger and asked it as he shook her hand. "Do we really require martial arts experts in your own building, Dr. Herger?"

She laughed and pointed to two comfortable, plump chairs. Bess noted this was not her private office. Was multi-media easier to deliver here?

"You two have raised quite a stir in important circles." Margie let the statement dangle long enough for someone to take the bait.

"It was our CEO's idea. He figured out a way to let people actually see with their own eyes what's going on?"

Dr. Herger made a small temple with all ten fingers, resting her hands on the table in front of her. "Yes, and as it turns out, the location of where all this is going on has turned out to be the problem."

Bess cocked her head. "*Location*? What do you mean?"

"All of America and everybody else in the world got to see one helluva strange fight. I can promise you that no woman of child bearing age ever imagined that within her sacred body there would be such a battleground. And now a full three months after your record breaking appearance on the world stage, certain troubling results are in."

"Like what?" K.R.'s ears had become natural radar receivers, almost sticking out perpendicular to his head.

"If the American birth rate was falling off the charts, now it's like a skydiver whose parachute won't open. At least that's what the data tells us. Women are saying that if men's sperm behave that way inside their bodies, they just won't get pregnant."

"So…maybe we were too successful…it was too visually compelling?" Bess asked both questions with a cool slowness, as if the words dripped like molasses from her tongue.

Margie nodded vigorously. "I'd say so, yes, something like that Bess. If this projects out like we think it will, in two years we won't even be at half replacement rate. It'll be something like .7 children per couple. Oldsters will eventually totally rule. And they are enormously expensive. We're barely meeting their needs now, as you must know."

"Well, Dr. Herger, there is the option of fertilization in the petri dish. As you must know, eggs only give off the signal when they emerge from the ovary. The ones that are sitting in the petri dish are fat and easy targets for eager sperm. They don't act bizarre then."

"Yes, of course we are aware of that Bess. But there are certain political implications if we go around proclaiming that from every rooftop. We have enough social divisions as it is between richer folks and those who were once in the middle. Look at life span for instance. My God, your own company just recently perfected *Telomere Renewal*. With that beautiful artificial enzyme they engineered, telomeres inside cells can actually be lengthened. Boom! In the space of a couple of visits to the clinic, someone's life extends out to age 100 and who knows how much beyond? The poor slob who has no insurance certainly cannot get his telomeres extended. Now is not the time to tell the common joe, 'Hey, it's not so bad that you can't have kids. Just stop by the Baby Clinic and pay another big fee to get the baby started in a petri dish! Such a message does not ring well in light of so many people problems."

He sat bolt upright slowly nodding and mumbling. "Of course Dr. Herger. That's probably correct. If I was a woman, I'd certainly be concerned about it. Women also have the information about the great increases in ectopic pregnancies. They no doubt believe there's a correlation here."

"And they'd damn well be right! I have the figures right in front of me. All this warfare is damaging Fallopian tubes. Even if an egg manages to get fertilized in all that chaos, most of the time it cannot drop properly into the uterus. It latches on instead to whatever soft tissue it may encounter in the Fallopian tubes-a disastrous place indeed for any growing embryo to begin life."

Bess's two hands shot up into the air. "So what can we do? The cat's already out of the bag. Women are making their minds up based on the actual data."

Dr. Herger paused, the tiniest of smiles playing around her lips. "Maybe you could go back to them, to the people of the world. They believe you. They like and trust you."

Bess recoiled, both hands pawing at air. "And tell them what? That it's really ok to have sex?"

Margie drew back in her chair keeping the laugh well hidden. "That's an interesting thought Bess, and do hold onto it. But, no, I suppose that would be too direct. Surely there's something the smart people in your vast and rich company's public relations division can dream up for you to say. Something to reassure these women. Say things to get them over their fear."

"Tell you what Dr. Herger, you say this very thing to Bill Kim our CEO. He'd hear you out. We take our marching orders from him. We cannot possibly go back on television for any other reason. The last time almost killed me." K.R. now stood to his full height.

Dr. Herger walked both of them to the door. "Indeed, what you just said is worth considering. I guess we'll know where we stand soon enough."

They heard from Bill Kim at a strangely inopportune time. Bess and K.R. had agreed to briefly speak at a gathering of medical researchers in Atlanta, and just as Bess was leaving the podium, in strolled Bill Kim himself. Amiably, with little fanfare he sat himself in the front row of seats just as K.R. pulled his notes from his suit pocket.

He tried valiantly not to look in the direction of his boss, who most definitely kept a gaze focused directly on K.R. After twenty minutes of talking, another ten of taking questions, K.R. finished, but then he saw Bill Kim with hand held high, as if he were a kid at school wanting to ask the teacher one last important question.

"Uh, yes. Uh-everyone the man wanting to ask one more question is Bill Kim, the CEO of *Samsung Biometrics International.* My big boss."

Bill Kim stood up amid a smattering of claps. "I know all of you in this room are proud of the accomplishments of Bess and K.R. your colleagues, and my friends. But we have one more task ahead for them, and I thought I'd tell you all first. Women all over the world are worried. More than worried really. Many have become obsessed with what happens inside their bodies if they have sex. I know what we revealed was not a pretty sight. So much slaughter. A real battleground. Our reality show has perhaps turned out to be far too high on reality, and so we must find a way to offer reassurance to women. So we are buying a block of time and once again the world can see our two wonderful people here K.R. and Bess Lee. But this time there will be no *SpermCam,* no drama from inside a woman's body. This time, our pair will merely answer questions; pre-selected questions to be sure, and they will be spread out from every corner of the earth. There will be a minimum of multi-media for this important event."

Bill Kim turned to face K.R. whose jaw perhaps had lengthened toward the floor. "One more time into the breach, my friend. One more time."

Neither K.R. nor Bess ever got the chance to ask Margie Herger just how she'd gotten to Bill Kim. For the next month they worked tirelessly to promote every detail of this next television project. Everything would be scripted. The questioners would be pre-selected with questions that had one purpose: Reassure the world's women it wasn't so bad. Appearances might be deceiving. That would have to serve as the strange theme for the twins' second appearance to the people of Earth.

In that space of a month when K.R. and Bess could barely attend to matters of research, their research assistants hit on an intriguing bit of information. It was only the sub-class of Killer Sperm called *pyriform* sperm-distinguished by their odd little pear-shaped heads-that went berserk when the siren call of the egg amplified. Their close cousins, Killers called *tapering* sperm-those with more cigar-shaped heads-tended to behave more like *Egg getters.* They would greatly slow down and maybe stop altogether while the egg's call amplified, but it seemed not to be their way to make crazy right turns and spit their poisonous loads on whatever they touched.

And curiously, confirmed the researchers, it was only the *pyriform* sperm that had flecks of iron hard against the membranes of mitochondria. K.R. made certain this information reached Margie Herger's desk, and after this next television special was finished, he couldn't wait to schedule an appointment with her.

This time, K.R. actually managed to smile when the green light came on. Maybe it was easy for him to smile-the first set of questions belonged to Bess. She spoke slowly, carefully, as if it was only her speaking to one woman at a time, anywhere, everywhere.

"How can we prevent ectopic pregnancies?" came the first question. "What is making sperm behave this way?" This question was launched to her in more than one form, and she answered each in a slightly different way.

"There's no way to tell exactly. Some rumors are going around that that the terrible sunspot activity of the last two decades has something to do with it. Sunspots would imply more cosmic rays and that does damage DNA. As you probably know, we are more inclined to go with the *Dance of the Red Queen* hypothesis. Much has been written lately about what might be called 'destruction' or 'pillaging' of the Y chromosome's genetic material by its corresponding mate, the X chromosome. We think this could have a lot to do with the matter of the egg's strange changes in its siren call to the sperm. It is entirely possible that the Y chromosome has hidden certain critical genes or lost them entirely, and they simply do not 'hear' the siren call of the chemical signal emitted by human eggs the way they used to. Consequently, in response, eggs have or are changing the call, trying to find a better frequency for the sperm. They are not 'deliberately' trying to evade the sperm, quite the opposite is true we think."

Bess set the tone for K.R. to step in and feel quite comfortable. "Is there anything a man can do to help his sperm out, so they won't be so aggressive inside the female?" K.R. smiled broadly, fully thankful there was the built in cheat sheet for a quick and funny answer to such a question. "Yes, sir there is. Before you have sex, if you can separate your *pyriform* sperm from their *tapering* sperm cousins, you won't have any problem at all." He paused, letting the chuckles ripple through the audience. "We know now that these two types *of Killer* Sperm although closely related, do have differences that may be directly associated with the *Dance of the Red Queen*. Our research, along with the CDC, could give answers to that within the year. If so, it would be very helpful in answering a question such as yours."

K.R. knew Jade had managed to finagle a seat in the very front row. She applauded loudly and happily at such an answer, and her beaming smile could have bored a hole straight through the invisible glass barrier.

Close to the two hour wrap-up, Bess was ready to field the final question. Did she have a clue the person would be able to so easily wedge in such an incredible follow-up query? Bess never told anybody if or how she let the Scottish woman have her fifteen minutes of fame.

"Is this going to mean the end of the human race?" Part one seemed straightforward and simple enough. The plump but serene-faced lady from Edinburgh clearly was sitting at her kitchen table with a cup of tea or coffee bellowing steam.

Bess shook her head boldly in disagreement, still managing to smile in the midst of another doomsday-type question. "No. Not if we're smart. But for the time, we probably must employ methods of fertilization outside the human body much more than we would like to. Sperm do not exhibit unusual behavior in petri dishes or test tubes. One sperm easily fertilizes an egg in the artificial environment of a Fertility Clinic. Once it proves itself viable, that embryo can be put into the mother or into a surrogate. Governments everywhere will have to do their part to help fund this effort. It will be worth the money, and if people demand it-well, there you have it. Start demanding! We also will be working hard to find out more answers. Maybe if we helped out the *Dance of the Red Queen*, it would be the smartest and most effective thing, instead of just fighting it. Bucking Nature is never a good option."

The Scottish lady immediately launched her follow up question even as the studio technicians tried to cut her off. But Bess waved them off and the flickering form of the woman in Edinburgh came back on. Her red hair came down in long, rolling locks, spilling over her shoulders, and she smiled impishly.

"When are you going to have your own baby? What are you waiting for?"

Bess paused for many seconds. She glanced toward K.R. who only stared ahead cooly. Then Bess blew a kiss out toward Jade Lee. She was the first person to stand, looking as if she was ready to burst across the barrier. "Actually, in about 8 months I'll have my baby! I decided last month to do it. The egg was implanted and there's a tiny fetus inside of me. The baby will be a girl."

The audience exploded. Every person stood, faces keening in smiles, faces red with joy. Tears streamed down cheeklines from more than one person. As one, the people of Earth rose and shouted toward the ceiling, or toward any handy compatriot.

Exactly why this was so, had less to do with Bess Lee's personal good fortune, and far more to do with her example. Bess *was* the symbol required for these difficult and strange times. She showed a way, especially for womankind. She'd offered herself to ease the fear of so much unknown.

K.R. stood by his sister and watched her, eyes focused in raw disbelief, even as he clenched both fists tightly. What *exactly* he would say to Bess, and how he would say it, was yet to be determined. Even so, he was human, and it took only a few seconds to become totally caught up in the frenzy of admiration for the courage of his sister.

K.R. understood it innately, didn't have to ponder at all. His own sister was telling the frazzled, puzzled women of Earth: *Follow me. Watch me. Do as I do. Don't be scared.*

K.R. smiled when Bess stepped his way. He wrapped both arms tightly around her waist, mumbling so that no one might hear. "You got me sister. I'm stone cold shocked. But congratulations anyway."

Like two bullfighters who'd jammed the lances into the bull, brother and sister stepped forward and made a simple bow. It really had nothing at all to do with anything they'd done. It was just this-both K.R. and Bess's heart overflowed with love for them-for those people out there-those citizens of the world. To the ones who required the most help, K.R. and Bess offered their genius-and their basic humanity.

THE END

Is it true that the end always justifies the means? How much trouble do people go through to maximize this rationale? How much can they really learn when they discover what fools they have been all that time? When horror merges with what people call 'truth', then we seem to truly have an intractable problem. Humans made it. They have to solve it.

August Rose

This story has already received acclaim and high ratings published by Pandora Project Publishing, and appearing as an E-Book novella.

At the heart of this mystery is a supposition that in the general election of 1968 the incumbent LBJ did decide to run again, but lost to Richard Nixon. The problems lay in the fact that the election was close, partisan and bitter, and people wondered about the rumors of 'deals' Nixon made with special groups to get their support and gin up his right wing base. Recall that in that time, America's cities were burning, racial unrest and discord had never been more strained, and many rural Southerners were still aghast at the Civil Rights Act, and the subsequent desegregation of schools. Distrust between groups of Americans was at an all time low and sinking fast.

⁂

Dr. Richard Spell drove through the sleepy Mississippi town on an afternoon that was only special because a tropical disturbance was moving in from the Gulf of Mexico, forcing the late summer temperature into moderation. Thunder boomed in the distance as he found the correct road that led him out of Baxter City.

Nobody gave the slightest look or nod his way. Even though he was a well dressed black man in a late model Cadillac, this apparently interested no one. This suited Dr. Spell as his sole mission was simply to go to the charred remains of the old RoseCrest Baptist Church about five miles away. The Negro church had sat atop the knob of a hill there since just after the Civil War. It had seen good and bad times. The bad times centered mostly around it getting burned to the ground. Such a thing had happened again last year - under mostly uninvestigated circumstances.

He slowed the car where State Highway 44 met Gerald Bend Lane. Slowly the car crawled up the hill. He was surprised at the steep attitude of land here. He'd always thought about Mississippi in the most negative manner -- dwelling in his writings and commentary on the horrible disparity of wealth that existed in the Delta. But this part of the state lay more toward the Tennessee border and sizeable hills were the order. In this hill country whites and blacks had an uneasy co-existence, but the nice homes and clipped fields belied any undercurrent of social injustice.

Dr. Spell walked up to the chalky cinders of wood. In his mind, he could imagine the men who'd occupied the preaching arena here. He could see in his mind's eye many Sunday meetings where some gifted black shaman would stomp and stalk about, maybe performing a healing every now and then, always shouting, and responding to the swaying and chanting of his congregation. Dr. Spell innately understood how blacks needed that kind of religion. It gave them a balm, a sedative, albeit temporary, from their constant suffering from laws that slapped them hard, in every backhanded way possible that the white majority might contrive. And now this -- a burned building, blackened hopes and dreams, and no justice to show for the crime.

A dark low cloud scudded toward him, but still he ventured toward what was the back of the old sanctuary. Somewhere out that way, toward a meandering stream they called Bear Creek, Dr. Spell was told of a three acre cemetery. The church land went down a steep ravine and took in maybe 100 yards along the creek bank. He'd been told about lots of caves in the vicinity but that held little interest for him.

Once again Dr. Richard Spell examined his belief system. He'd told the Committee of Six that they had found the right person for this job. Even so, he knew some elements of information had been denied him, not everything had been laid out clearly. This much he did know: He had been pronounced the new pastor of what would be a restored RoseCrest Baptist Church, and something very special was to come with this appointment -- some kind of special cross, maybe one of gold, was to be at the heart of his church and represent a new beginning for its parishioners.

As to the Committee of Six, he knew of their shadowy reputation. He'd been shocked when they requested his audience, even more stunned when they rescued him from an occupation that made him little money. At least now he could serve his people in a way that was more traditional. Let's get this church rebuilt was his thought as the first raindrops fell like little peas on his starched cuffs. I will grow into this job of country preacher and agent for that incredible group of folks on the Committee of Six. They were known to back projects that upped the level of racial equality. They'd picked him for a reason. His mother would have been proud.

Sheriff Juniper McHewn watched the train of lumber trucks go back and forth from the grounds of RoseCrest Church. There had been no rumors of an imminent church rebuilding and he wondered about that. Everyone in these parts had crooked ears that always caught the slightest whiffs of interesting information. He'd noticed that in early morning, a crew of workers tended to leak away, as if going down the wooded slope toward Bear Creek. What could they be doing down there?

Hadley Writt had radioed his nearby presence and Juniper wrinkled his nose at the thought of having another conversation with the fellow. Writt was of the opinion that the Sheriff should exert a more take-charge attitude up on that knob of hill, even though it was none of his business at all.

He eased from the patrol car and joined Juniper in a deep well of shade. "When you think they'll be finished with this little project?"

Juniper grunted, "Sooner than later. They got good organized workers out there. It's not your little country carpenters stopping by whenever they can lend a hand. Both men paused to consider the loud clunks of sound bouncing down the hill. "Say, Hadley, you went over to see Muley. What'd he have to tell you?"

Hadley tugged at the belt that held back his ample belly and removed the hat to scratch an itch on the forehead of his crew cut. "Muley says that a Dr. Richard Spell has assumed the pastorship but he hasn't actually met him yet."

Juniper casually nodded. "A Dr. Richard Spell you say? What's a real educated man like that doing down here at a church that can't collect funds to get its timbers replaced?"

Hadley frowned as a truck loaded with pine planking stopped and turned to go up the hill. "They don't have to do this. It's the fancy niggers who are funding it -- it has to be. All this is gonna do is stir up the hornet's nest again, and nobody will get any peace."

Juniper's scowl let Hadley know he cared little for the slur, but Hadley knew little of political correctness. They'd known one another their entire lives; had perfected cheat sheets which got them through high school science courses. Hadley possessed decent lawman's instincts, but from his upbringing he'd been taught the very worst things about folks different from him. Hadley might go way past any point of fairness at any time; thus, Juniper kept a close watch on him.

In the course of his busy life, Juniper ran his county jail as properly as he could. There was endless paperwork, arrests to make and decisions that affected people's futures. Such a decision had come only yesterday, in the case of Marvis Landis.

Marvis Landis had the unfortunate job of trying to be a good husband to Betta Younger. Juniper knew her family well; they had fine lands, good Holstein herds and profitable corn fields. At the same time, there was not a den of folks more litigious than Betta's mother and father. They preyed in legal ways upon the less fortunate, and like successful legal vipers, knew when to strike. It was they who'd financed Betta's divorce against poor Marvis.

The problem had come when Marvis came to visit his kids at the home he'd been forced to give to Betta. She'd forcefully slammed the door in his face, even though it was his right to be there. Marvis made the mistake of plowing through the shut door, unhinging it, and then knocking Betta down against the brick fireplace. For that, Juniper had to arrest Marvis Landis.

So as the drama of everyday life played out, RoseCrest Baptist arose. When Juniper came back to study the construction, he was amazed to see a building almost glowing in the September sunlight. The special delivery was coming now and Dr. Spell had asked Juniper to be on hand.

So the golden cross came into their lives. The workers used a special crane to take it from the flatbed, and crane worked and strained to get it positioned over the place in the roof from where it would be bolted in place just above the baptistery. Juniper was happy Hadley Writt was not present to see this -- a spectacle unlike any other. The cross was simply too huge to comprehend. And the way the light bounced off its ultra smooth surface -- its golden surface -- seemed bizarre for this place and time.

Richard Spell made his way to where Juniper stood. "It looks fantastic doesn't it Sheriff. But I was told it is not pure gold. However, it is convincing."

Juniper watched Spell through his Ray-Bans. "How much of gold is it then?"

Spell didn't return his gaze. "Frankly, I don't know. I didn't ask that kind of question."

Juniper continued his questions, surprised that the same alarm bells apparently were not going off in Dr. Spell's mind. "Then how much is it insured for?"

Now Richard Spell took a long look at his Sheriff, the one who'd protect him from another church burning. "I haven't checked on that yet, Sheriff. I'll have to get back to you. But I can tell you this, the building is fully insured. You will make sure that this time no people get over this way and make another bonfire, won't you Sheriff?"

Instantly Juniper's arms folded over one another. "There was no proof anybody set a fire here, sir. The building was old wood. Those structures go up in smoke over time. Accidents happen."

Indeed they do." Spell turned away when he said, "But this time we have the golden cross to protect us."

Everyone in the county and beyond was invited to attend the first sermon. But the congregation then and later consisted only of black faces. And they watched in both fascination and boredom as Dr. Richard Spell learned the art of being a preacher. When they were too bored to behold him any longer, they cast their gaze on their golden cross -- and it seemed to watch over them in return. Ten feet tall, six feet at the intersecting beams, on bright days when the light filtered through the long skylight on the roofline, the pastor seemed like an angel moving about, resplendent with brightness, receiving the beams from heaven. If only his words could match up. People there wanted to really believe they were special, but after several weeks went by, membership leveled out then slowly declined. Juniper set about to check why.

Muley Calloway had always been his favorite black citizen. More than seventy years old, every stitch of it spent around Baxter City, Muley's eyes always danced, even if one was green and its mate was blue. "How's your church work coming along, Muley?"

Muley tugged on his suspenders and laughed. "Truth be told Sheriff, it's not so easy to listen to our new pastor. And he hasn't promoted Sunday school at all."

Juniper acknowledged with a nod the tall glass of tea Muley had set before him. "Is your Dr. Spell too political or something -- a firebrand type who gets away from true Bible teaching?"

Muley shook his head. "Nawsir, I would not say that. His problem is that he does not yet understand how to blow out a sermon. We like it thick and simple. He reads from his outline and looks at his notes more than he looks at us."

Juniper could follow Muley easily enough. He could almost imagine the entire group snoring through a Sunday sermon. If so, it would not be much different from the Methodist church he'd always attended.

Our membership is languishin' Sheriff, kind of going down hill."

"But you have that golden cross. It's mighty attractive for such a small church."

"Yessir, yes we do have that." He smacked his lips together. "It's a beautiful thing, but by itself, it can't get the job done."

Hadley Writt sauntered into Juniper's office, grazing up against the private space on his wobbly office chair. "Have you heard Juniper, that three people left RoseCrest's membership last week? Joined some other church. So they are down to just 19 regulars. Pretty damned odd, ain't it?"

"It ain't a crime to resign from a church Hadley. What's your angle?" Juniper dropped his pen atop the mound of papers for the moment.

Hadley rubbed his chin as if discerning some puzzle before him. "The situation is this; here's a rebuilt black church with strong if unknown funds behind it. They've got this golden cross that's got to be worth thousands of bucks, and the tiny congregation is led by an unpopular, fruitcake kind of pastor. That's my angle."

Juniper reached absently into his shirt pocket for a cigarette and then realized Sara had taken them away again. He was eager to finally keep his word to his exasperated spouse.

Hadley continued daring to sit at one end of Juniper's desk. 'One of the ladies that quit coming told me that Dr. Spell insists he's allergic to fried chicken. Whoever heard of that?"

Suddenly guard Tom Burrell burst in. "Sheriff you may want to see this."

The sight was sorry for any day and Juniper wanted to turn his eyes away. He'd heard and approved of putting Marvis Landis into solitary confinement for his own safety. Such a thing was not supposed to happen like this. "Somebody tell me how my prisoner is like this."

The new person stepped forward with the information. "We put him in here after midnight you know Sheriff, and he must have started just banging his head up against the bars. We thought it was old George over there, you know, clanging his coffee pot like he always does. Mr. Landis told George that if he couldn't live with his kids, life was not worth living anymore."

"Naturally." Juniper scowled at the crowd before him and the pool of blood the man had been wallowing in. Juniper knew he couldn't keep Marvis in the regular cells because of his fits of crying, and the guy was so broke he couldn't make bail. Betta certainly wasn't going to help out.

"Let's get this man attended to, get his scalp sewed up." A stray thought came through Juniper's head: Is it possible to love your family too much?

But no such thought came Hadley's way. He'd just stepped in, saw the spectacle and went over to the moaning and sobbing Marvis Landis. For good measure Hadley kicked him in the ribs. "See you in Parchman."

December's weather had turned gray and miserably cold. An ice storm just before Christmas was the topping on the cake. Juniper turned into the Noonley driveway because the old mother reported her two boys missing, and there was no reason they would venture far from home. Juniper noted the frozen water on the porch, and saw Les Noonley slowly working to make the repairs.

"Pipes busted again. I know the boys got cold the other day. I thought they'd went to their buddies since they got a nice fireplace. But the buddies never saw 'em."

Juniper nodded. Those twin boys weren't bad, but they'd dropped out of school as juniors and became associated with some shady elements lately. "Ok Les, I hear ya. A deputy of mine will be along to get the exact particulars." He tipped his hat to this nice citizen and thought about the added burden a missing person report would make on his fat overload of paper.

Richard Spell had taken the surprise call the day after Thanksgiving and wasted no time getting to Atlanta. He'd been summoned. The Committee of Six wanted to see him.

As before in an Atlanta skyscraper he ventured into a room that was shrouded in both light and secrecy. He sat on a simple stool right before six silhouettes. He'd never seen their faces, and from the research he had gathered nobody before him had seen them either. And of course, the names were unknown. They seemed to be six rich and focused people who targeted salvoes against injustice in many varied and original ways.

A head bobbed and the man in the middle with a fine resonant voice spoke to Richard. "Thanks for coming again. You have done a good job so far, and we appreciate that you have not prodded us to tell you much about the golden cross. But before we go on, before we tell you any more, we'd like to once again ask you Dr. Spell, are you the kind of man who reacts against injustice and will take firm action to counter it?"

Richard answered: "Yes sir, I will."

"Wonderful, Dr. Spell." A woman on the end clapped for effect. "So we can tell you this now; word is leaking out where you live that the golden cross at RoseCrest is formed from pure gold. We think this will attract certain elements there. They won't dare show their faces in daylight, but like true vermin will creep up at night. They will have evil intentions, and will come to the very face of the golden cross in an effort to desecrate it. But we have devised means that will deal very effectively with such vile people."

"What means is that, may I ask?"

A new member spoke up, his voice shrill and high, "Actually, you may not ask. Enquiring about the mechanism that will help enforce justice and make your membership numbers soar to new heights, will do you no good. Remain dumb and ignorant Dr. Spell. It's the best thing to do."

Richard let the words come out slowly and squarely. "What am I supposed to think about such unusual developments like this?"

Then someone in the middle stood up. A lady with hair that flipped up on the ends and who used hard gestures to back up a craggy voice. "You deserve to know what we think will happen in the next few months. The lawmen of Crowder County will begin to press you about white people who are missing from their homes. You will know nothing. But the more you insist you know nothing, the harder they will press. If more and more people come up missing, you might begin to be persecuted in a more literal way. These lawmen will be under pressure to supply answers to the white community, and it will seem unfair to many for you to undergo this kind of scrutiny. As things spiral, you will have more and more ammunition for wonderful sermons, and blacks will come to you from far and wide. Pretty soon your little church Dr. Spell will be the center of attention. And still, you'll be constantly badgered by the local lawmen. After awhile, some point will be reached when your people cannot bear this any longer. What could possibly make this kind of persecution stop? You are only a small rural church, already burned down. Your golden cross may afford a rallying point, not only for the local people, but for an entire nation. Can you follow this reasoning?"

He felt a tremble move down his spine. Something fantastic or fatal was afoot. He was to be a pawn in a movement on some grand chess board. Was he up to it? "There will be no errors, no mistakes. You have my word on it."

"Fine. And when you leave the room there will be a paper on the table outside. Memorize the number on the paper then tear it up right there. From time to time, call the number and you will get more instructions. We won't need to meet again like this. Today was the last time."

Juniper had already tired of making the late night rounds. But at the holiday season and with his staff so overworked, he'd had to do more and more of the grunt work. Crowder County citizens were murmuring aloud about more young men who had gone missing.

He found himself on the road that led to RoseCrest. He turned off the lights on the patrol car and eased up the hill. He'd gotten in the habit of checking out the doors. For some reason, Dr. Spell had switched to simpler locks. Any kid could pick these. And the other change baffled Juniper. From time to time, strobe lights came on in the sanctuary. It became bathed in arcs of vibrating zebra strobes. Across the way, the golden cross received the strobes and regenerated the light back. The one room church appeared thus to be either the abode of gods or demons when this happened.

Everything seemed to be in line except that an overwhelming desire to smoke had raptured from nowhere. He resisted by running back to his patrol car and soon he was zooming down the highway. Cigarettes be damned. He needed to stay clean this time.

It was then that he paid attention to the light bulb flashing in his mind. At once he slammed on the brakes, and turned back to the church. Something had been afoot right under his nose, and his sixth sense just hadn't caught it right then.

He went straight to the front door. It was indeed ajar. Inside the church he advanced slowly, cautiously. Did his presence make the strobe light suddenly flip on? And what was this smell, maybe of old dirty clothes. He made it to the front pews and sat down. It was the first time he'd ever seen the golden cross at night. Some moonlight came in through stained windows and combined with the fiery intensity of the zebra strobes. Was this the brainchild of Dr. Richard Spell? How had the congregation approved such things?

Juniper considered how his subconscious brain had led him back here. He'd heard some owls hooting in the distance when he got out of the patrol car the first time, around midnight. At the same time the urge to smoke struck, he heard some other bird sounds. This time they were not owls. The sound that came to his ears was the distinct *bob white, bob white* clacking of quails. But these birds never sounded off at night, only in the heart of day. Someone or some people were using the bird calls as signals, so he hadn't caught them in their mischief.

A few footprints on the carpet led him to get up and walk toward the baptistery. A foul smell greeted him there. Had some raccoon gone off and died underneath the church? Juniper backtracked and in some brambles just off the church grounds he found a car -- someone's transportation obviously left unattended. But why? Where had the owner gone? He wasn't in the church. Juniper copied down the tag number and knew the next day might produce some lead they so desperately needed to make a breakthrough on these missing people

Pastor Spell made his office in the most simple way. He merely unfolded an old table that was easily stored, and spread his papers out right there two long steps from the pulpit. His chair was nothing more than the wooden rocker he preferred to sit in as the choir made their music on Sunday mornings. Juniper knew of his work habits by now. As Juniper made his way down the church aisle, Richard Spell stopped his activities and glared sourly. Juniper noted Spell's dressing habit as well; a full suit and tie even on Thursday morning. Juniper stared at the golden cross again. There was no way not to. It demanded the eyes strip it of its essence. Beauty of a kind never seen in these backwoods. And dangerous. Juniper felt it, knew of it even if such a thing as a cross was never meant to be that way.

Spell met him solidly. "You've been asking lots of questions to our church members. One wonders if you aren't harassing them. Such a thing is still against the law in this country."

Juniper made the motion. "May we sit? Richard Spell made a point of sitting very close to Juniper, almost touching a knee. "Are you aware Dr. Spell, that you had an intruder last night? He very easily picked the lock on the front door."

Spell retorted very quickly. "Thanks for that Sheriff, but do you hear of me filing any kind of request to you? Am I asking you to do anything for us?"

Juniper looked away. It was very true that this was his church and nobody had lodged complaints of any kind with the Sheriff's office.

Juniper spoke as softly as he could muster. "The fact is sir, is that this lack of security and the fact of a cross like this being here so available to anyone, could create a helluva lot of trouble. There's bad people out there. They could come here after a good drinking spell, come right through that door there. Some might even want to take a chunk of your gold with them."

Spell motioned grandly in its direction. "Look over there Sheriff. Do you see any of it chipped off? Is any part missing? Do you really believe for one second that any professing Christian would dare desecrate a cross of God?"

It was an easy answer. "Yes I do believe that. Some would."

Spell had slowed down now, made his gaze fasten on the Sheriff's jawline. "In fact we do want and even encourage people to come here anytime. The golden cross protects itself Sheriff. You have no need to worry about those who will steal it. Its beauty and its purpose will become evident to all -- even to those bad people whose motivations are suspect. The cross is for all-black, white, brown."

Juniper didn't care for the oratory. "One more thing Pastor, do you keep any video of people who might come in…after hours…to meditate here?"

Richard wagged a finger, almost laughing. "No such thing exists. How large do you think our operation is here?"

When Dr. Spell arose, Juniper knew he'd used all his time. Nothing had gone amiss; the church had not asked Juniper for anything. He was treading on a fragile line here. There was no need to mention Gary Goff to Pastor Spell. It was Goff's truck he'd discovered last night. Goff was another one of those poor crackers that Spell would never meet. But he wasn't at home or work. Nobody knew where Gary Goff was at the moment. Juniper knew where he'd be in a few days -- on the growing list of men missing. And the general arrow pointed right this way, to the small black church with the amazing and strange golden cross.

Juniper asked all of four deputies to attend the meeting. February had come and gone and four more men, all poor cracker types, had come up missing. Now nine menfolk sat like cold cases on Juniper's missing person's list. Nobody demonstrated in Crowder County, but elements of discontent were bubbling up. "Ok people, let's jump outside the box and think in new ways. What have we got to work with?"

Two deputies chirped together, “They’re all poor white males.”

We know that Gary Goff had an accomplice. Gary went inside to check out the golden cross and the accomplice stayed outside as a lookout.”

“Yes that’s right. And what did the accomplice finally admit?”

Tom Rosen, the newest hire, spoke up. “He said that Gary Goff went inside, but never came out. Bennie Thigpen was chirping their quail signal from the brambles and thought you might have been Gary.”

Juniper nodded. “So why didn’t Gary Goff come back outside?”

It was the question of the day, it always had been. The deputies looked at one another mutely. At last Hadley Writt stepped forward. “I think it’s the devil’s work. I really do. They’ve got it rigged somehow so that Satan himself is involved. We are told devils can appear as angels of light. RoseCrest is not really a church at all. It’s a demon’s haunt posing as one of God’s churches.”

The others looked at Hadley askance, shaking their heads. Juniper followed up: “We may as well say fairies inhabit the sanctuary and wave magic wands around. But thank you Hadley for a foolish answer like that that does us absolutely no good. Meeting over. Go out and do your jobs.”

They tromped out, heads hanging low. Hadley lingered. “You wanted me to stay boss?”

“Why didn’t you tell me Hadley, that those Noonley kids were new converts to the local Klan? I had to find out myself the hard way.”

Hadley preferred to study his shoelaces. “I told you Juniper, I don’t go to many meetings anymore. I really don’t know who is in or out these days.”

“So your membership in the Klan does not in any way affect your job with me?” Juniper gave him a look of steel.

“Not a bit. At first I admit I took this job as a kind of hobby, but the last year I’ve grown very serious. It’s what I want to do the rest of my life. The KKK is a kind of club where I can see friends every now and then, but I don’t get stoked up on their message.”

“But many do, Hadley, many younger, less educated, ill informed kids do get stoked up. Maybe somebody is telling these highly impressionable young men to go into the church and do some scouting, to see if maybe that golden cross can be taken down, stolen in the night. You think so?”

Hadley stood as straight as his six foot frame would allow. “Juniper I haven’t heard such talk. It could be going around, more in whispers than directives. The Klan operates that way sometimes, when they don’t trust even their own kind.”

"Well you keep your ears wide open and let me know anything that might be useful, ya hear?"

"Ok Juniper." Hadley paused, and Juniper's ears became bat-like. "I know something else. May as well tell ya now. Our last missing person you know is Lewis Pardee. He was initiated into Klan membership only two weeks ago."

Juniper shook his head. "Naturally. And now he's missing too."

There was no time to feel sorry for himself, no time for puzzlement. Right after Hadley left Juniper placed the call to Sheriff Joe Breedlove. Maybe he'd be the one to finally know something useful. When the low growl of introduction came, Juniper quickly berated himself for doing zero due diligence on Sheriff Breedlove. The last thing he expected from a Kentucky sheriff was for him to have been a black man.

I heard about your little dilemma over that way. Imagine a simple cross being such a problem for people."

"It's not that simple Sheriff. This cross is huge, possibly forged from pure gold. Worth who knows how much."

Breedlove had a style of cutting straight to the point. "And you must think the Azzioka family is behind it."

Juniper cleared his throat. "Well they had immigrated to the USA from South Africa, where they were part owners of a gold mine or two. Rumor has it that maybe they shipped some product here for safekeeping."

Breedlove's deep bass voice mingled with his Southern drawl. He must be an impressive stump speaker. "Of course Sheriff McHewn you had no way of knowing that the Azziokas are as much Japanese as they are black African. Theirs is an unusual melding of genes I'll admit. But over there in South Africa they were ultimately regarded as black and thus could not keep ownership of any gold mines. We are proud to have them in our county. They benefit the community a lot."

Juniper's pause allowed Sheriff Breedlove to continue, now more gruffly. "So why is my office graced by your call today. Can you get more to the point sir?"

"My source tells me that the Azziokas have some shady ties with various groups that might like to cause racial friction. Down this way, that's bad medicine indeed. This past election got people fractured up one way or another. It won't take much to put them at one another's throats. I have to try and prevent that of course."

"So where is the FBI in all of this? The kind of deal you describe sounds like it's really their investigation, not strictly the domain of a small town sheriff."

Juniper shut the office door with a swing of his big foot. Big ears outside did not need to hear the way this banter was headed. “Therein is the sticky part Sheriff Breedlove. The church has filed no charges, made no complaints, leaving us kind of hamstrung. And yet a good deal of the evidence points that way, straight to the sanctuary where the golden cross resides.”

“Well that may be, but don’t look to the Azziokas to be involved with your peculiar problem… And by the way, of what purpose would it be for them to forge their precious gold reserves into a cross for a small Mississippi church? You got an answer for that Sheriff McHewn?”

For once Juniper ended a phone call to a colleague with stone, dead silence. A fist smashed down hard on his oak desk. It was another hard day.

Muley Calloway saw the Sheriff’s car round the bend on the gravel lane and had already poured the lemonade by the time he’d sauntered over to the chair on the front porch. Muley placed the cigar box on the ledge right next to where his right hand would be. Juniper used Muley for inside information, and Muley used the ten dollar tip for almost anything.

“What was the subject of this past Sunday’s sermon Muley?”

“Sir, it concerned the salvation of my soul.”

“So did Pastor Spell convince you? That you are really going to heaven?”

“Yes he did Sheriff. But I already knew that fact. So he just reinforced the belief.”

Juniper chuckled as he waved at two flies that were vying for a perch atop his lemon wedge. “How about anything unusual over that way. Any strange smells or sounds?”

Muley leaned back in his chair. It had two good legs left, both of them in the rear. “Well I know this. For the first time Pastor Spell has begun to participate in the joys of eating our fried chicken. He did so at the church dinner on the grounds. Our sanctuary is nigh unto exploding with folks, even on Sunday nights. Pastor Spell is getting’ good at talkin’ on the persecution complex God’s people have to endure.”

“Hmm.” Juniper rubbed his chin. “But nobody ever persecutes you do they Muley?”

“Other than askin’ a lot of questions, I suppose not. Oh, and I must ask you to please attend a special baptism service next Sunday night?”

“You want me to come? Why so?”

“We is to have eleven new converts to our church baptized then. It’s a record that may never be broken. We wants everyone to see it so to know our little church is to be reckoned with. Eleven of God’s newest people. It’s great news to us.”

Indeed, Juniper attended and brought with him a guest Marvis Landis. Marvis had at last bailed out and since he had been banished from his old church, he came to this one to spite the hateful hypocrites who used to be his friends.

When the short sermon finished, Pastor Spell stepped into his special baptizing wardrobe and one by one, dunked the eleven new members under the water. When they came up, the dazzling presence of the golden cross pierced their eyes, and the Pastor encouraged each one to reach up and skim their fingers across its silky smoothness, and make a silent prayer. Juniper could not help but feel joy for each of them. And he had to admit, there was something about that golden cross that made a body feel good. So why did an aura of dread also accompany the joy? Just how big a gap was there, how much could he possibly be missing?

⁂

She came into Richard Spell's life most unexpectedly, far too suddenly for his senses to use any logic on the matter. He answered a knock on his door one morning, and there stood Jewell Fairly. She said somebody told her that she should pay him a visit and the best time was in the morning when he was in a good mood. So Richard playfully laughed at the very first thing that came from her mouth, and she smiled in a pleasing way that brought her to morning coffee more often. In only two weeks, she was making the coffee herself and Richard busied himself cooking the bacon and eggs.

Their engagement announcement greatly pleased the growing flock. Every pastor needs a helpmate, and Jewell Fairly showed off all the reasons why would make a fine wife. Pretty, accomplished, graceful and talented, she made Richard's face glow with pride. So when Jewell finally decided to part with her biggest secret she did so just after the morning coffee session.

"Richard you know I came to Baxter City because they had only one good stenographer."

"Yes dear, you told me so."

"Well, there's another reason I'm here. Actually, this is the truthful reason. The stenographer stuff was a ruse, a front to make me more believable."

His glasses were immediately to his face and he focused an unbending gaze upon his fiance's pretty oval face.

"It's the Committee of Six. They wanted me to come here and get together with you from time to time. But I can tell you with every fiber of truth that falling in love with you was never, ever in the equation."

For almost a minute he simply stared, first at her, then at the window. "What do you know of them -- the Committee of Six? No lies today. I must know exactly."

She made a little temple of ten fingers. "Like you I am appalled and disgusted by our regression. America will go backwards into a pit of no return unless somebody -- that's you and me for starters -- start to do something about it. I had practiced law and somehow caught their attention. They gave me a mission, I learned of it in stages. The last part, I learned at the very end...when I was in it too deep to get out. Some things, I already greatly regret having done Richard. But not falling in love with you. Not that."

He got up to hold her hand, to brush away a tear or two. Anger did not belong here, and he kept up a strangely felt detachment.

If you don't mind, I'd like to hold off on telling you the specific part of my mission. It's...rather dreadful. May I not tell you dear? Not now."

"Yes later, by all means, not now." He patted her hands. These days Richard was in touch with his emotions better than ever before. This discourse had blindsided him for sure. But one good side effect-he knew for certain her feelings for him were true. This truth-telling session was a direct result of the right kind of love that had grown between them.

⁂

J.D. Sasser was alone now. He slowly stirred a whisky sour round and round. He had to be very careful with strong drink. Especially on nights like this when crystal clear clarity of thinking was an absolute necessity. First, he'd met with the local small fry. He couldn't help but smile again when he thought of what crazy ole Forrest Younger told him about his ex-son-in-law. Forrest wanted some of the local Birch operatives to pay Marvis Landis a little visit in the middle of the night because he'd had the nerve to actually go to a black church service. Forrest could understand a little of the sheriff's need to go, to get some valuable time appraising the situation first hand. But Marvis went only to make Forrest and his daughter look bad in the community.

J.D. reveled in his membership of the Birch Society in Crowder County. But he was soon to be Imperial Wizard of the Klan for the entire state. That was the prime purpose tonight, to get together with the Big Boys, the out of state folks. What was the big picture like, where were they all headed? He half nodded to himself. With the cities of America on fire, and radicals of every kind coming out of the woodwork, they apparently were going to be left alone out here in the wooded heartland. Sasser's boys could pretty much write their own ticket it appeared now. That was the story the Big Boys told him.

So what to do about RoseCrest Baptist Church? It might be foolish to put it to the torch again. Better to make the heist first, then later maybe a good church burning. Not only would the message be sent loud and clear, we take what we want, but when the blacks rioted and did what blacks did in sheer rage, the heavy hand of the law would come down on *them*. And then, with the golden cross locked away in some sweet, secure location, he could decide its fate. But all in due course. J.D. took a nice long sip from his glass. Sometimes he worried he was too good at this. They were all so easily led.

Words flowed from his mouth to stick like a knife in their malleable little minds. He could make them up hardly without effort; make the fiery oratory that forced his minions to lift their arms heavenward. If the Almighty were really on their side, it was all that was required to get his country back.

⌘ ⌘ ⌘

In the middle of the night, Juniper's mind came onto something. He jotted down a few notes on the writing pad he kept handy, and early the next morning began to connect the dots. At breakfast he tested a few morsels on Sara.

"What do you know of gold, Honey?"

Sara ambled over to the grits pot and dumped some on a plate already festooned with charred bacon and scrambled eggs. "I know that being married to you guarantees that I will never have any. Anything else?"

He patted her ample backside. "Very good. Go back and join the drama club. Now, tell me any of gold's properties that you know of."

She sat on a stool at the bar and dredged up a fistful of Fig Newtons. "Well gold is shiny, flexible and useful for jewelry. I know you can add something else."

"Sure can. Gold is one of the best conductors of electricity that exists. Even better than copper."

Sara eyed him suspiciously. "I know this has something to do with that damned golden cross, but you best keep it to yourself." She winked at him and muttered, "May your newest theory solve the problem so we can finally get some peace around here."

By late afternoon he had it all together. He'd told nobody, did not want anything to leak out. He might be so wrong; he'd get laughed out of town. If he was right, it would at least answer the simplest of questions -- how much was the golden cross actually worth? If it were indeed forged of gold, the current would be unencumbered with the highest possible reading. The less gold that was present would mean the current number would also be lower. Simple, brilliant, but possibly unworkable.

The problem was this: For the voltmeter to work he had to attach the clips properly. He could tape them to the ultra smooth surface. It would take some effort and he'd have to stand in waist deep water. To get to the cross you had to get wet. There was no other way.

He waited until close to midnight. It was no problem to pick the lock, a baby could do it. Now the strobes turned themselves on. They behaved like some kind of sentry, Juniper thought. They never came on during church service or in daylight. Maybe they only came on when movement activated them. He came to the baptistery and stood over it. When he stepped into the water and moved toward the golden cross he had to fumble around to get his headlamp turned on. The strobes stopped. There was blackness tonight, no moon, no starlight, and even the golden cross projected an aura of gloom.

He paused and leaned against a front pew. Some kind of eerie feeling seemed to be washing over him just now. He certainly believed in angels and demons. Which one was it that was screaming in his ear -- "don't go on, don't go on!" The golden cross took in the beams from the black and white strobe patterns, almost absorbing them before spraying them back. For a fleeting moment Juniper's mind played dire tricks on his eyes. Who was that hanging there just now? A person? Yes it was. Could it be the Savior himself? Juniper stared hard trying to see through the darting zebra stripes imposed on the cross. By god no! It was not the Savior hanging there. It was he, himself, Juniper McHewn! Certainly this illusion must come from hearing so much preaching about Jesus and the Cross. Blink and it should go away, he thought.

His habit was to place one foot in front of the other. He waded slowly toward the baptistery. The job was his and his alone. Just now he was sorry he violated the one big rule he preached to his deputies about always having immediate backup.

Directly underneath his feet, a weird grinding vibration. He thought of wheels turning reluctantly. And then the noise so utterly out of place in this sancturarial tomb. A -WHOOSH. Waves came at him from both ends of the baptistery. But his feet had left him as well. Water coursed into both nostrils. Like a reverse tsunami, it was impossible to resist. Some kind of funnel had given way and he headed down, down. Juniper's two thoughts grabbed his brain and hung on. Hold your breath! Land on your feet!

How many feet down would he fall? Impact was a split second in the distance. One foot crashed onto the voltmeter he'd dropped. The other ankle smashed straight down and what was this thing that had rammed itself through boot, sock and flesh?

The pain stabbed instantly. He bellowed like a bull struck by a spearshot. His agony reverberated round and round, as if he'd descended into an echo chamber. The thought of being dead suddenly seemed acceptable over this kind of pain.

Juniper managed to adjust his badly sprained right ankle, the one that had landed on the voltmeter. But as to his left ankle, it moved not an inch. He bent down just low enough to feel out the bed of iron spikes. This was his landing site but to have lost his balance and landed stomach-first would have guaranteed a rapid death. His foot had impaled itself on at least one spike. Was this the space for the corpses of all those poor missing white crackers. Now the same for him?

The headlamp still worked its magic and when his eyes had adjusted he found himself astride a field of graves. He was like a stationary pawn on this morbid turntable of spikes. Next to him, other permanent occupants, what was left of them. He instantly retched as smoky columns of smells unfit for Hell, saturated his olfactory. Some of his vomit draped itself over a flesh draped skull right beside him making the bones seem like they'd suddenly sprouted soupy, green hair.

All around him death paraded in a gory, silent spectacle. Bony parts were etched with pieces of torn clothes, and here and there some putrid rotting flesh. So this was the game at RoseCrest Baptist Church! The caves underneath its foundation solved the entire mystery. Juniper knew of mazes of caves in the general area, he'd explored some as a boy, but nobody had told them they intersected with church land. And so he was trapped here, about to die from the sheer agonizing pain of being crucified in his foot. Along with these other small fools, Juniper McHewn's legacy would shrink to nothing.

Growls! Huffing sounds embedded in the black spaces just beyond his feeble light. If Dracula himself were to appear, drape himself over Juniper's neck and quickly suck away his life's blood, maybe it would be the quickest way to avoid further awful suffering. Then he saw, thinly at first, through eyes that had first to blink away salty tears, an army of long tails flicking is quick s-turns. Tails pumping, they came on quickly.

Rats! Too many for this to be an accident! They hesitated only long enough to allow the pecking order to work. Some alpha males wanted to be first in line. Their black eyes danced, and they showed teeth that clanged like two spoons snapping together. These weren't the ordinary rats of field and barn. Juniper had ported in Singapore during his Navy days. These rats were like those down there. Rats born of the urban sewer. Now they were right here, pure predators out to do some kind of grisly work in rural Mississippi. Hand on pistol, withdrawn in a heartbeat. But where to shoot? How to shoot straight down here with the kind of pain that made every muscle shake in astute agony?

Something jarred his head from behind. The feasting was on the verge of commencement. One had already clambered up his body like some kind of silent tick. And it wasn't content to just lick up the blood all around. It wanted to finish off its prey the fastest way possible.

⁂

Hadley Writt had waited in the blueberry bushes for Juniper to emerge from the church. But something had made the sheriff tarry. Some kind of danger? Hadley twitched and strode quickly to enter the same door as had his sheriff. The strobes danced on. Hadley knew of them but had never been in the sanctuary when it happened. He heard water flowing, and half ran toward the baptistery. It was refilling itself. How was this so?

Hadley knew something about Juniper's general plan because he'd tailed him to the hardware store. Old Man Monroe couldn't keep his mouth shut about the voltmeter and when Hadley learned of Juniper's plan to switch up with Carlton for late night duty, he knew something was up. It was just a matter of tailing Juniper and not getting caught.

He sat down in the Preacher's seat to gather himself, and then he heard them. Shots rang out from somewhere. One shot. Then rapidly two more. But from where had they come? He spun his ears around for a radar lock, but that was all he'd get. The shots seemed both muffled and distant and Hadley wracked his lawman's instinct for answers. None came. He knew, could feel, Juniper's terror. The man had been right here, right where Hadley stood now. Still, Hadley could not make a connection between the voltmeter and the golden cross. He had to have help, and fast. He knew where to go.

Hadley was only mildly surprised when Jewell Fairly opened the door. She had been sleeping on the couch right here in the small living room. Richard Spell emerged with a face plastered with alarm and mistrust. Hadley cut off the emerging question expertly. "It's an emergency Pastor Spell. Maybe you and Miss Jewel could save a life tonight."

Whose life?" Jewell wasted no time bolting into her jeans and sweater.

He removed his hat. His face became drawn tight, chin dipping in full austere mode. "It's Sheriff McHewn. I know he went into the church sanctuary trying to get a lead for…an ongoing investigation. But before I could help him, he just literally disappeared right then and there. Maybe you two are the only people who know something about that golden cross…its powers…so I beg you to help me…help him."

Richard darted for the keys to the church and his car. "If I have the power Deputy. Jewell, shall you go with us?"

She gnawed for an instant on a knuckled fist. "I'll meet you there. I'm coming on my Harley."

Instantly, Richard gathered in her game plan. She would try and save the good Sheriff however that might be. Richard had to keep Hadley Writt off her back if he could.

It was tricky enough to navigate dark roads at night, but she also had to find the trail that would lead her down the steep bank behind the church. Once there, she ditched the Harley and sprinted toward where she thought the covered, secret door to the cave maze lay. It was socked in by artificial plants, and thickly enough to keep sharp eyed squirrel hunters from discovering it. But she went straight there, turned the key on the lock and swung it wide.

She hadn't come here since early December when she'd received a stark directive: Stop feeding the rats. She'd never dared come at night. If her lantern were to die, she'd be stoned with fear in this maze of death. From a distance she heard the sound. It rang out like ivory tambourines. Then she saw the army of rats. They were clacking their molars against upper fangs, almost in unison, as the flesh and blood feast dangled from some oak rafters the cave redesigners had left there.

It was Juniper! Jewell saw the blood trail and small pieces of flesh that stretched all the way to the deadly spike forest. Somehow, he'd ripped himself up and tramped to the only spot that might save his life. How he jumped up there she could not guess. It wasn't that high -- just barely high enough to keep the starving rats from his shredded lower parts. But for a wounded man such as him, the feat seemed most incredible to her.

Jewell flung a wrapper of meat she'd extracted from Richard's refrigerator. Most of the rats scurried there, howling and yelping at a chance to get meat. She shone her lantern onto Juniper's bloodshot eyes. They bore the face of terror, but in a strangely calm way. "At this moment I am the only human being who knows where you are. If you walk out from here tonight Juniper, I need an immortal promise extracted from you. A promise that could dwell in eternity. God Almighty himself would expect you to keep it. Do you follow Sheriff McHewn?"

He could only groan at such ridiculous talk. Jewel took in this marvelous man's incredible will to live. Right here in modern times was a man hanging with his last strength from oaken crossbeams, that themselves, were directly beneath a fantastic cross of gold. The religious ironies pecked at some part of her inner mind, but there was little time for that now. A man was about to die. What would be her role here today?

"Alright, Ok, You are here. You made it just in time. Now get me down and help me get out." When his calf suddenly spasmed, bright red jelly sprayed everywhere, sending the rats into further uproar. "I'd advise you to run over that way and get my gun that's on the ground. Shoot a few of these little bastards to let them know their place." His raspy voice, like his body, was almost gone.

"There's no time for that and beside…I don't know how to shoot a gun. I can knock them off you. But Sheriff…there's a promise you have to make first." He could not see her mouth move, only heard the words.

"What in holy hell are you talking about. There's not time for a speech right now, Miss Fairley. Look around. Hell can't be much different from here."

She grabbed his feet to steady his groaning frame. She tried to regulate her voice but it came out too much like yelling. "You cannot tell the story of this place. Its purpose or location. You have got to take it to your grave Sheriff. If that's too hard, let me know right now."

"How do I explain these injuries? My people aren't that stupid." He watched with half closed eyes as Jewell moved around and expertly fought off three little monsters that tried to use her as a springboard.

"Well…it's a long hard fall down that clay cliff that's directly behind the church right above Bear Creek. I would imagine if you fell by accident, the tumble would hurt you a lot, and if you were knocked out for a spell, it may be possible that some night animals would want to feed on you. Your people would understand that…if you were to say it convincingly."

He grunted and nodded, barely hanging on. Those arms must be incredibly strong. "What about those poor boys over there, what's left of 'em? How can they get their due? What's justice for them?"

Jewell adjusted her lantern to better fight off the gathering army. "There can be no justice for them Juniper. They made their mistakes and paid for them. No redress there. There's barely any for you, none if it were not for Hadley Writt."

Juniper nodded and knocked dollops of clay from the cave roof. He'd played a lot of poker in his time. This was fold up time. "Ok Miss Fairly I will agree to silence on this…death trap. But there's one extra item and it's a big one. If you do not agree, then just let me stay here and die. I'll rot right along with these good old boys."

"Hurry Juniper. There's not much time." It came in a whisper. She'd been bitten. Her blood flowed.

"You must agree that I will be the last person to come into this booby trap. No more people are to die here. Hell, Jewell, there's a church of God right above us. What would that God you know exists think about this joke of justice? It's my only term, my only condition. If you can't meet it then leave now, and I'll rot here. You'll have another secret to keep. But you have to know I'm right on this one. What do you say, Miss Fairley?"

Jewell shifted position again, both to fight off rats and try and shield Juniper from falling. If he collapsed now, they'd be upon him and she'd be totally helpless against them. How much sense did his lawman's words make? Actually, way too much. Her version of truth could not lie here, not this way. There was no lightning bolt from heaven; her decision to agree with Juniper was more a melting away. A melting away of the hard stony core she'd cultivated as she tried hard every day to pull the ends of the same rope together. Sewing Justice together, she always liked to think. But maybe the ends would never join. Juniper moaned, his last strength crashing.

Let it go Jewell. Let it go. She asked Juniper to release his grip and moments later they were dragging one another away as rats hopped on and off like they were on some kind of two-headed bus. Their fangs hurt but something else dawned on Jewell's mind, like a picture from a medieval tapestry she'd once seen on some ancient church wall.

Juniper's wounds of the body had suddenly become hers of the soul.

⁂

Jewell nuzzled against Richard's skinny chest. "Your time as a lonely single man is just about up. When we're married it will be under that same golden cross that just about wrecked us. What immense irony, Richard!."

"Yes, of course. But we don't own that cross. The Committee of Six does. They can remove it any time they want to, and then what?"

Jewell sighed and tapped her long fingers on his wrist. "Given all that's happened, they would be idiots to make big changes at RoseCrest. If we are here at RoseCrest simply promoting the church, a normal church now, we won't attract any more attention. I've told them as you have, we intend to keep our mouths very much shut on all that's happened. Sheriff McHewn has given me his word of honor to keep quiet. I believe him. I told the Committee of Six exactly that. They were not so happy I could tell. But they'll take a stalemate given all their exposure. They have a ton of potential liability. It's a stalemate for now. Justice is neither advanced nor enhanced."

"So for now..." Richard's voice tailed off. "No checkmate for anybody. No winners, no immediate losers except... They will remain in our own private nightmare. This is not how I ever thought it would end. I guess my dreams of vanquishing the evil-hearted people of this land are...have....". She drew him closer to her breasts and for a moment, Richard hushed. Suddenly his nose became the overactive organ. "What's that smell?"

"I have been in the rose patch again. That's what." He eyed her carefully, admiring the combination of common sense and strength within the woman of his finest dreams.

"I picked a bundle for Juniper and put them in that beautiful vase his wife bought. He should be out of the hospital next week."

"I can't get over all those roses growing on our trellis. My mother grew roses back in Iowa. She said they hate hot weather. I don't know about Mississippi roses though, maybe they're special." Richard moved aside to let her take up the two small wine glasses she'd posted on the lamp table.

She reached for the jug of muscadine wine and poured another dollop for her lover man. "My dear Richard, here's a toast to life. A toast to roses that are not supposed to bloom in August."

They drank even as forces of gloom and desperate darkness continued to gather across the face of the great land. If the evil men would ever go away, it might be the result of smaller victories won over time, such as just happened in Crowder County Mississippi. And what exactly was evil? Could it really be defined? Neither knew the answer to what before they would have shouted from any handy rooftop.

Both Richard and Jewell suspected communication in this arena would remain unspoken for a good long time. Now they knew all too well that there will always be those people who make grievous mistakes, even compounding problems which arise from possessing too much blind faith. But such people always possess a secret talent; they can turn from their errors just in time. In so doing, it is proven beyond a doubt that even in the depths of August, when things are the hottest and most hateful, roses can bloom.

THE END

Just how dangerous can cloning be? If it can make the life of common people all over the world a better and more loving place, could there be a role for such advanced science?

Prodigious

Warning! This is flash fiction! It's just what your short attention span needs right now.

Bioli entered the room at the exact appointment time and was pleased to discover that indeed, the rogue billionaire of biomedical fame, Carmen Carradoza, had kept his word. Carradoza watched the journalist pad his shoeless, sockless way across the bamboo flooring. Bioli only glanced at Carradoza's almost peasant cotton shirt and ruffled surgeon pants. For a billionaire and a genius, he dressed like a slob. Carradoza was nothing if not a man of simple tastes and he was well known for possessing an overpowering almost cosmic desire to be of benefit to not only Chileans, but to people everywhere.

Bioli plopped his writing pad and pencil upon the hardwood table. Carmen fixed an appropriate gaze upon the one journalist he had chosen among thousands. Bioli had barely had time to fly from New York City, and Langley, his producer, was just now huffing his way up the stairs in this elevatorless building.

"Thanks for coming Mr. Bioli. I hope my restrictions aren't too tough on you?" He spoke in accented English, and as he always told people, he'd managed to learn English only in his spare time, and at a time when the language brain of his youth had shriveled to a speck of its former self.

""Not at all Dr. Carradoza. I always prefer my own little special brand of shorthand anyway for interviews like these."

For a number of moments, neither man flinched. Dr. Carradoza's bulldozer staring act forced Bioli to place his pencil between two fingers and gently tap against the table top. At length the older man's wizened face softened. Bioli heard the sigh, almost inaudible. Whatever plan the crafty billionaire had devised for today, he now was irrevocably committed to it.

"As you know, I've always despised the public spotlight. But by the nature of my work, nowadays I am thrust into it."

"The world wants to respect you," replied Bioli. "What you are doing largely serves the public interest."

Dr. Carradoza made a huffing sound. "And it makes me a very wealthy man." He leaned forward. "Did you suspect Mr. Bioli, that I have no idea how much I am worth? When I die all of my money is donated to a dozen worthy projects here in Chile. Money is perhaps the main reason this conservative country has embraced modern views so suddenly. If wealth spreads outward, rather than concentrates, society is motivated to change."

Bioli gambled on the move, made it without questioning himself. "And your pending human cloning projects will make you more money than ever. And no doubt help Chile to mature as a modern democracy. But the clones have to serve other purposes as well. They simply cannot exist in a vacuum."

Carradoza leaned back into the soft cushions. "Ah yes. I knew you would bring that up. In fact, I had hoped you would." Carradoza's soft grey eyes did not match a face riddled with extraordinary dips and rises from wrinkles that were far from ravishing. This wasn't an old man yet, and yet he took no measures at all, many of which he'd perfected, to give illusion of deeper youth.

"Word is Dr. Carradoza, that a human clone is already out there, waiting as it were, for you to present him to the world."

Carradoza's hard face unwrinkled the tiniest bit when he smiled. "Even in Chile, as advanced as we are in these matters, it's still against the law to clone a human being." Now he leaned forward, the words barely audible: "And how do you know that's it's a male who is the first clone of human history?"

Bioli kept a fixed look on the Doctor's chin while his active heart pounded in his chest. "I see. So you chose me because...you trust me just enough to reveal sufficient details to the world, without anyone knowing *for sure*...You need attention in dollops, not waves."

Dr. Carradoza nodded. "Something very close to that Mr. Bioli." The man suddenly looked to a corner of the room and snapped his fingers. A door opened and staff wheeled in a television on a stand. A receiver unit posted atop gave Bioli a clue to where this might be heading.

"Shortly I will leave this room. You will then be in attendance with a person of whom you will only see his silhouette. You may ask him questions, but be discrete. When you become too bold, a red square is displayed. Three red squares concludes your interview. At any rate, you will have a maximum of ten minutes. Do you understand Mr. Bioli?"

In a few moments everyone had cleared the room. The television turned itself on. Against a white background, a person's face appeared. Someone was right there but in blackened silhouette facing forward. He cleared his throat. "It's nice to meet you Mr. Bioli," came a juvenile voice.

Bioli blinked as the room's lights dimmed. "What do you call yourself?"

"Oh I have a real name. It's Richard. But of course, I must withhold my last name."

"Is your last name the name of your mother or your father?"

"It's of my father. I am his clone in appearance. But my environment is very different from what his was when he was my age. It may seem odd to you that I know a great deal about clones, and yet I don't consider myself to be one. I have my own ways of doing things and thinking. I'm not mindless or stupid."

"So you see your dad often?" Bioli scribbled frantically, his method of shorthand was being tested today if only because both hands were shaking in fantastic appreciation of this moment.

"Only by online means. We talk twice a day. But I cannot meet him or live with him yet."

"When will that day come?" The first red warning square came down and hung there. Bioli's last question bore offense to unknown censors and monitors. These parameters were becoming more apparent with each passing second.

"That's up to Dr. Carradoza. But it will be pretty soon I think. It will be a happy day for me. My dad agrees."

Bioli scratched at his fledgling beard. "Richard, tell me how you will feel on that day when you come out before the world. Do you think you will feel awkward at being regarded as so special?"

"Probably a little. But since I was a tiny boy, I've been encouraged to be independent. Nobody has ever forced me to be like my father. Of course, I do resemble him perfectly when he was my age."

"May I ask your age?" Bioli cringed, but no second red square appeared.

"I am ten years old." Carradoza's team had cloned the first human being. They'd managed to sequester the most special boy on earth without placing him into overt isolation. Dad was even a regular feature in the boy's life in a virtual sort of way. As for his mom, Bioli knew enough about cloning to realize she was of utterly no consequence to Richard.

"So if you show the world who you are, say, in one year, you will be eleven. How can people really know you are your dad's clone? He would be older than you by maybe thirty years I'd guess. Appearances may not convince people very much."

Richard laughed. "Even though he's forty years older than me, there is a built-in guarantee people will know we are the same."

"How so? They will see an identical genomic profile?"

"Sure they could do that too, but there's an acute visual clue that anyone will easily relate to." Richard chuckled lightly, betraying an airy lightness. The child was certainly comfortable in his own skin, this first boy clone. "If I were to turn my profile sideways, you'd be given a huge clue what I mean, but it may cost you a penalty."

"Well, I accept that risk, Richard." Bioli leaned forward, as if something were about to jump out from the television screen.

Richard raised up slightly and turned his neck. A thrill of discovery rippled down Bioli's spine. Now Richard was perfectly sideways in his chair. The residue and legacy his father had given out in that cloning exercise ten or eleven years ago, that sure-fire double indemnity gene shone like Betelgeuse's last glare. Bioli's natural detective prowess lurched into high power. Simply by the way Richard looked, Bioli knew Carradoza had a gambit. But now, so early in the puzzle game, Bioli only stumbled around the puzzle.

Three strikes, three penalty squares. Richard's image bolted from the screen. Bioli had seen far too much when Richard turned himself sideways to the camera and yet, Bioli suspected everything had gone precisely according to plan.

The lights stayed dimmed, and nobody came back into the room. Bioli was left to shuffle out on his own. In the anteroom, his producer paced. "Did you get it? How'd it go? Will Carradoza come out for the photo shot tomorrow like he promised?"

"Yeah, I think so." Bioli glanced around the room. "He did not know in advance we'd meet exactly here, in this little room, did he? Let me try and lock this door. I've got to know right now if our plan worked."

Bioli removed his bifocals. From a humped center he extracted a small, nearly invisible nodule. Carefully he took the nodule and placed it into a special crevice on Langley's I-pad. Indeed, Bioli had managed to outfox Carradoza. Whatever Bioli had looked at in that room, the tiny, special camera had captured both the sounds and the action. This, of course, directly violated Carradoza's prime directive. There was to be no extraneous information distributed without his permission. Even so, the world would never see this. It was solely for the two men's benefit in this room. They knew that Carradoza's specialty was to lead the media around by their noses, as if they were the dumbest of dumb bovines. At such manipulation he had become expert.

The interview with Richard had concluded after only six minutes. It was enough. Langley whistled softly and stared at the last frozen frame. His head bobbed from side to side. "Poor kid. Imagine having to go through life with a proboscis like that. It's enormous."

"Yeah. Like father like son. Dad's clone is unmistakable for sure. No need to educate the public with boring genomic maps. There really *is* something about having an enormous nose that jars someone's emotions. In this case, it's virtually inconceivable people could be confused."

Bioli's fingers stalled at his stubble-flecked chin. "That's true enough. But Carradoza's gambit must be deeper. It's got to lie at the heart of making money from human cloning. It's the best game that movitates Carradoza. When he gets endless new bankloads of new cash it will prove he is winning again. Sniff out the money trail as it's most likely to exist when the clone is revealed. What's most likely to happen? They both go to jail?"

"Unlikely," said Langley, rising to the puzzle Bioli was projecting. "From what we see here, Richard will be regarded with both awe and pride by his people. The government will likely forgive Carradoza for his sins. Money will easily grease the pockets of those who would give him the most trouble. He'll be free to move to his next stage."

The men searched each other's eyes. Langley paced the floor while Bioli sat down in a chair and made his face into a blank slate. Langley's fingers snapped first. "How does this sound? Carradoza will exclaim to Chileans and to the world, that it's ok to have flaws. He actually does not *want* to clone the perfect person, the most beautiful woman, the smartest genius. His cloning centers will be open to all, even to those who want to propagate prodigious noses."

Bioli arose and pounded Langley's large shoulder. "It will be the first official shot fired over the bow of world public opinion by God! Carradoza's declaration to mankind would be equally bold and sacrilegious: *There is little to fear from massive human cloning if the average man could get back a beloved son, daughter or wife, lost too early.* If the great middle classes of the world perceive benefit, who could really oppose him?"

Bioli paused and let Langley digest that last load. Langley's brows arched as he cocked his head sideways. "Could it really be that a child's simple, prodigious nose will be the driving factor that gives human cloning an appeal it never had before? If our guessing is even half on target, you gotta give Carradoza credit. He has genius."

"*Uncommon cloning for the common man.*" How's that for an advertising header? Over the space of the next twenty years, how many people would go for it? How much money would be made?" Bioli whistled softly.

Langley handed Bioli his two socks. "Not to be facetious my friend, but we both already know the answers to those questions." Langley propped his ample form down in the only chair in the room. "Enormous numbers of people will go for it. It could be the spear tip of a new revolution in biotechnology."

"And the money to be made, with Carradoza's companies at the center of the hub?" Bioli placed one hand on his friend's large shoulder.

Langley tapped three nervous fingers on the tabletop. "It can't even be imagined. You are talking about appealing to massive numbers of people dealing with their most visceral, basic emotions that center around love, family, relationships. How much money to be made you just asked? Inconceivable amounts. Huge money. In a word- *Prodigious*."

THE END

So you have plowed Ten Golden Fields. What did you think of this kind of varied, character-driven fiction? If you were reading the E book, was the format ok? If you really want a hard copy book, would you let me know? I'll see if I can ship you one right away.

whenaganace@gmail.com

THANKS SO MUCH FOR READING! Wen

About the Author

Give me a tennis racket on a beautiful day. Let me take pen in hand after that and write. That's ME!

Wen Henagan is a Louisiana native who will always be captivated by certain things like LSU football and any sport played outdoors. But as a kid he also had a big imagination. He wrote stories and poems and his teachers noticed. Wen has consumed the interesting material in books the way a pelican takes sardines. So when he took a job abroad, he had more time to put together finely woven stories that went to the very limit of his imagination. These days, Wen jets back and forth between Northeast Asia where he is employed as a Professor to teach English language, and resides in his home in Florida in summer and winter.